KT-523-714

THE LAST OF US

THE LAST OF US

Rob Ewing

WITHDRAWN

THE BOROUGH PRESS

The Borough Press
An imprint of HarperCollins*Publishers*
1 London Bridge Street
London SE1 9GF

www.harpercollins.co.uk

Published by HarperCollins*Publishers* 2016

1

Copyright © Rob Ewing 2016

Rob Ewing asserts the moral right to
be identified as the author of this work

A catalogue record for this book
is available from the British Library

ISBN: 978-0-00-814958-1

This novel is entirely a work of fiction.
The names, characters and incidents portrayed in it are the work
of the author's imagination. Any resemblance to actual persons,
living or dead, events or localities is entirely coincidental.

Printed and bound in Great Britain by
Clays Ltd, St Ives plc

All rights reserved. No part of this publication may be
reproduced, stored in a retrieval system, or transmitted,
in any form or by any means, electronic, mechanical,
photocopying, recording or otherwise, without the prior
permission of the publishers.

MIX
Paper from
responsible sources
FSC **FSC C007454**
www.fsc.org

FSC is a non-profit international organisation established
to promote the responsible management of the world's forests.
Products carrying the FSC label are independently certified
to assure consumers that they come from forests that are managed
to meet the social, economic and ecological needs
of present and future generations.

Find out more about HarperCollins and the environment at
www.harpercollins.co.uk/green

For Karin

Acknowledgements

Thank you to Karolina Sutton, Norah Perkins and Lucy Morris of Curtis Brown, and to Katie Espiner, Charlotte Cray, Suzie Dooré, Cassie Browne and Ann Bissell and all the team at the Borough Press. Thanks to Claire Ward for her fantastic cover design. Thanks also to Donald Sinclair for checking my Gaelic; and to Jamie and Elspeth Traynor and Miranda Barkham.

Special thanks to Karin for all her support and encouragement over the years, and to our three children, whose book title suggestions – *Life's a Beach, Staying Alive* – were better than any I came up with. Thanks also to the real-life Elizabeth, for the gifts you gave. And thank you mum, for everything.

A final thanks to the people of Barra and Vatersay, for their warmth, humour and kindness during our stay there.

Behind the Back Bay

Date – lost count

I have become skilled.

For starters let's talk about dogs. When dogs die after being trapped inside you usually find them at the front or back door, or near the toilet if it hasn't gone dry, or next to the water melted out of a freezer. I imagine them running between the two choices: water and escape, water and escape, until it's too late.

Cats are usually by these too, or by the window if there isn't a cat flap. But you can't predict as well with cats, maybe because they had too much of their own mind back when they were still alive.

Being an explorer you get skilled at knowing.

I know what a cup of tea left for months looks like: dried muck. Bowls of fruit turn to furry glue. Cupboards jump with mice when you open them. Plants all die, apart from that one cactus we found, because trapped indoors was a good enough desert for it.

And dogs are more often found at doors, cats at windows. That's the rule. Plus dogs smell worse than cats, though neither of them are very nice.

I say I've become skilled – but the truth is everything has got more difficult. So I can't wait here for ever for my friends to come back. Can't keep imagining new friends out of thin air. Can't keep hiding in the same old sleeping bag without noticing the bad stink of it.

Even with skill you can't truly smell yourself. If you came home Mum, magicking yourself out of the wind in the bay, this is what I think you would smell:

1. *Old food*
2. *Dog-smell from the dog-friend (gone now)*
3. *The smell from my glass-cuts*
4. *Clothes & bedsheets*
5. *Pee smell (Alex's bed before his illness)*
6. *Smoke (from the bad fire)*
7. *Shoes (seawater + shoes = epic fail)*
8. *Cheesy crisps (strange, we didn't have any of them)*
9. *Cold wet air*
10. *Earwax*

Still, there's the worry about smells you can't know, and there's no way to come wise on that. So this morning I went outside. I went holding onto doors, chairs, cardboard boxes. Rubbish piles. And I collected the yellow bits of gorse from the field at the end of the street, and brought them in and put them in saucers all around.

Now they shine like fires far away, like when the crofters set fire to the heather and you saw it at dusk.

My eyes go slow around the room. It's half-bright from the skylight, even though we taped cereal boxes over the glass to keep out the sun. Here in the high north, now that it's summer, our sun hardly goes away. Underneath the skylight is Elizabeth's bed: still made, with the edges neat the way she liked. Her rules on the wall, her survival books in a tower. Alex's drawings and toys scattered like he always kept them, like he got grabbed in the middle of one last fight. Which I suppose he did.

I can see the stain on the carpet. Red food dye. That mark tells where it started to go bad for us.

Then the clothes that Elizabeth got out but didn't have enough room to take. Her toys, which made me uneasy, because she was meant to be the one in charge. So uneasy that I wrapped them away from seeing.

If anyone is listening: God, or Mum, or the devil: I should say that the only obstacle from taking the bad tablet is me. That's not a pretty thought, right? Except I was too busy with other plans for escape to notice when the thought came. When it sneaked inside me.

You see, I did one bad thing. But that bad thing led to lots of others, which grew like a crowd of dogs when you're holding warm food.

Now it hurts too much to think about. So I'll think about this, instead: how Alex used to ask, 'How many more sleeps?' How some mornings he'd wake up convinced he didn't sleep at all. How he was sure he just went to bed and woke up and it was light. Nothing in-between.

3

How you used to give imaginary directions to someone driving a car over the sea to our island.

Turn southeast at Greenland. Down a bit from Iceland, up from Ireland, up and across a bit from England or Wales. Our island is one of the Western Isles – not the Outer Hebrides, which is the wrong-sounding word that mainlanders use. (Nobody knows what Hebrides means – not even our teacher, Mrs Leonard, who's dead now, though you can still see her if you want to.)

Know what *that* means, Mum?

'Course you do – you are up there with God, and can see it all. Only I dare you – dare you to come down into the village, then go past the lifeguards' station, and on to the houses that look like someone coloured them in with white chalks.

Go ask her yourself. Go on.

Mum, if it's you that's listening – even though you never give me any sign these days – then I have to tell you one more thing. Don't take it the wrong way, but – your last look was a look that meant nothing.

I don't mean that there was nothing there at all. Being skilled these days I know what a real true empty face shows – there's usually too much teeth, plus no eyes you can figure on. And I don't mean it didn't mean anything to me – because it did, else I wouldn't be forever harking back and going from one detail – *creased mouth* – to the next – *half-wide eyes* – to the next – *eye-wrinkles not happy or sad* – and thinking: but what does it add up to?

No, the problem about your last look was – I'm still not big

4

enough to read it. That's the law of faces: you can read kids younger, but older kids get hard. Adults, even harder still. If you get words as well, that can help – except when the look is sarcasm, which doesn't go true and has no law.

But you didn't give me any words – just a look, which might be somewhere between surprise, or all-time giving in, or not caring, or caring too much.

So I'm trying to work it out. Hopefully I get there before the time I've got runs out.

And now that I've told you that one thing – now that we're back on talking terms – I need to ask a favour.

If you are in heaven, and seeing everything – like the crumbs at the bottom of my sleeping bag, like the gorse spread around the room or the sea's sparkle in the window – then you need to blur your eyes for once. Stop paying attention to stuff that doesn't matter.

Instead: help my friends.

Three weeks ago

This morning I noticed Elizabeth's rainbow. She put water in a saucer on the windowsill, then a mirror in the water. I didn't think it'd work, but then saw that it did.

It's on the wall, beside the cereal boxes we taped over the big skylight. It wobbles a bit like the sea, disappears with the wind, comes back when the air is still. Just now it reminds me of a puddle with petrol spilt on it.

Elizabeth is still in bed. She's looking towards me with her eyes open. I give her a wave but she looks like right through, like she's thinking about the way things were before, which she usually is.

I hear a yowling noise from out on the street: one of the cats, or their kittens. They still roam around, for all days mainly, only now the bigger group is broken up into just a few stragglers who feed on rubbish like the gulls.

Saw two of the kittens taken by an eagle. The MacNeil brothers saw the rest go. Saw a crumple of fur and bones on the shore-walk next to the sculpture of the seal. The cats stayed in their house for a while after that, but I guess they got their courage working again.

Elizabeth gets up and begins to ribbon my hair without saying anything. Alex sits forward, rubs sleep from his eyes. His trousers are damp. Elizabeth gets him to stand and strips his sheets, tumbling them into a ball to be put in the garden.

Alex washes himself with a flannel then says, 'You get up?' His voice is dry and croaky; Elizabeth recognises the warning signs so plonks a bowl of cereal in his lap and orders him to eat. She pours ten toty cartons of cream in a glass, adds yellow sterilised water, pours the lot on top and hey presto – he's got a normal breakfast.

Our clothes are already in three piles. Elizabeth puts on a CD – *Winnie the Pooh*, which we listen to while getting dressed. Then she takes the balled-up sheets and puts them in the garden beside all the others.

Alex: 'It's only sweat. I just sweat the bed.'

Me: 'Don't worry about it.'

Alex: 'I just have a weakness for sweating . . .'

Me: 'OK, I believe you.'

He's scared of going to the toilet alone, so I take his hand and go with. The flies on the ceiling do their mad angry dance when the door opens and closes. The porch door's stiff, not broken like the one to the kitchen.

Outside, there's the smell of dewy grass and moss in the sun. I jump over the screeching fence, do my daily business. Alex is about to go by the door when I warn him to come away a good bit: 'Stop being too close,' I hiss. 'You're always too close. Come over by the fence.'

He comes in by the fence, pees. He looks around – to the street, to the bay, to the road going west and to Beinn Tangabhal, our big hill at the far end of town.

Alex: 'Is it smoke?'

He's pointing at the hill. It's only cloud. I tell him.

'Cloud isn't smoke then?'

I think about it, then decide I don't know the answer. I'm pretty sure I used to know the answer. Or maybe he's half asleep, and it's a kid's question.

He's less bleary when we get back in. By now Elizabeth is doing her routine. She turns the two radios on. One has a dial which she circles all the way, going through the stations. The other has buttons. She takes her time, slowing on the dial at the places we marked with gold stars. Then she gives Alex his injection. He already has his jumper up ready, so it's done quick.

She holds up his pen and looks in carefully at the glass window on the inside of it.

'Just half of this one left,' she says.

After this Elizabeth writes our shopping list: *Sheets – for 1 week. Breakfast. Batteries. Bags. Tins.* Hearing a noise, she turns down the CD. We all listen. But it's only coming from the street, a lot of yowling and screeching – it's from the House of Cats. She turns the CD up again.

We've finished the funny milk that doesn't need a fridge, so I have cartons too, and they're not bad. There's apricot jam after this. We dip pink wafer biscuits in, rather than using our spoons and having to wash up. Then there's digestive biscuits, toasted over the gas-burner flame, then hint-of-mint hot chocolate.

I comb Alex's hair. He doesn't like wiping his face, plus he always forgets to wash his hair, so I take him to the mirror to show him how it looks and the damage it does to his appearance.

I get the toothbrushes out, brush mine. 'Dreamt I had a wobbly tooth last night,' I say, remembering.

Elizabeth is cleaning our cups in the bowl. 'You missing any new ones? Or old ones, mean to say?'

I put a finger in to test: 'All just the same.'

'Why do we brush our teeth again? Can anybody remember?'

'Oh *not* this again . . .'

Alex wrinkles his face at our talk of teeth. He doesn't like having his brushed. He had a sore tooth when it was still dark and stormy, and his face went big for a week. After that he lost four of his baby teeth, all at once. He cried a lot, and it took him ages to get better. Now he has a big gap in his top teeth, with no adult ones in yet.

Me: 'Remember all the good reasons?'

Alex: 'Elizabeth says gum disease means sickness going in the blood. Plus, if you swallow a tooth then you don't get a coin.' He sighs and looks around for his clothes, which I know is just a delaying tactic.

I push down his chin, which doesn't usually work but does today.

Me: 'Firstly: chewing surfaces.'

The saying of this makes us stop. We both look at each other. Then we ignore ourselves.

*   *   *

It's only a short walk to school. The skinny cats follow us, so we scare them off. It rained last night, but it's sunny now, which makes the road shine.

If I almost close my eyes this brightness joins up with the shine coming from the sea. When I tell Elizabeth about this, that it's one way of making everything look back to normal, she nods and does her distant look.

We sit down in our usual classroom seats and unpack our bags. Alex is very fussy about how he sets out his pens: he has to get the colours right before it's good. Elizabeth sits beside Alex, then we wait for the MacNeil brothers.

I wait until the clock shows 9:02 before starting. We do reading first – this is Alex alone. Elizabeth leaves it to me, so I give him plenty of praise and tell him he's a Good Communicator. I put a star in his reading book, then get him to read it again in his head. Then we do writing – I draw two lines in Alex's book, ask him to do his best vowels. After this we do words, then sentences.

While he's doing a story I take myself aside. In my head I think: All right Rona. Read this page to this page. Then do a story where you use plenty of Wow Words, and especially these – Frog, Dainty, Wolf, Tiredly.

Elizabeth is about to start her lesson when Calum Ian comes in, with Duncan following after him.

Duncan is wearing his hood up high today, the way he does when he wants to be invisible.

They take a seat as far from us as possible. Calum Ian takes out his pencil and sharpener. He starts to sharpen his pencil onto the floor in one long unsnapped strand.

10

'Martin far,' says Elizabeth.

I know she can't help it, but she never gets it right. She says *madainn mhath* like there's a Martin who's far. The first time she said it I nearly went – 'All right, where?' I've tried to correct her, but there's no chance she'll come wise.

'*Pòg mo thòin*,' Calum Ian replies.

This is very rude and should never be said, not even to your worst enemy.

Elizabeth: 'I know what *Poke Ma Hone* means.' She gets the sound of *that* right at least.

Calum Ian looks like he knew she knew already.

'What is it, Duncan?' Elizabeth asks. 'Why are you hiding yourself away?'

Duncan's jacket scrunches.

Calum Ian: 'He's being quiet. He only wants to sit in peace and quiet. That's right isn't it, Duncan?'

Duncan doesn't answer.

Elizabeth takes the teacher's seat. There are ten empty places, five filled. She writes our names in the register, then hands around bits of paper.

'We'll start with an activity,' she says. 'As part of our remembering. It's the thing where you choose a colour, then a number. All right? Then there's a message. We can all make one. Who wants to have a go?'

She calls it a fortune-teller for our fingers. It's like a beak with four spikes, made of paper. My first try ends up wrong. Alex can't do his and he ends up getting offended. Calum Ian does his but looks grumpy about it, while Duncan's hands are quick and skilled.

Me: 'Choose a colour.'

Alex: 'Blue.'

Me: 'B – L – U – E. Choose a number.'

Alex: 'Four.'

Me: 'One two, three four. Open this up. And the message is – Keep calm and keep playing.'

In the end it's a good enough project. We laugh at some of the ruder messages, then Alex finds one which says You see a ship! And we stop wanting to play.

We have a break, then Elizabeth says we should change activity: to real remembering.

'Who wants to go first?'

When nobody volunteers she begins:

'Dad used to talk about memory. He said there was short-term, and there was long-term. Can anyone tell me what the difference is?'

Nobody wants to say and get it wrong.

'All right, so short-term's the thought you just had. It doesn't last, unless you remember it again. Long-term lasts, but some-times you need to remember it to keep it strong. Otherwise it can fade, and you forget.'

She waits for us to understand. I try to remember what I had for dinner – no, it's gone. I should've practised.

Elizabeth: 'Who'll go first?'

No one answers. Calum Ian looks up at the cracks on the ceiling, then stretches out his arms and collects back like he's years after being bored.

'Will you try, Duncan?'

Duncan pretends to be reading his jotter. But then, to

12

surprise us all, he stands. He stands for the longest time, even past the point of my being nervous for him.

'Dad used to have a game where he pretended he was a robot,' he says in a hurry. 'You'd control him, except he might attack.'

He waits for us to say anything. When nobody does he goes on: 'I remember he was friendly after the pub. If he'd gotten drunk he had a joke about people annoying him to give him a trophy. He didn't want it. They'd run up the street after him, chasing him. It was sort of stupid . . .'

He looks out at us, seeing if we're still listening, looking like he's sure we'll be bored.

'I thought he was trying to make himself out to be important . . . I thought he was worried about being too ordinary as a dad. That's why I always practise my fiddle: so he can see how good I am when he comes back. So I can make him proud.'

He stops. Elizabeth makes a go-on face. We're meant to be writing it all down for Duncan to keep in his diary, but I mostly prefer just to be listening.

'Mam, she played I spy. She said it in the Gaelic. Said it with sounds, as well: I hear with my little ear. You could hear the kettle, or the wind. Or the fridge. Once she did it for her stomach rumbling. Then for her baby.' He stops for a while, picks at some fluff on the edge of his sleeve. I can see all his face now. There's new scabs on his chin.

'Dad didn't play the robot game when everything went bad. There wasn't much I spy then either.'

After a long time and with a quiet voice he asks: 'If a baby isn't born, does it still get up to heaven?'

13

Calum Ian stops writing. He leans across and raps Duncan hard on the arm.

'That's you finished. You've done your bit. I don't want you talking about them, all right? So, you're done, *suidh sìos*. Now get your arse in and sit.'

Duncan wants to stay standing – but when Calum Ian gets up and folds his arms, he sits. His big brother looks annoyed, or maybe sad, I can't tell. He gives Elizabeth a look like she did a stupid thing for encouraging Duncan.

'Know what I think?' he says. 'There's just as much stuff we need to forget. So get on, Big Brains, answer that: how do we *stop* ourselves from remembering?'

We wait on Elizabeth.

'Remembering is all we've got,' she says.

It feels like the right time to change topic. Elizabeth writes down Duncan's memories then gives them to him.

'Let's move on to sums,' she tells us.

It's my job to hand out the workbooks. We all know the pages, but I say them anyway because that's what happens in a class. My lesson is counting money. I have to count picture-bundles of spending money in under a minute. I use the clock on the wall. It takes me two minutes, but only forty seconds if I cheat.

Alex, who's young, has to read *Kipper's Birthday*, which he's done before but this time with feeling. Duncan's the same age as me, yet he won't be encouraged. He mostly lies head-down until it's time to go. Calum Ian is one year below Elizabeth, so he copies her mostly.

I turn the pages and stare at the sums I know I did last

year. The book is very good – giving examples, sums that are worked through, but even so, it's not enough. I don't want to tell the boys that I don't know. The last time I did that they called me *Gloic,* which means brainless idiot, not even anything to do with the truth.

Then the sun starts to shine on my desk, and now I want to be outside. I think of the gardens we saw on the way here, with flowers I haven't the name for, either in the Gaelic or English. I recognised some very big daisies, but the rest I didn't know. Daffodils? Roses, maybe? There might be a book in one of the houses, or the library. For learning there can't be a better place to start than there.

'This is dumb,' Calum Ian says.

I look up at Elizabeth, who pretends not to hear, at least not until he says it for a second time.

'Why is it dumb?'

Calum Ian scratches his pen across the lid of his desk. 'It's the same page, over and over. Plus I never cared about sums in the before. How can they help us now?'

Elizabeth lines up her jotter and pencils. Then says, 'Sums are needed for lots of things.'

'Say some.'

She tries to think of examples. In the long run she says, 'Sums can tell you what the date is.'

'No they don't. All you need for that is a calendar. And there's plenty of those in the post office.'

Me: 'People used to tell the time by the sun. True. There was a shortest day and a longest. The olden-times people used sums to work it out.'

Calum Ian: 'We've got calendars.'

Elizabeth: 'Which nobody can agree the date with.'

Calum Ian: 'Because *you* got *your* count wrong.'

He takes out his can opener – twirls the head of it, squinting his eyes at Elizabeth.

'Why'd you get to be teacher? It could just as easy be me, or Duncan. Or Alex sitting quiet there. Or her. But it's forever you.'

Elizabeth puts her pencils back in her satchel.

'It's not even as if we learn anything. We've been at this same page for days. *Weeks.*'

Elizabeth leaves the teacher's seat and goes to sit beside Alex. Then she takes out her things and looks patient.

I know Duncan will never get up to replace her: he's too shy. Alex is both shy and too young: he's only six.

We hear Calum Ian's chair screeching. He scrumples his pages then goes to the teacher's desk.

On the whiteboard he writes his name, then underneath:

I AM A BOY NOT A FUCKING TEACHER

'There's no point pretending to be a teacher, because I'm not,' he says. 'There's no point in any of us pretending because none of us are. The – bloody – end.'

After this he draws an arse on the whiteboard, and I have to admit this is kind of funny.

But when we start to laugh he gets furious; he rubs off what he's written then shouts: 'Shut your traps! *Sguir dheth sin!* That means you as well, Ugly-face!'

He's talking to his brother, Duncan.

16

Duncan hides as deep as he can in his jacket, to match the quietness of the rest of us.

Now Calum Ian looks worried to have said what he did. He goes back to his seat, rolls down his sleeves – but they're clarty, so he rolls them back up again.

'Duncan could teach us the fiddle,' Elizabeth says in a quiet voice. 'We could get them out of the music cupboard?'

'I'm going home.'

Calum Ian begins to pack his bag. Duncan begins to collect his things, too.

Elizabeth: 'We could do messages?'

'Another crap idea. Who's looking out for them, tell me that? We send and send but we never get any back.'

'And never will if we don't keep sending.'

'*Fine*, you do it then. See if I care.'

'But we have to stick together. Remember the saying: "What's going to work?"'

This is Elizabeth's saying. She always does it when we're struggling, or disagreeing, or needing a boost up.

When nobody adds on the next bit, she has to add it herself: 'Teamwork! That's what's going to work, right? We're all going to be a team. Right?'

'Do your stupid sums for the team, then.'

After this Calum Ian gets up, scraping his chair, and leaves, with Duncan hurrying behind.

I look across at the drawing Duncan left on his desk.

It's the same drawing he always does: of a face with black scored-out holes for eyes.

*   *   *

17

Elizabeth goes into one of her quiet moods. She walks me and Alex to the swing park, then leaves us.

'See you at home,' she says, her voice sounding like we've not to follow too soon.

Sometimes if I'm not concentrating I still think we're living in our last house. We've moved twice now, usually when the mess gets too much. Elizabeth isn't sure if this means we live like kings – having a new house when it suits us – or like orphans. I prefer the king choice.

It's only Calum Ian and Duncan who've stayed true to their old home. This gets me the big envy sometimes, when I think of my old home, abandoned.

Alex and I sit on the swings for a bit, eating rice crackers with mango chutney spread on top.

The wind mushes the water in the bay, and the sun makes the mush glittery. The wrecked trawler out on the rocks of Snuasamul looks like the world's biggest whale. I hold it between finger and thumb. It's tiny.

Alex: 'Do you think there's a ghost on that ship?'

Me: 'As usual – too much imagination.'

Alex goes back to nibbling his cracker. He frowns at his chutney then says, 'Don't want more of this. If you eat the same thing over and over you get a heart attack.'

'Who says?'

'No one. I just think it.'

'Well you shouldn't think it. It's crazy! That's only if you eat too many chips and you get a fat arse and you smoke. If this isn't you, don't worry.'

18

He still looks worried, though, so I decide we need to do something brave, just the two of us.

First of all, I command us in getting an offering. We pick some of the flowers we don't know the names of, plus dandelions from the grass strip by the History Centre.

Then we go bit by bit closer to the side entrance of the big kids' school.

No one likes going here. They made it different to the little kids' school because of who they put in it.

It takes a while to get our confidence up: so we kick the rainbow-painted stones along the pathway, then run up and down the slopey concrete.

After that we go in.

The wind goes in first, fluttering leaves and bits of paper by the door. There's broken glass outside one room. Dirty black stuff in spots trailing up along the corridor. On both walls are the message boards. Some of the paper displays have come down. I hold one up: there's a bit at the top called 'Our Wall of Achievement', but the bit underneath has fallen away, so there's nothing. I think this is kind of funny in a dark way, but Alex doesn't.

He walks ahead of me, trying not to step on the black spots, or the rubbish.

He's looking at me for braveness, but I don't feel massively brave without Elizabeth.

Going through double doors, there's another corridor. Skylights making it go bright, dark, bright. A broken window inside one classroom: maybe a bird hit it, or the MacNeil

19

brothers throwing stones again? Rows of posters about bullying, some about road safety, some about littering. Along the corridor on brightly-coloured card, with a wiggly blue border, are the pictures of all the kids who went to school last year.

I'm there, in P4, alongside Duncan. Elizabeth is in P7. Calum Ian's in P6. Alex, only in P2. We didn't really know each other then, but we do now, for sure.

There's a short bit outdoors between our school and the big school. We get to the playground. It's marked up and ready for games: basket- and netball. The hill rising away behind, the rocks going silver with sun.

It's like going underwater. We put on our nose-clips, wait behind the door. Then I count to ten and go in.

Top corridor, heading to the gallery above the gym.

We put our perfume-hankies over our faces.

Going inside we hear a noise like the world's biggest bee. Millions of the world's biggest bees.

I run forward, and throw our flowers onto the dried and drying pile of old flowers – then we get out fast.

As the door slams I hear the flies buzzing up into the air. They're down in the gym. The noise is giant.

Back outside I smell myself for the stink that stays. It feels like we got away with it, just.

Elizabeth started the offerings. But she doesn't always like us doing it on our own, in case the dead down there make us sick. Still, I figure as long as we stay up in the gallery, run in and out, we'll be fine.

Alex doesn't look too much happier now that we've done a brave thing. His hands shake, only this time I don't think he needs food, or medicine, just fresh air.

Leaving him outside on his own I take a minute to go back to my old real classroom.

Its windows are broken, and the floor's wet; there's a shelf swollen from water. Some birds must have come in, because there are new trails of bird shit everywhere.

There's a rack with books on it. New books on it, neatly placed. 'Can I have a book for reading practice, miss? And for Alex? He's just started out.'

When I relax into it the teacher is there. She's sitting down, reading her own book. She takes off her glasses.

'Go on,' she says.

I sit in my old seat. Beside me is Anne-Marie. On the other side is David. In front is Margaret-Anne, and behind, Kieran. We take it in turns to read a bit of story. The teacher says, 'Very good: now it's Anne-Marie.' Then it's my turn to read, which I do while everyone else listens. I've always been a good reader in English, so it's easy, and I enjoy it and probably read longer than I should because the teacher forgets to ask me to stop.

When I can't read any more I close my eyes. I put my ear on the desk, ignoring the floor-noise, and try to hear them. I listen hard. Usually someone sniffing, or making a cough, or the sound when they move, a chair grating, a book opening, a pencil-scritch, anything.

But there's just the wind.

Sometimes the quiet gets on your nerves. You can hear

21

the whistle in your ears. The dogs and sheep are turned to dinosaurs. When it gets bad we turn on the CD player and listen to music. It's one reason we collect batteries. The MacNeil brothers I've heard tooting car horns for the same reason, and once I stood beside the War Memorial above Nasg and screamed just to be rid of it.

I get up, walk around the class. Some of my art is still on the wall from last autumn. Paintings of what our summer holidays were going to be this year. We were going to Glasgow, me and Mum, then on to a big water park in England which had blue and red slides, and a kids' club and face-painting, and bikes and lakes and all sorts of fun.

So this is what my painting shows: a water park in a forest. Except I never saw it in the end.

Alex looks fed up with me when I get back outside.

Alex: 'You leaved me alone.'

Me: 'You look like you're facing your worst enemy.'

Alex: 'A dog came and sniffed me. At least the dogs remembered to be my friend.'

Me: 'Was it in a pack? Was it a collie? Remember Elizabeth told us to stay back from them.'

Alex: 'Wasn't.'

We walk along for a bit, but he won't be encouraged. Soon he wants to just sit and stare at nothing. Knowing the warning signs I take four pink wafer biscuits from my emergency supply and stuff them in his gob.

After ten minutes he's less grumpy. I take a wet wipe and wipe a window in his dirty face.

He says, 'Sometimes I don't know why I get scared. I know I've got an illness, but it can't always be that, right? If I'm scared that's when I start thinking about zombies.'

Me: 'Well you shouldn't, because there aren't any.'

Alex: 'Not even new ones?'

Me: 'Not even.'

Alex: 'Not even of people?'

Me: 'Stop asking the same question differently.'

To cheer him up I show him the book I got in the library: it's called *Dr Dog,* and it's about a dog who's a doctor and who has to cure the Gumboyle family. The book is good, and makes him laugh. Job done.

Elizabeth is nowhere around. But anyway, we don't want to meet her because she'll just take us New Shopping, which nobody likes.

Instead we go Old Shopping, normal shopping, this time to the post office. I decide it's a mission, so we have to take out her list of rules to remind ourselves:

1. Stay together, and do not wander far.
2. Keep warm.
3. Put out something bright.
4. Look bigger.
5. Use the whistle for emergencies.
6. Don't eat anything you're suspicious of.
7. Stay away from deep water.

She always has rules, which I don't mind, though Calum Ian got fed up with it, and anyway said he was too wise for instructions coming from her.

The post office door is blue, with peeling paint. For old time's sake we knock on it. It's open anyway, like all the doors around here; even the doctor's surgery is open, though someone smashed the door for that.

Being in the post office gives me sad memories. Alex, however, likes playing with the ink stamps behind the counter, so I put up with it for him.

I borrow a sheet of first class stamps to take home for when we're drawing. Meanwhile Alex stamps his hands, his cheeks where I wiped, his knees, his nose. Now he's covered in POSTAGE PAID and looks chuffed.

Me: 'You're a weird kid.'

We leave the post office and go to the butcher's, which sells butcher's meat yes but also everything else. I mostly preferred the sweets. Mum likes the papers and rolls.

Each time you look at an empty shelf something new comes out. This is a skill I've learned. At first we didn't see the batteries – but then we did. Next came the tin of stew. Next came the big sausage of dog food (for befriending, not eating, Elizabeth claims). Next came the serviettes and cupcake papers (spare toilet paper). We used food colouring to mark the water we'd sterilised: that was Elizabeth's good idea. Drinking red water isn't so bad when you're used to drinking juice. But Alex thinks too much colouring makes it look like blood.

Now the shelves are empty. Nearly. There are two farmer's

journals with red scribbled names on them. There's swim-goggles, knitted jumpers, gloves. There's a plastic cricket set no one ever wanted.

I tug on the string of the cricket set. It's jammed. No, snagged at the back. Alex helps me push the shelf. It's easy to do cos it's empty and not stuck or nailed.

Dust, cobwebs, lentils. Then lucky kids on a mission: a packet of icing sugar! Squashed, yellow, but still sealed.

Me: 'The latest gossip is – I got a plan!'

Alex: 'I know your plan!'

We heave away the rest of the shelves. Some of the metal arms drop clanking. There's more cobweb-dust – then treasure. A tin of Scotch broth (unbuckled). A tin of hot dogs in brine. A packet of pastry mix. A packet of balloons. A plastic box of paperclips.

The pastry packet is open, mouldy. But the tins are good. Eager beavers, we pull all the shelves. We can't move the ones around the walls, they're fixed.

Still, it's been a good mission, one of our best.

'We got *so* lucky,' Alex says.

Calum Ian and Duncan are on the main street. We hide the things in our schoolbags, then shout on them. They're on a mission as well: with the cars, sucking petrol for their bonfire. Duncan still has his hood up, zipped up high so it's hard to see his eyes. From side-on I can only see his mouth: his lips are cracked and red from the petrol.

Calum Ian's lips are red as well. He wipes his mouth and spits like a granddad. '*A bheil am pathadh ort?*' he says, to

25

Alex, joking, while holding up the plastic milk bottle he uses to collect. Then says to me: 'You do it.'

He uses a stick to prise open the nearest petrol cap. When he gets the cap off I feed in the tube and suck, but I don't have enough suck to get it going. Calum Ian gets it started – but when he hands it over it spills past my mouth and I'm nearly sick with the smell.

'*Gloic!*' Duncan points at me and laughs.

Calum Ian demonstrates perfectly how it should be done: suck, finger on the end, drop the tube down, pour. Once it's started the petrol pours all by itself, and doesn't even want to stop. It fills three bottles.

When he's done Duncan uses gold spray-paint to write an *e* on the windscreen, for *e*mptied.

Seeing my bag he asks, 'What you got?'

Trying not to sound boastful about it I show them our treasures. Both of them whistle, then look very interested. Calum Ian checks the dates on the hot dogs, then the broth.

'Share and share?' he says.

I look for getting something back. But all he does is take the hot dogs, and the broth, and the icing sugar, leaving us just with the balloons and paperclips.

Alex, looking disappointed, asks if he can dip his thumb in the sugar just once.

'We'll need it for emergencies,' Calum Ian says, waving him away. 'All right then – swap you for petrol?'

'We don't want petrol.'

'All right. So have nothing.'

They pack our treasures away in their bags.

We follow behind, hoping to share back over as they suck more cars. It gets to me that I'm the smaller kid, and thinking of our reinforcement back at home I say, 'Why're you mean to Elizabeth at school?'

Calum Ian rubs his red mouth. 'She's fucking stuck-up.'

'No she isn't.'

'Aye she is. She's an incomer. Thinks she knows it all because of who her mam and dad were. But what did they do? Sat on their arses in the end. Never helped anybody. She only pretends being leader, I can tell it.'

'*You* aren't better.'

'*Gloic,* you should stick up for the island folk.'

'Stop calling me *Gloic.*'

Duncan gets between us. I think he's trying to get us to stop arguing, but I can't always feel he's on my side if Calum Ian is standing near.

'Just tell us your real nickname,' Duncan says, 'the secret one your mam used. What was it again? Then we'll stop using that one.'

I think it might be a trick, so I don't tell.

In the end it becomes a big deal. Duncan puts his hands together like he's praying for me to tell any answer: and I get so annoyed at him for this that I say, 'Your nickname is Scab Face.'

It makes him pull his jacket up high. He kicks at the wooden post of a fence, rather than me.

Calum Ian doesn't stand up for him with his sadness, which makes it worse, really.

They put the plastic milk bottles they filled in a shopping trolley, then begin to push it home.

We follow them for a bit, and I say they'll not be wanted if they come to visit later. Calum Ian makes an O with his mouth to show he doesn't care. Duncan has gone back to being invisible.

'Why'd you even collect petrol?' I shout. 'Your last fire didn't work.'

Calum Ian: 'So we're going to make the next one bigger. Plus I got a better idea for how to start it.'

'Your ideas never work.'

Now I get annoyed that they won't share food or plans. So when they're not looking I throw a stone which whizzes past Calum Ian's head. He just waves back.

Elizabeth is waiting for us at home. We tell her about the badly shared hot dogs and broth and icing sugar. She doesn't say much, just tells us how clever we were with our mission in the first place. Turns out, though, she's been New Shopping – and on her *own*.

There are new sheets on Alex's bed, plus tins of fruit and peas and carrots, and packet soups and biscuits. It's a very, very good result!

We don't ask where she went shopping, and she doesn't offer to tell. We look through some of the other things: candles, raisins, ancient treacle, coffee filter papers, even two packets of Jammie Dodgers.

Alex: 'Were these from a good house? I mean, were they opened already or near to—'

'All houses are good,' Elizabeth says quick, holding up her hand for no more questions.

'Can there be poison that gets—'

'*Shut up*, OK?'

For dinner we have to put all the food we might eat in a square for choosing. With the power of three we decide on chicken soup, beans on crackers, then raisins dipped in treacle. I like to spend ages reading the sides of the packets. Ingredients. Contents. Est weight. Best before.

Me: 'You know why they call them ingredients?'

Elizabeth: 'What's your idea again?'

Me: 'Because it's the stuff that makes you greedy. In-GREEDY-ents.'

Elizabeth does a half-and-half smile.

I go on reading the packets as she makes our soup. Wheatgerm, rice syrup, flavourings, colourings, E116. This is how clever the world once was! Not just cream with chicken. Your statutory rights. What about statutory wrongs? Customer queries, call this number. I've tried to call these numbers before, on our spare charged-up phone, but there's never any answer.

Just when I think Calum Ian and Duncan aren't coming because of the stone I threw, they do come.

They smell of bonfire. We don't ask what they've been doing. Their knees are scuffed and dirty and Duncan has black scorches on his shoes. In the shadows made by our torches his skin looks even bumpier.

We've all got scars: on our faces, on our backs and necks, from the sickness. I remember a lady on TV saying that the worse your scars, the worse the illness.

Duncan got the worst of all of us. After that it's Elizabeth, then Calum Ian, then me, then Alex.

Adults and littler kids had the worst scars of all. That's why they became so sick. That's why we have two separate places to go and remember them. See them.

We eat dinner, which is great because it's warm, then Calum Ian takes the best seat on the couch and says, 'Press play, Bonus Features.'

Alex gets called Bonus Features because that's what he thought the seventh *Star Wars* film was called. He's in charge of our battery-powered DVD player. Tonight he does adverts, by using some recordings we found, and then we get a film: *Tin Toy* from the *Toy Story* DVD.

It's very short though, and awful soon it's over.

Elizabeth: 'OK, batteries out.'

Both Duncan and Alex thump their arms and feet on the carpet.

'No no no!' shouts Alex.

'You're not the ruler of me!' says Duncan.

Alex becomes unmanageable for a bit. We try to ignore him but then Elizabeth remembers: his injection. He's in a different mood from this morning, though, and he struggles and cries and Calum Ian has to get involved to hold him down, which only makes things worse.

Afterwards Alex rubs his stomach and cries.

'I forgot not to be angry,' he says.

For a treat he's allowed batteries in his DS. For me, I decide to draw, so I tear a stamp from the book of stamps we found, and stick it in my drawing jotter. Beneath it, under the Queen's head, I draw a fat body with an old woman's stern hands and knees. Mum once said that the Queen had jewellery dripping

30

off her, so on her wrists I draw pearl bracelets with richness oozing.

Alex: 'The Queen lived on a farm in London.'

For some reason Calum Ian and Elizabeth find this funny. I find it a bit ignorant.

'D'you think the Queen died?' Alex asks.

'She was old,' Elizabeth answers. 'But her doctors would be the best. So maybe she didn't.'

Alex puts down his DS. 'I think she did die. I think she got sick. I think there's no Queen.'

Calum Ian: 'What about the Prime Minister? I bet they put him underground, miles under where there was no bad stuff could happen. I bet he's still there, eating apples, drinking milk. And I hope he chokes on some of that milk, and a bit of apple gets lodged and kills him.'

He chucks a rubber ball against the wall. When it comes back he catches it, nifty.

'Who's stronger – Santa or God?' Alex asks Elizabeth.

'That's a hard one . . .'

'Do you think Santa died?'

'*No*, of course he didn't. Santa can't die.'

'So then why didn't he come last Christmas?'

Elizabeth sits forward, sighs. 'I suppose I could say . . . well he's a supernatural being, like a god really, so he can't truly die. He's protected by force fields. He'll come this year, just you wait.'

Duncan makes a sound of spit in his throat which is disrespectful to Santa. Elizabeth does her frown at him to tell him not to give the game away.

31

Alex goes back to his DS for a bit. We hear swooshes and a beep-countdown then the game-over theme.

'I absolutely hate Santa,' he says.

Elizabeth: 'No you don't.'

'Yes I do. I hate him and I hate God. And I hate baby Jesus and I hate the tooth fairy.'

'You forgot the Easter bunny,' Duncan says, doing his sound of spit again.

Alex says nothing.

'Who wants a bedtime snack?' Elizabeth asks.

By bedtime snack she means supper. By dinner she usually means tea. And when she says lunch, really that means dinner. It's her own habit. I learnt that Elizabeth is in a separate country, and time, when it comes to food, because she's from England.

Now Calum Ian calls her an incomer – which is kind of true, but not truly kind.

'*Incomers* like their own name for food,' he says.

Elizabeth looks away sadly, so I decide to stand up for her at once: 'When Elizabeth's mum and dad came to the island, they decided it was too risky for babies to be born here,' I remind Calum Ian. 'This meant that I got born in Glasgow. Same with all the other kids at school. So we are *all* incomers. Which makes *you* the odd-one-out.'

Alex claps; Elizabeth smiles. Calum Ian gives me the rude two-finger sign.

We turn on the gas fire. It dances blue when I blow on it. I almost prefer it to the real fire. Elizabeth gets out the sleeping bags, and we gather in to toast biscuits.

In the fire-dark her skin looks bumpy like Duncan's. You can't tell where the black or the blue of her eyes are, which is kind of scary, so I try not to look.

'Do you think your mum and dad are dead?' I ask her, without even knowing I was going to.

This is against the rules. Nobody says so.

Elizabeth burns and burns her biscuit. The smoke of it gets up my nose. She could be waxwork.

'They are dead,' she says.

The ask was my fault: my bad idea. So it's my job right away to make her feel better. I say, 'When my mum comes back from the mainland, the worst thing will be telling her about Granny, and the cousins. And my aunts and uncles. It's going to be terrible. I'll be glad to see her, but it'll be terrible all the same.'

Elizabeth says nothing. So I try again: 'My school book last year said three new babies are born for every two people dying. So at the gates of heaven it's: hullo, hullo, hullo. Goodbye, goodbye. That's the rule.'

Elizabeth just stares at her singed biscuit.

'Don't know where my mum and dad are,' Alex says, licking his biscuit. 'The last time I saw Mum, she was just away for a minute. Wish they'd come home.'

'Our dad's away on his boat,' Duncan says, before Calum Ian can stop him. 'He was gone away to bring food back from the mainland. That's why we can't be staying with you lot. We were told to wait at home. Sorry, but he ordered us there.'

'Always do as we're told,' Calum Ian says.

This makes the MacNeil brothers remember about leaving.

33

They want to get back before it's dark. I ask Elizabeth if I should follow them and get back our food, but she tells me just to forget about it.

Our house is the shape of a loaf tin. It's good because it doesn't have any wrong smell. Also, there are three beds in one room, so we can sleep together. Also, it has a gas stove (Calum Ian changes the cylinders) and thick walls and a roof with flat bits for collecting rainwater.

Also, it's not any of our old homes. This helps us to become a fresh family. Which is especially good for Elizabeth, who has no family of her own.

Before bed it's tick-check time, then we do the routine with the radios.

Same static-noise as always.

We unpick the cereal boxes from the skylight, and lie heads together under the window. I forgot that in the summer stars don't exist. In wintertime you can even see them going to school in the morning.

Now Elizabeth tries to remember all the things her dad said about the stars, and the sky. It doesn't last very long. Usually if I've run out of memories I make stuff up, but she has a rule for herself against that.

'The past is precious,' she says. 'It has to be correct.'

It's when she starts remembering about planets going around the sun, and moons going around the planets, that I remember – the riddle that Mum told me. And because it's a true memory, I want to tell it.

It must be a good one, a good riddle, because it gets them quiet. I know the answer but I won't tell them.

'You could give us a clue,' grumbles Alex.

'OK, here.'

For one clue only, I hold up my drawing of the Queen.

When Elizabeth puts on the night light I promise to tell them the next day if they still haven't guessed.

Back Bay

Time – now

It's not a very good day for seeing far out to sea. I sometimes forget to keep watching.

This morning the rain was marching adults in my dream. Mum used to call that sort of thing 'wishful thinking'. She never said if wishing worked.

Then there are other things: things you didn't wish for. Like the Gaelic weather sticker at the end of my bed. It said, '*Tha i grianach*'. I had to tear it, right through the happy face of the sun underneath.

All around the ferry building I put cups. Some of the plastic ones blew over, so I put round smooth stones from the shore-line in to steady them better.

Then I waited. And waited. I saw the sky go bright in a place I'd never seen bright before. So what did that mean?

Did you think it was a good idea, Mum, or not?

After the light got halfway I could see my reflection in the water under the pier.

A girl with long hair. Looking like she had a beard: her hair down in straggles, covering her face.

A reminder of who we found after we saw the painted dogs.

'Looks like you're facing your worst enemy,' I say to the girl. But she wins in the end by hiding herself in ripples.

Later, I went to put flowers on the sea, to remember my friends, but the tide got me, up to my waist. That was a slip-up. I have to be more careful nowadays.

I have to think of everything.

It's too easy to make mistakes. Two days ago, when I was on watching duty, I accidentally looked at the sun with the telescope. Since then there's been a black moon in the middle of what I'm seeing.

Even so, I'm a smarter kid for having it. I won't make the same mistake twice. Because the more mistakes I make, the smarter I'll get.

Still, the thing to worry about is this: how many mistakes is a person allowed? How many mistakes can a single person make and still *be*? There isn't a rule, or none that Mum ever told me.

She's telling me the answer to her riddle. It's time to pay attention: everything else can wait.

Now I see her, and I bury down to the bottom of my sleeping bag as the sound of her starts to become real: '*What goes around the world but stays in the corner?*'

Mum's wearing her red and blue post office jacket. She asks the question in English so we know it's a riddle.

We pass by Mr MacKinnon's blue-eyed collie, the one that's always on guard. Then the phone box. Then the forest of fifteen trees, then Orasaigh, the island where the rats used to live. Floraidh MacInnes once told me that there was a storm and all the rats came ashore and ate the annoying cats, but she's a liar, I never believed her.

'A shy man on a boat?' I answer.

'Works fine. I accept it works fine, but it's not the answer I was looking for. Try again.'

It's my work to get the bundles together. Mum's fingers are inky from the packets. She whistles up for hills and down for dips. She keeps spare elastic bands in a coil around her wrist which make her hand go puffy.

'My stand-in is coming tomorrow,' she says. 'He's not been before. Early ferry, with any luck. Then that's you and me are away on our Christmas shopping. How good is that?'

I give her the thumbs-up. It's damp, but the heaters blast dryness. We go on the east road first, because most people live on that side of the island, then onto the north road.

My favourite postbox is the one which fills with sand in a west wind. It crackles inside like a shell.

Mum hands out biscuits to all the dogs that bark. She says that if we give enough biscuits to the barking dogs they'll be too fat and soft in the head to chase us.

'*Chan ith a shàth ach an cù*,' she says, testing me as we drive away from another one. 'Your mother wants to know the English translation – go ahead.'

'None but a dog eats his fill.'

'Apart from auld Eric in Cleit who wants to dig his ain grave with his teeth – well done.'

Mum said she learnt everything at school but the old sayings; now she wants me to know them, too.

'Look, will you,' she says. 'Washing out in the rain.'

The washing is Mrs Barron's. Mum chaps on her door. Mrs Barron is OK. Mum gets permission to take in her sheets, and when she comes back she smells of mist. Mrs Barron has handed her a letter for posting. The letter has a lovely stamp: hummingbird, green and gold.

She hands the letter to me and I put it in the going-away postbag.

'Using up his collection,' Mum says. 'Since Mr Barron died. Last year it was Jubilee editions. I'm forever telling her that it's like tearing up ten pound notes – but she has her ain mind.'

I let my fingers sift the letters in the bag. Some are smooth, others pebbly.

There's a sheep scratching its arse on the last postbox before we get on the round back for home.

'Fine day for it,' Mum says, as she unlocks and empties the postbox beside the sheep. She's mostly polite to animals in case they're the departed returned.

When she gets back in the car I answer, 'Stamp.'

Mum draws a tick in the air. 'Full marks, *a ghraidh*! Around the world, yet stays in the corner. You got it perfect.'

'But that doesn't work, Mam. What if you posted a coconut? Or any round thing, like a ball? There wouldn't be corners then.'

'*Seadh?* When did you hear of anyone posting coconuts or footballs? Is that even likely?'

'It's exactly where your riddle doesn't work.'

The ribbon road shines with sun and rain. Eilean Mor shows through rags of cloud.

On the drive around to the south road Mum stops to ask the cows if they've ever heard the like of posting coconuts.

The cows look up for a bit, before going back to their usual grass-chewing.

It's like stones you find on the beach. Polish them, make them shine. Keep them warm in your hand.

Make a new ending. Where nobody gets sick, and the electricity comes back, like it should've done, like it always did when there was only a storm.

Nineteen days ago

It's a clock which wakes me, which means I'm in trouble, as the alarms were meant to be turned off.

There's a big mess in the room. I only notice it when it gets bad enough to hide nearly all the floor. There's dirty clothes belonging to Alex: hanging in fankles from the pram we brought in last night. I think the pram was from a game he was playing: another game where he fell asleep and had to be lifted to bed.

We began shopping for clocks to keep time. Best of all is the radio-clock which Calum Ian found, which even tells the day of the week and the date. Still though, it doesn't remind you of what dates are important, or the dates you might forget. Alex couldn't remember his birthday: was it the 11th or 12th of March? Then when the lambs came nobody knew if that meant it was Easter, or spring.

We found a diary in the post office which gave us the date of Easter. But what about spring? Then Duncan noticed we'd passed a day called *British Summer Time Begins.* That told us

41

it was summer, and that we were already in it. But where had spring gone?

I looked in the library, but there wasn't any useful books on it, not even in *Space & Time*.

Elizabeth is writing a new sign. She adds to the bottom of it then pins it between our beds, next to the posters for *Health and Wellbeing* and *Food Groups* and *How We Grow*.

Alex stands in front, reading slowly with his finger.

RULES FOR OUR HOME

1. Tidy as you go.
2. Share food & don't waste food.
3. Paper plates save water.
4. Make your own bed. ~~I am not your mother~~
5. Don't go to the toilet too close to the back door.
6. Dog poo on shoes indoors – bad!
7. Save batteries – don't leave torches on at night.
8. Matches, matches do not touch, they can hurt you very much.
9. Ghosts & zombies are not real.
10. If it smells – don't eat (main exseptions food in tins, vinegar, food in jars, mushroom soup.)
11. Teamwork will work!
12. Alarm off on every clock!!

Alex and I stare at the rules, wondering who's to blame. I decide that the rules fit most for him – apart from the mushroom soup and vinegar and alarms bit, and the bit about dog shit, which was anyway a mistake.

Me: 'All we needed to do was check our feet. And paper plates, they get mushy after a while.'

Alex: 'A minute after you put me to bed I'm asleep and the torch stays on all by itself.'

Me: 'All flavours of soup stink.'

Alex: 'Would we get a dog? If we had a stray dog we wouldn't need to waste a single drop of food.'

Me: 'You can't trust dogs to watch your food. Anyway, Alex always stands in dog shit. It's disgusting.'

Alex: 'You're a dog shit.'

Me: 'You're the *king* of dog shits.'

Elizabeth: 'Stop it, both of you! OK? All I want is for you to help me a bit more, that's all.'

We go back to staring at the rules. Most hark back to something that's happened. It's hard to get everything right all of the time. Still, Alex does need to be reminded about matches. That's a big fascination of his.

We get up, get dressed, do the routine: radios (fizzing noise), teeth (gums fine). I put batteries in the portable TV/DVD player. Snowstorm. Alex takes his injection without fuss this morning, then we have our breakfast. Today for a treat it's creamed rice, which I used to hate but now love, especially with jam. Then when we're done Elizabeth goes through the cupboards, making notes of anything we need. I have a suspicion of what she's going to say before she comes out with it.

Elizabeth: 'There's a big issue I kept off the rules. It would be great if you'd help.'

Alex's eyes swing up from sucking his sleeve.

'It would really help if you'd come New Shopping. Even if

you end up staying outside, it doesn't matter. It'd just be a help to have the company.'

Alex switches from sucking his sleeve to the neck of his T-shirt. The drool on his clothes makes him stink like a dog's bone. I tell him to pack it in.

Elizabeth: 'I'd appreciate it.'

Alex: 'What about Duncan, and Calum Ian? Can they not be your sidekicks?'

Elizabeth: 'Maybe they've decided to do their own shopping? I didn't even ask. All I know is I can't do ours all by myself.'

We think about it. Alex looks very doubting. He plays a blasting game with the lightsaber I made him out of yellow card and tinfoil.

Alex: 'There is actually a black lightsaber.'

He says this when he's trying to put you off. Usually the conversation goes: There is a black lightsaber – No there isn't – Yes there is – No there can't be because light is not black – Yes there is cos I saw it in my *Star Wars Clone Wars Encyclopaedia*. And black light is radiation. So there. This is what he says when he's trying to pull the wool over.

Me: 'Can we do something fun first?'

Elizabeth: 'Like—?'

Me: 'Can we go to the rocks and chuck bottles?'

Elizabeth: 'We don't just *chuck* bottles: we *send messages*. There has to be a purpose to everything.'

Alex: 'Why?'

Elizabeth: 'Because we lost our adults. Because we're alone. So we do all we can, every minute of every day, to get help. Agreed?'

44

It isn't always nice when she spells it out. Anyway, school's cancelled. To make the agreement proper I head up to Elizabeth's rule list and add underneath:

13. All go shopping (after nice stuff.)

This settles the business for the three of us. Then we shake on it so nobody can go back on their word.

We take the shore road towards Leideag. Some birds flap around like flags. Out to sea, those islands I can't remember the names of. We always look for boats, though our eyes are getting used to not finding them.

Further along we join the beach. There's a lot of mess on the sand, though nothing new. A jumble of rubber tyres with faded labels on them. Hundreds of kids' plastic chairs, the sort you'd find in a playhouse. There was a skeleton in oilskins, now there's just oilskins. Now and then the beach changes and a bone sticks out. Calum Ian and Duncan hate this beach, because they're scared the bones and skeletons could be one of their uncles.

We come to the life jacket that used to be around the skeleton. It's got foreign writing on it. It might be Spanish, or French? Anyway, it isn't a local fisherman. Elizabeth has told this to the boys, but they're too superstitious to even come close and they won't ever listen.

A track takes us to the end of Leideag, to the radio mast and Message Rock. Calum Ian worked out it's the best place to launch bottles: because it's the bit of land sticking out, it's outside the bay, and also, the island Orasaigh stops the bottles

45

coming back in again. He even put out two markers – yellow wellie boots – at the best launch-off.

But now he won't come, because he got cross last time we all came. The argument began with Alex:

Alex: 'Don't want to throw mine in.'

Elizabeth: 'But you're not losing it. You're telling your wish to the sea by sending. That's the rule.'

Calum Ian: 'A lot of rubbish, making wishes. *Seadh*, I bet they won't come true. I bet we all end up wishing for the same thing. That would be dumb.'

Elizabeth: 'We might not.'

Calum Ian: 'So what'd you wish for? And you? And you? Aye: you all wished for everyone to come back, didn't you?'

Me: 'How did you know?'

Calum Ian: 'Stupid fucking rubbish, wishes.'

But this morning it's just us three. For my message I draw a picture of me with realistic hair standing beside our house. The house is a deliberate kid's version (lots of square windows, a pig's tail of smoke from the chimney) for extra impact. Alex has drawn himself holding a black lightsaber. No details. Elizabeth has done all the details of herself: address, age, name, family name, class at school, hair colour, cos she's like that.

We get to the sticking-out edge of Message Rock and chuck them in. My one seems to wait for a bit – then it hurries off. It always seems to be mine that gets washed back up on the beach, which makes Alex gloat. He says he has a better throw than me, but I think it's just luck.

At school we learnt about St Kilda. The people there ran out of food and they got tetanus and anyway there was no

46

TV so they sent sea-mail. Sea-mail from St Kilda doesn't get to America, it gets to the mainland. It's a law of nature for all time. When the rescuers finally got to St Kilda the men had waited so long they'd grown beards. No one wanted to stay after, so that was the end of St Kilda.

We watch the tide as it starts to cover the rocks guarding the bay. There's seals on the rocks, curled up like black bananas, not caring about what happened.

Me: 'To the seals it's all normal. Except for the rubbish, and the oil slick, which anyway didn't last.'

Alex: 'I used to think there was a plughole and the sea was a sink. That's why the tide went up and down.'

Elizabeth: 'It's a good idea.'

Me: 'It's eejit-talk.'

Alex: '*You're* an eejit.'

Me: 'Do whales not hibernate?'

Elizabeth: 'I don't think so. I never heard of that.'

Alex: 'Why don't people hibernate? Bears do. And squirrels. And birds.'

Me: 'Birds don't hibernate you eejit!'

Elizabeth: '*Nobody's* an eejit, OK? It's a good question. I don't know why people don't hibernate. We're mammals after all, and some mammals hibernate.'

Alex: 'Do you think my mum and dad might be hibernating?'

Elizabeth looks away to the wrecked trawler.

If the sun's low we can watch the bottles bobbing and shining for a bit, until they pass over to the sound. This morning it isn't long before they disappear, which makes me think about how big the sea is.

Big enough for the nearest island to be blue. The mainland, to be gone.

Back when we used to take the ferry it was five hours to Oban. It never seemed too far when there were TVs and DVDs and games and dinner and showers and friends to run around with. But now the sea goes on for ever.

Alex: 'Goodbye bottle.'

Me: 'It can't hear you, it's a bottle.'

Alex: 'Are you sure there's no ghosts on that ship?'

Elizabeth: 'Positive.'

Alex: 'My bad dream is when everyone starts to come alive. I see them coming from the boat. They walk along the bottom of the sea. Then they start to come up the beach and I'm running and crying. But I'm not proper running – my legs are too slow. Are you *really* sure?'

Elizabeth: 'Yes.'

Alex: 'How sure?'

Elizabeth: 'Listen: Dad said there was no such thing as ghosts. He said ghosts were just a figment of the imagination.'

Alex: 'What's a figment?'

Elizabeth: 'A part that's not real. A part you ignore.'

There's no hazard tape on the door. Elizabeth's rule for this is: Be aware anyway. Someone was digging in the back garden: there's a pit, lined with tatty plastic. There's no broken windows, and the door's unlocked.

Elizabeth goes in first. 'Hullo?' she shouts.

No answer.

The carpets are red and gold in patterns like a king's robes.

No smell. So far. Stairs with a metal chair for going up and down on, for someone old, or with a bad back, or broken legs. Elizabeth signals us in.

Downstairs there's a front room, kitchen. It's very untidy. The walls are golden from smoking. Out the kitchen window we see a back garden with gnomes. Some of them are fallen over, sleeping. Windchimes trying to wake them up.

In the kitchen cupboards of old people you'll usually find golden syrup, gravy powder. Good finds today: oatcakes, digestives, lemon curd. Hot chocolate to add to our hot chocolate supply back home.

The fridge: shut. I wear my perfume-hanky and open it. Instant pong. The food inside gone slurpy black. Elizabeth works away behind me, collecting all the worthy stuff I can't be fashed getting: hand-spray, mousetraps, gloves, hats, scarves, clothes. Alex comes back from the cupboard under the stairs with new bedsheets.

'This is good – we're working as a team,' Elizabeth says. 'See? It isn't so bad, is it?'

Alex: 'It *is* so bad. I'm never wearing those. That's a scarf for an old dead lady, it's poisoned.'

'You won't be saying that when it gets cold.'

'It's summertime. It won't get cold.'

'It will in winter.'

'But we won't be here in winter. We'll be rescued by then, won't we?'

Elizabeth doesn't even answer, just packs her New Shopping into plastic bags.

Upstairs, there's a bathroom, two bedrooms. The bath and

sink are unfilled. The main bedroom has one enormous TV. Nobody in the bed, but we knew that because there was no smell. Pill packets, dried-out cups, plates. A cross on the wall. Loads of old-fashioned DVDs, which Elizabeth says are of a type called westerns. *Shane. High Noon. The Magnificent Seven.* It smells of dust. There's a dressing table with loads of pairs of crinkled tights hanging from its mirror.

The bed feels warm where the sun was on it.

Alex: 'Dust is skin. Every single second skin is falling off you. But how does dust fall when nobody's home?'

Elizabeth: 'Dust is other things as well.'

By the end, we've got a good haul. Elizabeth finds creams called Elocon and Eumovate and Liquid Paraffin, which she says are good for skin. Alex finds a ship in a bottle, plus the bedsheets. I find another clock to add to our collection. The clock is called a barometer. Elizabeth says it measures air. Right now the air is 𝕱𝖆𝖎𝖗.

We almost go right into next door. But Alex stops us.

'That's my auntie's house.'

'Are you sure?'

''Course I'm sure! I always came here. That's her name if you want proof.'

We read the doorplate. Then Elizabeth finds a scrumple of tape by the step.

Then I notice a **B** sprayed in gold on the doorframe.

Me: 'I think . . . Calum Ian's been in.'

Alex: 'He can't do that! He shouldn't be going into my auntie's house!'

Elizabeth: 'Look . . . let's just move on to the next house, all right?'

The tape makes a ripping then a sucking noise as we pull it off. Flies come out – we wait for them to stop. There's a smell. Elizabeth pushes the door, but it's stuck.

We know already what the problem is. There's someone behind it.

Actually it isn't a someone, it's a some*thing*. A dog. Gone flat, like dead things usually are.

It's easy to push aside. Once inside we find a carpet to cover the dog over with.

You can hardly even see it, once it's covered.

Duncan used to reckon that dead things went flat because their souls had left their bodies.

He told us that Father MacGill once mentioned an experiment where they tried to measure the weight of a person's soul, by taking their weight before and then after they had died. The difference in the sums, he said, was how much the person's soul weighed.

Calum Ian, however, thought it was rubbish.

'Flatness is the difference between sheep and sheepskin rugs,' he said. 'It's fuck all to do with souls.'

The carpets are grey, the walls white. It feels like a dentist's. In the front room there's a fishtank. The water has turned green. The dead fish are floating in stringy black bits of mould. I go to dip my finger into the water just to hear what the plop sounds like.

Elizabeth: 'Don't!'

51

She comes and sprays my hand with soap.

There's a big mess in the kitchen. Wood splinters, dust, bits of ceiling. The roof's broken down. Amongst the dust and splinters are lots of black bags, tied. I check inside, but they're empty. They feel damp still.

Me: 'What happened?'

Elizabeth: 'The roof caved in.'

This person was starting to get prepared. We find pots filled with water, but not covered. The downstairs bath got half-filled, but still not yet covered. The windows of one room are blocked with cardboard and sheets.

Then in a hallway cupboard we find food hidden in a cardboard box – enough, maybe, for weeks.

Alex: 'We can eat and eat!'

Me: 'And eat and eat!'

At the back of the cupboard there's plastic tubs with the most complicated labels I've seen. The tubs contain pink stuff, brown stuff, yellow stuff. They are called recovery drinks. Elizabeth sniffs, tastes, then mixes some with her water bottle. She tries it, then gives me some.

'Maybe OK?' I say.

We find chocolate bars called *Maxifuel Protein*. In a big box. Meal replacement, it says. Hooray! We can eat just bars! No more tins! But they don't taste much like chocolate, more like bad fudge. I don't like them.

Me: 'They safe?'

Elizabeth: 'I think they are. Still in date.'

We find the person upstairs. I was expecting a man, but it's a woman. She's a mystery. She's on the toilet floor. The floor has fallen through to downstairs. Her mask has slipped to her neck, with lots of brown spots on it: sick, or blood. There are towels laid out on the floor. The towels are dirty. There's broken glass. There's little red and white pills spilt in the bathroom. They're stuck to the tiles like they got glued on. She's wearing clothes like an Olympic runner. There's mushy spots on her skin.

We gather our shopping on the front step. Elizabeth takes her blue spray-can and sprays a **B** on the door.

Alex: 'No more New Shopping. *Please.* Can we not just stay outside now? I don't want to do any more.'

Elizabeth: 'You've done really, really well. Thank you. No more for today. We're done.'

Alex: 'Are you being truthful?'

Elizabeth: 'Yes.'

Alex: 'Why do we have to bother?'

Elizabeth: 'Because we need to do all we can to survive OK? Remember? Anyway, I didn't ask you to come upstairs with me. You should've stayed downstairs.'

Alex: 'It was too late. I was there.'

I fill my backpack while Alex frets, and while Elizabeth adds the house to our map of food-stores.

People are mostly dead in bed, or in the toilet, or between the two. They smell the worst of all things, worse than cats or dogs. So you get in and out fast. And you don't look at them in case the memory of the way they look becomes long-term.

Mum always said about bad stuff on the internet: 'Never look for bad stuff because you can't unsee it.'

*   *   *

On the way back home we stop at the cool box. For the past month, since the world started to feel warm, Elizabeth has kept Alex's injections in a cool box in the stream beside our village.

Now she takes the foil packet out and stares at what's left inside. When I try to be nosy, she shuts the box.

As soon as her back is turned I sneak a peek inside.

Me: 'There's hardly any!'

Elizabeth: '*You* . . . We've loads. OK? Enough for months.'

Me: 'But just one packet . . .'

Elizabeth: '*Shut up* about it.'

Then it's sandwich time: crackers, corned beef. Corned beef is the opposite of a Wow Word as it doesn't taste of corn or beef. Today Elizabeth has made jelly-water. Our water on its own tastes of coal and chlorine, but add a packet of jelly cubes and it tastes like sweets.

After this she gives us each a tablet, which she says is a vitamin. Alex looks very suspicious about his, and so do I.

Me: 'Where – honestly – did you get these?'

Elizabeth: 'Shopping.'

Me: 'New or Old?'

Elizabeth: 'Just shopping.'

Me: 'Did you get them from a bad house?'

Elizabeth: 'Just because something comes from a bad house doesn't mean it's *actually* bad.'

Me: 'I'm not keen.'

Alex: 'Is it safe for diabetes?'

Elizabeth looks surprised, like she hadn't thought of this. She digs out the boring book she always carries and reads it, frowning. In a long time she looks up.

'It doesn't mention vitamins . . . truthfully then, I don't know. I think it'll be all right.'

Me: 'Polar bears have too many vitamins in their livers. You should check it isn't made of polar bear.'

Elizabeth: 'I think it would say on the packet. Like with cod liver oil for instance.'

Me: 'And hot dogs, for instance.'

Elizabeth: 'Smart arse.'

In the end we flick our vitamins into the stream. Elizabeth looks sad about it, but doesn't stop us. It's good fun, and I want to flick more, but she won't allow.

'We're not getting enough fruit,' she says. 'I did a project last year about sailors in the olden days. They got something called scurvy. That's where you need vitamin C. Your gums and skin start to bleed. Well, Calum Ian and Duncan have very red mouths, don't they?'

Me: 'That's because they're always sucking petrol for their stupid bonfires that never work.'

Elizabeth doesn't disagree.

Me: 'Know something? I got reminded there about our hot dogs. Remember, that the boys took? Well I want them back. It still gets me fed up that they stole them.'

Elizabeth: 'Best forgotten.'

Me: 'No it isn't. I bet they have hundreds of stuff in their house. I bet they eat all night until they're sick.'

Alex: 'If I get sick the thingamabob that hangs down my throat comes out.'

Elizabeth: 'Rubbish, it only *feels* like it does.'

Me: 'I think we should go to war with them.'

Elizabeth: '*Nobody's* going to war. We all need to stick together. Remember – what's going to work?'

We deliberately don't say – *teamwork*.

When Elizabeth and Alex go back home I lie and say I'm going for a walk.

It's not usual for me to go alone, but she looks fed up or in a sad mood again so I get away with it.

I know their garden right away. I know their street even, because of all the black bits from fires.

Six of the posts along one fence, charred and burnt. Burnt black spots of grass, like a spaceship landed and bounced. A whole front garden, burnt in a square. A kid's plastic go-kart half-melted into glue.

They haven't burnt their own garden. The nameplate says R. MACNEIL. I spy around the windows like Ruby Redfort on a mission. They must be upstairs.

A sprinkled heap of coats in the hall. The carpet looks worn, but then I see it's dried mud. Two pairs of wellies, neatly together. There's a family smell, stronger than Duncan's even, sort of like gammon crisps.

The living room's a mess. Bits of fishing rod, nets, lines, lumps of metal. There's a lot of empty cereal packets. Standards are slipping, Mum would say. There's shopping baskets on the floor full of games, DVDs. Some of the DVDs have been melted, by Duncan I guess.

A jar on the table, full of brown muck, with darts in it. What's that all about? It smells bad.

They must be out. I do an actorly halloooo up the stairs, but nobody shouts back.

I go upstairs. The first room must be Duncan's: it's a mess across the floor and smells of socks. The next room is very tidy, with even the bed made. Posters of football players, blue bedsheets, boxing gloves.

But then I realise that they're not sleeping in either of these rooms because there's another room: with a big bed for adults. On top of this bed are two sleeping bags, with a pillow at one end and a pillow at the other.

So many beds, they didn't know which to choose. Calum Ian's teddy is a monkey. Duncan's is an Eeyore with all the stuffing coming out. Their pillows are manky, with brown bits and spots of blood on Duncan's.

I look around the room. Duncan's fiddle books, like he was reading them before bed. Then inside Calum Ian's sleeping bag I see a drawing book.

The first drawing is of five kids, made up like a family. A man and a wife, one big son, middle daughter, little son. All holding hands.

With a longer look I see that the family is *us*. And Calum Ian made himself the dad, and Elizabeth his wife.

Feeling disgusted but still laughing, I punch Duncan's pillow. But it feels hard, nearly breaks my hand – I find a fishing trophy hidden under it.

The trophy has his dad's name, next to *Silver Darling – One Day Winner.*

Underneath Calum Ian's pillow – there's a camera.

It's got batteries. It's working. It takes me ten or twenty seconds to work it out. AUTO to get snappy, ▶ to look.

I take a picture of my knees, both feet, then my big toes.

Then the back of my throat to show the thingamabob that Alex was talking about. That looks weird.

I choose GALLERY, and find loads of other pictures besides the ones I just did. There's one of Calum Ian and his mum. Duncan and his mum. Then the boys and their little sister Flora, who was nearly at school. Then a picture of their mum on the front step with a big stomach, holding around it with proud hands.

I go through the photos, up and down. The dates go from March to November last year. By December everything bad had started to happen, so the family snaps here must be the last they took.

In a box at Calum Ian's side of the bed are some real pictures. A marrying one of his mum and dad. He's wrapped them in clingfilm for keeping good.

I put the camera back, and go back downstairs. Their kitchen is like after a bomb. Skyscrapers of dirty plates and cups. Maybe Elizabeth was right about using paper plates. And mouldy tins in a bin overflowing.

Then I find that the cupboards are completely stuffed with food – which they should have shared. There is about a hundred packets of digestive biscuits! Plus crackers galore! And UHT milk, in proper-sized cartons!

Then I see our tins of broth and hot dogs, already opened, eaten.

And I get very, very angry.

I've been told by Mum about anger. If you close your eyes and count to ten it either doesn't matter or you've forgotten. Anger is like adverts that way. Also, don't let your mum brush your hair if she's angry. And if she's angry and asks 'Do I look stupid?' do not answer.

I think about this, but I'm still mad. So I take one packet of biscuits and open them and stamp them into the floor. Then I take two cartons of milk, and pour them onto the biscuits. Then I take a tin of soup and open it and pour the soup over the kitchen chairs. Then I find crisps: when we thought crisps were extinct. I eat as much crisps as I can, then throw the rest around like confetti.

Then I get the best idea. I go upstairs and take the camera out from under Calum Ian's pillow. Then I go for ▶ and press OK then MODE MENU then CARD SET UP then ALL ERASE. ARE YOU SURE? GO →→ OK.

I take one picture of me smiling, then leave.

To put the cherry on the cake I borrow Calum Ian's spray-can and spray a big gold **G** on their front door, adding extra curly bits to show I was only joking: **G̵**.

When I get home I find out *that's* where the MacNeil brothers have been.

Everyone is standing around Duncan like he's become very important.

His face looks queer. It's red on one side and so puffy his cheek droops and you can't see his eye.

Me: 'You're turning into a pig.'

Duncan looks sad about this, but too tired for fighting. Elizabeth glares at me and kneels between us.

'Does it hurt?' she asks.

Duncan doesn't mention if it does. Calum Ian says, 'I'm always warning him, I'm *forever* warning him, but does he listen? His fingers were manky when he was picking at his scabs. He's an eejit; he needs back in Cròileagan.'

Nursery was years ago for Duncan – so it's not kind to tell him this. His good eye grows the spike of a tear and his mouth turns down.

Elizabeth goes to her bedside cabinet and takes out three of the books from her boring book collection. The first is called *Medicine for the Rural Doctor*. The second, *Clinical Medicine*. The third, *A Colour Atlas of Dermatology*. This is an atlas not with maps but with pictures, and of faces and bodies. Two of the books have her mum's name written on the inside. On the other she's written: *Belonged to Dad*.

Elizabeth: 'The redness, it sort of stops in the middle . . . Is there a problem where it can stop like that?'

Calum Ian: 'Look at *these*!'

Me: 'Some of those pictures are scary.'

Alex: 'I'll get a wrong dream . . .'

Elizabeth: 'Let me mark the page – stop, give them back.'

Me: 'That's rotten!'

The book is something you can't stop looking at, even if you close your eyes. The pictures make me laugh and gasp. But then Elizabeth is shushing us, and I realise that we must have forgotten about looking after Duncan. He's holding his hood up high over his face.

We look as seriously as we can. Elizabeth goes through all the pictures. Then she puts a plastic strip on Duncan's forehead which glows red for hotness.

Elizabeth: 'He has an infection.'

Duncan: 'Don't tell me it's bad, please . . .'

Elizabeth: 'Is your eye sore?'

Duncan: 'How can an eye be sore? It's just sore if you get a stick in it or something. Your eye can't *get* sore.'

Elizabeth: 'Around the edges? Your eye*lid*?'

Duncan: 'Oh aye. *That's* sore.'

In the end we can't decide if Duncan has *Rosacea, Forehead*, or *Acne Vulgaris, Cystic, Face*, or *Herpes Zoster, Ophthalmic distribution*, or *Erysipelas, Face* or *Impetigo Contagiosa*, or *Dermatitis / Eczema, Secondary spread face*.

Calum Ian: 'It all looks the same.'

Me: 'Could it be all of them at the same time?'

Elizabeth: 'I don't think so. That's not likely.'

Me: 'Then just some of them?'

Elizabeth: 'Don't know.'

Calum Ian: 'I thought you *did* know? I thought you were the doctor's girl, who had learnt everything before going to big school? That's what *we* believed. Or what you wanted *us* to believe.'

Elizabeth looks hard at the book. Then she asks us for an extra moment, and goes out into the garden.

Alex eats a biscuit and stares at Duncan as if he were a dinosaur in a museum. I look at Calum Ian and say, 'You actually like Elizabeth, don't you? Bet you draw pictures of her at home where she's the mum and you're the dad and we're the kids. Bet you do.'

Calum Ian's face changes and changes: the last change turning out to be the worst.

'Where you fucking been, *Gloic*?' he says. Then: 'You fucking stay away from our house, all right?'

Too late – I'm thinking.

For about the first time, though, I have doubts about what I did.

I go to the window. Elizabeth is in the corner of the garden. She's talking with nobody there.

When I go outside she stops. When I ask who she was talking to she says, 'Nobody.' She looks shy again when I ask if it was her mum or dad.

'Don't worry about it,' I tell her. 'It's natural. I talk to other people all the time.'

'I know you do,' she says.

We stand staring at her book. It's open on a page, of a sad boy with angry skin and terrible bumps on his face. The illness he has is called *Smallpox, Scarring of Face*.

Me: 'Is that the illness we all got?'

Elizabeth shakes her head.

'It looked a bit like that. But I checked before. The illness we had isn't even in the book.'

The wind hushes and shushes across the grass. Elizabeth looks at me funnily. Then she takes my hand and says, 'We need to go up to the hospital. He needs antibiotics. I don't want to go there on my own.'

The hospital was built on its own rocky shore. Mum used to call it a cottage hospital, but that's false because it's not a

62

cottage. It's not a hospital either: more like a long house, or a small fish factory. Part of it was a nursing home, which is where my granny lived before she died. Her window had a good view of the bay. You could spy kayakers or seals or birds or ferries from it.

We go in a side door. There's a glass corridor, where I waited once while Morven my cousin had her wrist set. Then some doors into the hospital. It used to look spic and span, but now it's messed up with bits of card and plastic and old clothes on the floor. There's brown spots all over the place, brown tracks where the wheels went. There are no flies inside; maybe the doors help with that.

The dentist's room is first. It has a big chair like a torture or captain's chair. The next room has big blue footballs and rails on the walls like gym-rails.

Elizabeth continues to the white room. The white room has white cupboards beside a bed for sick folk. The floor's a mess of smashed bottles, ripped-up packets. Nearly all of the cupboard doors are splintered or broken open.

There's a fridge. We open it only enough to know it stinks. Elizabeth opens the cupboards and begins to collect packets of pills. She lines them up in rows, so we know what they are. This is OK fun, especially when all the packets start to look like buildings in a city. I find a pen and draw wheels on one packet, then drive it crazily around a road in the street I've made.

Elizabeth: 'Could you *please* help? Stop it, will you, and pass that over.'

I pass her a boring book. She reads the name of each tablet

aloud, then drops all the ones she doesn't want into a plastic bag she has opened out on the floor.

Me: 'I found another packet, look!'

Elizabeth: 'What does it say?'

Me: 'The name on this one says . . . Warfarin.'

She looks it up in her book.

'No, it's a poison. Put it away out of reach.'

She goes back to checking her tablets. I get bored. The plastic bag at her feet fills up too slow, so I go back to playing cars, and I'm playing so seriously that I don't notice that she's stopped.

When I look up proper, Elizabeth is just staring at a book. It was open on the counter, yet I didn't notice it because it seemed like from a bank or something.

The book is a list of names, medicines, all in a row – beside her mum and dad's signatures.

'They were writing just here,' she says.

I try to think of what to come back with. It's not easy. It needs to be more adult than Elizabeth even.

'Are you able to smell your mum's perfume on it?'

She puts her nose down on the page.

'I can't.'

'Did they know how to use everything in here? All the complicated stuff, all the machines, the tablets?'

'Yes.'

'That's amazing. They must've known everything. I wouldn't've known how to even start.' I try to catch her eye. 'Do you know how to use everything?'

'Me?' She stops looking, now looks back. 'Me? How can you—' She goes back to her work.

After a long time of searching she has three packets that sound about right.

Only one of them turns out to be an antibiotic.

Someone has cut some of the tablets out, so the packet is shaped like an L.

Me: 'Will it make him sick if it's the wrong kind?'

Elizabeth: 'I really, really hope not.'

'Are you worried about Duncan?'

'Yes.'

'Is he going to die?'

'No . . . Come off it, don't be saying things like that. I thought we all agreed not to talk about getting sick? Yes, you remember. So let's not mention it again.'

She starts looking in the bottom cupboards for creams. Before we leave I click some switches on and off. I try the taps in the sink just to make sure they're dry.

'Elizabeth?'

'What?'

'Do you miss your mum and dad?'

'About as much as it is possible to miss anything. About as much as you miss yours.'

I have to think about this.

'OK then, but I never knew my dad. So it's hard to miss him to even start with.' I wait for Elizabeth to smile or show appreciation, but she's busy. 'Truly though, I do miss my mum. But I'm a lucky one. It'll not be long before I see her again. She's coming back. I know it.'

She stops searching. Instead she looks at me. She sits on a footstool and gives me an over-long stare.

'You believe that? That's really what you think?'

'Aye, I do.'

She goes to say something but I go first: 'She just left me for a while, that's all. So I just have to keep waiting. Keep looking until I've discovered her. It's called Pester Power. Which means not taking no for an answer.'

She holds up a packet.

'This is it.'

'It's the right antibiotic? Will it work?'

'I'm really hoping it will.'

'Is it the yellow stuff that tastes of bananas?'

'No, it's a pill. Called Trimethoprim. In the book it doesn't say it's for skin. But I can't find anything else.'

She sounds headed towards sad Elizabeth, so I take her hand and blow a fart onto the back of it.

'It *shall* work. You don't have to be grown-up to be a doctor. Remember our law? "Kids rule; adults drool." We can do everything they can. Or could. That's called teamwork.'

Elizabeth does her half-and-half smile.

When we get home Duncan is lying on a chair, still wearing his coat. He says he feels happiest when he's left alone. But Elizabeth won't take this for an answer; instead she helps him, moves him into her bed.

Once he's tucked in she tries to give him the antibiotic: but Duncan won't swallow it. She crunches it up, but the taste is bad and he spits the crumbs back at her. She mixes another tablet with water, and tries to gets him to drink that, but he refuses. To distract him I do my party-piece – rolling my eyes around until they go white – and Alex does his High Five – In the Sky – In space – In your face – routine, but Duncan just looks bored and Elizabeth says we should stop it.

In the middle of this Calum Ian comes in.

I know right away he's been back at his house, because his face looks very stiff. I don't want to look at him, but I can't stop myself. He doesn't look back at me. Elizabeth asks him over and over what's wrong, but he won't tell.

Alex: 'He says the tablet tastes nasty. Well, I didn't like my injections at first, but I got used to *them*.'

Me: 'I'm going to pray for Duncan. God can decide anything he wants so long as Duncan gets better.'

Elizabeth: 'We'll try and give him some more later.'

Calum Ian doesn't say a thing.

Later on I get Duncan on his own. Elizabeth has given him some soup, and he seems happier. I try to get him interested in reading, but he can't be encouraged.

Me: 'Will you not take your tablets?'

He doesn't answer.

Me: 'What are you doing?'

After a long time he says, 'Only thinking.'

'Thinking is never an only . . . what did you think?'

'I'm wondering why I can't remember.'

I lie beside him, sharing his pillow. His breath smells weird, like bad food, but I put up with it for being close.

Me: 'Maybe you've forgotten . . . listen, I can't remember plenty of stuff either. Like how adults sound . . . DVDs don't count, the words in them can't be a surprise.'

67

Duncan: 'I forget . . . my birthday, last. What was it? It must've been a party, but . . . can't think of it. Was it at the pool, or was it at home? Also, I can't remember much before I was three. Only that's not new, that's the same for everyone, Elizabeth told me . . .'

Me: 'Why do you need to remember? You're doing fine as you are now.'

Duncan turns his red face away.

'You remember what your mum looks like?' he asks.

'Easy.'

'Go on.'

'She . . . has got brown hair. A bit like mine. She's not skinny, not fat. She likes to sing. She has a neat voice. She's usually calm. She can be the boss, but also doesn't mind having other people be boss as well.'

Duncan listens, then says: 'I can't remember what my mum looks like.'

And this makes me feel terrible, like the worst devil: because I deleted the last pictures he had.

'She came to the school hall, remember?' I say, feeling desperate now. 'She helped with the Christmas decorations . . . She had the lights wrapped and wrapped around her arms . . . she was very jolly . . .'

Duncan looks at me, blinks, looks away.

'The earlier bits,' he says. 'They got jumbled. Like I'm not sure what truly happened. I try to remember how everyone went away, but I can't.'

Now I decide to tell Duncan what I did.

In a whisper I apologise for everything. But for some strange reason he doesn't seem to care. His eyes just look far away, and his words are slow.

'Equals,' he says in the end. 'This makes us equals.'

When it's dark I see Elizabeth getting up and down. I hear Duncan saying *No* lots of times. Then Elizabeth comes past, holding a mirror. She puts it in a drawer out of sight.

'Is he getting better?'

I go to her bed to bury in beside her. She looks weary about it, but too weary to argue against.

'Not yet.'

'Why did you hide the mirror?'

'Because Duncan's scared of them.'

'Why?'

'They used them on us – remember? To check if we were breathing. He's worried we'll do the same.'

Elizabeth waits for me to remember; and when I do she presses my arm to say she wanted not to tell.

She's holding two of her toys. I don't always like to see her do this – because I don't want to think that Elizabeth is just a kid like me.

When I mentioned this before she got angry and said: 'Some days I feel like being a kid too.'

I lie with my body in the warm spot she made. Elizabeth strokes my hair, not far from how Mum used to do it.

'You had another bad dream last night,' she says.

'Did I?'

'Don't you remember?'

'No.'

'S'OK. My dreams are often bad. See, that's why I need the toys. My worst dream – this is going to sound mad – is the one where I dream last year didn't happen.'

'That's a *great* dream.'

'Not when you wake up again it isn't.' She continues, 'I used to think it would be great if there were no adults around. But it's not. It's just boring.' She looks at me. 'I'd dream them back if I could. Only I'm not sure how safe that is: living in a dreamworld.'

We have a long night: waiting to see if Duncan will get better, or worse. Waiting to see if he's still there.

It's even after the glow comes in the skylight and the windows that I hear him calling out – for Calum Ian, for his mum and dad – and I can't get to sleep after this, because I can't stop thinking about the photos: wishing, like Elizabeth's adults, that I could dream them back.

Back Bay

Now

Mum – are you still listening?

This is the story of how I got to be here. But it isn't an easy story for me, because it hasn't ended yet.

It's become a war against giving in. Against forgetting.

For knowing how to survive.

As I told you already, I did a bad thing. So now you know what the bad thing was.

So now I need to tell you, please listen, that I was only trying to make amends. But is that the right word – are there bad amends as well as good amends?

Revenge is the wrong word.

Like Duncan said: I was trying to make us equals.

This is what happens when there isn't anyone else to talk to. You begin to forget things. Even though I'm meant to be young with a hungry brain, I always forget. So I added another rule to my longer and longer list:

23. Practise your words and memories.

And I was glad, because it gave me something to do, something new to think about besides the bad I'd done.

So I practised, and when it didn't work at first I got scared I might have to learn every single word over.

But words are like tides: they come back. All you have to do is wait for them to roll in again.

There are two times I remember where the new world was beginning but I didn't know it yet.

The first was in my class at school. Mrs Leonard was acting busily – we had a visitor coming, and she was trying to put up the classroom Christmas decorations before he arrived.

'Five minutes ago I strung up that tinsel,' she's saying. 'Now it's come undone. Is it ever possible to buy anything that functions on this island?'

After she says this Mrs Leonard thins her mouth, which means she's either thinking, or concerned. If she's concerned it's best to let her get on with it; if she's thinking then her next thought will come along in a minute, so say nothing.

'Ah children, our visitor has come.'

This morning he looks ordinary: no tie, jeans like any dad. Mrs Leonard shakes his hand and goes pure beetroot in the face like she did when the priest chose her for his dance at the end of the produce festival.

'Children,' she puts her hands together in a church, 'I'd like you to give a warm welcome to Dr Schofield, who has come along today to give us a talk on the very important work he does for our community.'

Dr Schofield waves like a film star – which he isn't – then goes to stand at the whiteboard.

Duncan MacNeil puts up his hand: but he's too early, Mrs Leonard makes her *watch it buster* face at him.

Dr Schofield lifts the silver box he brought – it's suitcase-sized – onto the desk in front. Then he points to the middle of himself and says, 'Eeshh – Meeeshh Brian. Tha MI ag ION-sach Gaelic.'

Everyone looks at Mrs Leonard to see if she understood a word of it. My bet is she's still waiting for the sound of his words to clump together like us – then she says,

'The doctor is telling you his first name: Brian. And he says he's learning Gaelic.' To Dr Schofield she says, 'I thought that was impeccably well put. *Is fheàrr Gàidhlig bhriste na Gàidhlig sa chiste* – it is better to have the Gaelic broken than dead, yes?'

I don't agree. I thought he was very bad.

Dr Schofield waits for us to settle down then says, 'You'll know me from the surgery, or from the cottage hospital. Some of you I have seen: yes, some of you in this room. Coughs, colds, cuts needing glued or stitched. Broken arms, pulled elbows. Sore ears. Sore throats.'

We look around for who it might be.

'Don't worry, you don't have to tell,' he says. 'And *I* would never tell. That's my duty of confidentiality. I would never talk or tell anyone else about your medical problems. Unless you asked me to do so.'

All quiet.

Margaret-Anne: 'What about our mums?'

73

'So – well yes, I suppose being the age you are, yes, apart from your mums.'

Kieran: 'What about the priest?'

'Not the priest.'

'I thought Father MacGill knew everything that happened?'

'He doesn't know about your sore throats.'

We look at Kieran – *duh.*

Dr Schofield puts his hands down on the silver box.

'Now, I wonder if you're curious about this. No? Does anybody know what I've got in here?'

Nobody does.

He gets us to gather in a half-circle up at the front. Using a quiet part-evil voice he says, 'In this box I have a person. True. I keep them locked up inside until I feel kind enough to let them out. Do you want to see the person?'

His eyes look mad enough for it to be true.

He unclips the lock. There's an *ouhhh* as we peer at the dark insides – there's a face! Blonde hair!

But then he lifts out: a big doll. Man or woman? Plastic yellow hair, shit-brown tracksuit, white cheap trainers.

Straightens the legs. Puts the doll on the floor.

'Say hello to Annie,' he says. 'Now can anyone tell me what we use Annie for?'

Everybody's hand up – it's Duncan's reaches highest.

'Yes, Duncan?'

'Dad has to do first aid, for on his boat. He says that fire is the biggest worry at sea. But he said your doll is for practising the kiss of life.'

It's stupid to be laughing at this, but everybody does.

'That's absolutely correct Duncan. And as Rona's serious face tells us – the kiss of life, or what we now call rescue breathing, has nothing to do with passion – and everything to do with the business of saving a life. Would anybody like a demonstration of how we do that?'

We nod for yes.

'Part of what we do is train for the worst. Annie's role is in teaching us how to save lives. She's probably one of the most important members of our team. Certainly, she has better hair than me – look.'

For showing this he takes the plastic yellow hair off the doll – it comes off in one blob like scrambled egg – and puts it on his head.

He just looks weird. Nobody laughs. We all turn around to the teacher to see if we should be laughing. She doesn't know either.

'Drop the hair joke,' Dr Schofield says.

In the next bit he tells us about his ABC – Airway, Breathing, Circulation – and Mrs Leonard gives in exchange our ABC, which is the first three trees of the Gaelic alphabet – *Ailm* for Elm, *Beith* for Birch, *Coll* for Hazel. It's a good share, though we have his learnt before he learns ours.

He's at the start of showing us the recovery position – which is easy, it's only lying on your side – when his phone goes.

'Work mobile,' he says. 'Just a moment.'

We have to return to our seats, while he sticks his finger in his ear to listen more easily.

'Hullo.'

Mrs Leonard makes her *be patient* face at us.

'Where?'

It's funny – a big doll on the floor, him there talking.

'Sorry?'

I'm tapping Anne-Marie on the arm to tell her about the big stupid doll and him talking. Mrs Leonard's mouth goes into a thin slit to warn me – *Behave.*

'This a hoax, you think?'

He listens, nodding even though the other person can't see him, then he says to Mrs Leonard – 'Look, I will maybe just take this call outside if that's all right.'

Then he leaves us.

We get bored waiting. Mrs Leonard leaves the doll where it is; she even has to step over it on her way around to the whiteboard.

It's weird – like a dead person in the room, which no one's even bothering about.

'OK,' says Mrs Leonard. 'Dr Schofield has obviously been detained with something important, so let's get back to the work we were doing with symmetry and shapes. Who wants to give us all the first example?'

When I excuse myself for the toilet I find he's still in the corridor – leaning against the wall by the back door.

Adults can lean on walls, it isn't fair. Like a sneak I stay in the cubbyhole space before the toilet door to listen in – creaking the hinges to make it sound like I went in.

'Which public places?'

The skylight window above – one shining speck. Planes fly over our island on their way to America, Canada.

'So nobody's got any idea? That was *weeks* ago. How long has it been since—? *Seriously?* That doesn't sound like – if the incubation *is* as long as that, but I never heard of any potential pathogen with—'

The speck: gone.

'What *is* the official line? We had the contingency for swine flu, didn't we? The health board were all over that, storm in a teacup and we stocked up even when there wasn't a scrap of bloody—'

His voice sounds: angry? Annoyed? Scared?

'I *know* that turned out all right. But what you're telling me doesn't bear comparison.'

I move back out and Dr Schofield sees me. I smile, give him a wave for checking things are OK.

'Go back to your classroom, love,' he says in a hurry, clicking his fingers and pointing at the door. 'You can't be listening, all right?'

Something doesn't make sense about his eyes. Did I do something very wrong?

'Back to your classroom,' is the last thing he says to me.

Twelve days ago

Duncan spent a week at our home: getting his energy back, growing strength enough again to walk around. His face went from red, to scabbed, to saggy. He stayed with us until two mornings ago, when Elizabeth wanted him to get dressed. Duncan preferred his pyjamas: said he would put his clothes on if he could sleep in them from now on. Elizabeth said no way. That started an argument: and when Elizabeth put up new rules about getting along and give and take, the MacNeil brothers left us.

Calum Ian never mentioned what I did to his camera: and Duncan seemed to forget I ever told him. So after they left I decided that everything was OK: but that I would still try to make up to them by sharing my food, and not minding if they stole mine or didn't share in return.

Now we're back in school, in the P5 classroom for Duncan's first day. This room works because it's not anyone's old class. Also, it has a picture-roll going around the walls with the

Gaelic letters on. My favourite is B, for *Beith,* which is birch. My least favourite is H, for heather, *Ur,* because that isn't even a tree, it's a bush.

Part of the ceiling got broken. Elizabeth says it's because slates come off and no one fixes them. But at least the windows are fine. I've learnt that once a window's gone everything starts to come to pieces.

'Facts and opinions,' Elizabeth is saying. 'Does anyone know the difference?'

We're looking through our folders: the stuff our teachers were keeping back to show the parents. I found mine in Mrs Leonard's cupboard. We spent too long already staring at the things we used to care about, and looking for the signatures of our parents at the bottom of the assessment sheets – so Elizabeth changed topic.

Alex: 'That is too hard to know.'

Calum Ian: 'It's *easy*. Facts are real, see? They can only be one thing. They're top trumps to opinions every time. Opinions aren't as high up as facts.'

Elizabeth: 'Examples?'

We each have a turn. FACT – the giant tortoise can live to over 150 years of age. But OPINION – hippos are pretty. FACT – koalas usually sleep during the day. But OPINION – everyone should clean their ears. This last one, put forward by Alex, gets us into bother, because no one can decide if it's a FACT or an OPINION.

Alex: 'Mum used to clean my ears on the edge of the corner of the towel. That's a fact.'

Calum Ian: 'My dad said you don't need to do it. Opinion.'

Me: 'It smells bad but is useful. Fact.'

Elizabeth: 'Maybe it can be both fact *and* opinion?'

Calum Ian: 'No way. It can't be both.'

Me: 'What about God and Santa?'

Calum Ian: 'God's a fact. Santa's an opinion that you only get with babies. So who's a little baby?'

I don't want to say that I am. Neither does Alex. He just looks at the dirt on the floor.

'Maybe Santa can be both?' Elizabeth says, as usual offering an answer to help us agree. 'Here's a fact: if you believe in something then it might just be true. If you don't: well, that's only your opinion.'

Alex: 'What about zombies?'

Elizabeth: 'The rule doesn't apply for zombies.'

Just for cheek we find lots of other exceptions to mess with Elizabeth's rule: like ghosts, werewolves and mermaids.

She gets grumpy and says to forget it.

'Is heaven a fact or opinion?' Alex asks. 'Because if Mum isn't still moving, she must not be breathing. I'm quite bothered if heaven is not a fact.'

Calum Ian: 'Don't worry, Bonus Features. If she's not in heaven then she's in hell.'

When Alex looks upset by this Elizabeth squeezes his hand. For distraction she asks instead if anyone wants to remember. When nobody volunteers she says, 'Duncan did it last time, for the group. That was very brave of him. If there isn't a person who definitely wants to go, then maybe I should?'

No one tells her not to.

Alex: 'Please don't remember any bad bits.'

80

'OK,' she says, and stands at the front of the class, folding her fingers like Canon MacAllan used to do.

'I remember,' she says, looking nervous. 'First I remember that Mum had green eyes. She had kind hands. Ach! How can hands be kind? Bloody crazy of me.'

It didn't sound crazy till she said it.

'Before we arrived, Dad looked up the island in his map-book. It was away right far off the edge! I could never believe that – I mean, going to a place that far away.'

'*You* were the one far from us,' Calum Ian says.

Elizabeth points his way as if to say: *fair enough.*

'Mum called it a Big Step. When we got here: best of all she loved the beaches. She liked it when I saw the seals on Curachan. And she was really pleased that I liked the school.' She winds her hands around to show it's where we are. 'Specially as you can do projects. This first badge here – see? I got that because I did the tuck-shop kitty. This one, because I learnt about wind turbines and hydro schemes and helped plant the wildlife garden.'

She passes around her two badges. The first one says **BANKER**. The second, ECO-STUDENT. When she sees that no one is writing down her memories for her, she stops to write them down for herself.

'Never minded winter,' she goes on. 'Christmas! Only Dad didn't like winter so much. He wanted to get back to Bristol, because it was less windy, less rainy there. But me and Mum had other ideas. He said, "We'll see out two years." Pretty soon we'd been here three.'

'Dad always said you could tell the incomers,' Calum Ian grumbles. 'They only last one winter.'

Me: 'Weren't you even listening? Didn't you turn up your ears? She said it was *three* already.'

Calum Ian: 'I can say what I want, *Gloic*.'

Me: 'You were speaking stupid.'

This becomes an argument. When we begin to shout loud at one another Duncan gets up, and goes to the fiddle cupboard and takes out a fiddle.

It's out of tune, so he scratches it like there's a monster coming. We all stop talking. We start laughing instead, until it's a funny sort of riot.

Duncan looks surprised to have made us laugh. He makes more monster noises, until it's past funny, then tunes up the fiddle proper.

When it sounds right he plays 'Puff the Magic Dragon', slow and sad.

I used to laugh at the kiss-face Duncan made when playing, but now I don't.

He plays through twice then stops. Then he cuffs the strings and plucks them without any tune or song.

'I'm going to be world champion on the fiddle,' he says. 'For Mum. For Dad. That's my ambition. Then I'll come back and teach all the new young kids.'

'Remember Mr Patterson?' Elizabeth asks. 'He was our fiddle teacher.'

We all think of him. I thought he smelt funny. Mum said his smell was the water of life.

'I remember him at the summer concert,' Calum Ian says. 'All the parents were in. It's crazy: thinking about all the mums and dads. Just sitting there.'

Duncan puts his fiddle away. He goes back to his seat. Elizabeth goes quiet as she writes out her memories, then pins her badges back onto her jumper.

'I'm remembering next.'

It's Calum Ian. He does a fake bow then goes to the front. Elizabeth looks pleased: she quickly tears him a new sheet of paper, and gets ready with her pen to write down every last detail of his experiences.

It takes him ages. Finally he says, 'So they're dead. They've all died. Or where the fuck are they? I've realised that Dad's maybe in hospital. That's why he can't get to us, right? He got sick, he could've lost his strength, or lost his memory? Maybe if . . . if he fell off his boat, when he got to the mainland . . . could've bumped his head. That's what happens with a bump, your memory goes until it comes back weeks later.'

He begins to breathe fast, like he's running. He opens his mouth, puffs out. Then he says, 'Want memories? Right. A big thing I remember is the first house we shopped in. Uncle Frank's. Who wants to talk about that? Aye? OK, me then. His front door was shut. So we opened it and his dog Mo ran past.'

Duncan is saying *no*. Alex pulls up his jumper and holds it against his ears.

'Well, it's a fucking memory, isn't it? That's what we're doing, you should listen.' He kicks up a torn bit of floor then says, 'My one true memory, write it! The dog had been eating him. She never hurt anybody, not before. But she had to eat him, to survive. Write it down, quick! It goes in the book. Before we all forget.'

Elizabeth isn't writing.

83

Calum Ian shrugs and goes back to his seat.

Alex is still too scared to uncover his ears, or take his head from the desk-top.

Nobody wants to talk.

I turn around to look at Calum Ian. He's like a drawing where the eyes don't want to be angry or sad but both. I watch him, only because I'm nervous, and not for being sympathetic.

'Stop looking at me, *Gloic*,' he says.

I turn back away.

Calum Ian's chair scrapes. He stomps to the front. Now he's glaring at me.

'Had a camera,' he says. 'With the last pictures ever of Mum and my sister Flora in it. Some of my best memories were there. Only now I've *lost* them.'

He's looking at me. My hands have gone cold, but my face feels red hot.

'Sorry,' Elizabeth says. 'I don't understand. Where did you leave the camera?'

'Left it in the sea.'

'You left it . . . how in the sea?'

'I *threw* it in the sea.'

'Why?'

Calum Ian keeps looking very definitely at me. Then he clicks his fingers at Duncan.

'Out of here, Sidekick. *A-mach à seo!*'

But Duncan doesn't want to go. He stays in his seat, until Calum Ian has to grab the neck of his jumper to pull him up and away.

*　　*　　*

When they're gone we decide school's over. We go to the library for a bit, but the darkness today is too spooky, so we go back outside.

Alex goes to the playpark, but none of us can find the fun in it. It starts to rain, so we hide under the chute. Elizabeth has made packed lunches for us: crackers, dried apricots and custard pots to drink. We get to eat the portions she made for Calum Ian and Duncan.

'Why'd he throw his camera in the sea?' Elizabeth asks. 'If he cared *that* much about the pictures? It's senseless. He can be too angry sometimes.'

To answer would be admitting guilt. I drink custard instead, though with only half my appetite.

We realise Alex is still thinking about Calum Ian's uncle and the dog Mo when he says, 'Dogs are as dangerous as wolves, for true this time.'

Elizabeth: 'I hope you can just forget about it. Anyway, dogs were bred for being tame. They don't just go back to being wolves.'

Alex: 'What about a hungry dog?'

Elizabeth: 'I think we should change topic.'

We don't want to go home, not just yet, so it's up for a vote. Alex doesn't want to send messages; and I don't want to go shopping, Old or New. In the end Elizabeth takes charge and says that, because we're close by, we should go and pay our respects to the Last Adult.

She's in the Community Centre. This has the Cròileagan, where we went to nursery, but also has the soft-play room and the café, where you can buy the best fish and chips in town.

The Last Adult is in the soft-play room.

The main door went stiff. Inside the hall are lots of Christmas decorations. There's a silver tree with baubles and tinsel on. Some of the red tinsel has fallen off. A reindeer and a sugar-plum fairy are on the floor.

There's a blue face-mask on the mat, with spots of blood on it, gone black long ago. Heaped along one wall are lots of boxes, orange bags. We opened a bag once: inside were plastic sheets and aprons and cartons of gloves, old and used. Some of the bags smelt very bad.

We go in on tiptoes. Elizabeth opens the soft-play door. There's a smell, though only faint. There's the ball-pool, in the far corner, heaped with dirty blankets and towels.

We found her on a sleeping mat, beside the pool.

Back then none of us understood about bodies. You just leave them alone – apart from flowers – and close the door so dogs don't get in. We wanted to bury her, but nobody could pluck up the courage to touch her. So we found a pile of stones outside, which the adults were using to build a not-ready car park.

With plastic buckets and trolleys from the Co-op, we carried in the stones, and covered her up.

Now all we can see of her is this pile of stones. Our cards and presents are there on top, with our old flowers. I notice that the last of the flowers are already dry, and I feel a bit sorry for her. It's been weeks since we came.

The room has orange curtains, nearly shut. A sharp line of sunlight finding the pile of stones, like God keeping an eye on her.

Alex: 'Tell me how you knew she was the last adult again.'

Elizabeth: 'Because she was still breathing.'

Alex: 'Did she say anything?'

Elizabeth: 'No. Like I said before, no. She was just breathing. It sounded . . . bubbly. She was the woman who looked after the last of us. I knew her face. It was her.'

Alex: 'How did you help her?'

Elizabeth: 'I left her some juice, crisps. And water. Because that's what she did for us.'

We stand around the pile of stones. I wonder again who the Last Adult was. Elizabeth just says she doesn't know.

Alex goes back to the Christmas tree. He returns with the sugar-plum fairy and lays it on top of the stones.

'Wasn't she my mum?' he asks.

'No, she wasn't. I've seen your mum. I mean, I'd know her. It wasn't her.'

When we pay respects we have to stand and say nothing. During the time this takes my eyes get used to the dark. There's things left by the Last Adult: Bible, photos, dirty plastic cups, scrunched tissues, a water bottle. The water inside went brown. Plus a packet of tablets, the same type we keep seeing in people's houses.

There's also a pad of paper with all the last-alive kids' names on it. Our names are there. The other kids' names have been scored off. There's numbers next to the scorings-off. I ask Elizabeth what the numbers mean.

'The dates that they fell asleep,' she says.

There are other rooms in the Community Centre. But nobody wants to go there. That's where *we* were sick. Where we nearly died. Where the others died. And what if the thing that made us sick is still there? No way.

It's a relief to get back outside. As we cross the not-ready car park I ask Elizabeth about her afterwards memories. She's told us before, but still I ask: just like when I used to ask Mum about being born, over and over, just to hear about things that happened and I didn't know.

'It was very cold,' she says, 'so then . . . so I woke up, it was dark. All the lights were not working.'

'After that?'

'Then nothing. Maybe I fell asleep . . . I woke again and it was light. I remember having crusty eyes, not being able to see. I remember going from room to room. And then I heard someone crying.'

'Who was that?'

'That was Alex. He had on his Cròileagan orange vest, the ones the little kids used for crossing the road. There was a label on it with his name. Alex. He was beside Duncan. Duncan had a label too, though not a vest. Duncan was very sick. But he got better, so that's great. Calum Ian was in another room. He woke up as soon as I talked to him. He said he was extremely thirsty.'

'Then?'

'We found a torch. We found some food. We got boxes from the cupboard, they used to be full of paper towels. We got inside them. They kept us perfectly warm. That's why I never ever throw away cardboard boxes.'

'You found me.'

'Yes. We looked around the rooms. You were in the last one. You were hiding under a table. Didn't see me. Or you looked right through me, I don't know. We gave you some biscuits, juice. You didn't say anything. You didn't have a label or a vest, so I had to find your name on the list of kids that the Last Adult had beside her.'

'I remember dogs barking.'

'For true. There were dogs and cats trapped in houses. We let out as many as we could.'

'And I remember the cows, from way over at the farm. They were making a racket.'

'Because nobody had milked them.'

'The only thing I don't remember is when Mum said goodbye. Don't remember her telling me to wait. Is it just going to be a test of patience?'

Elizabeth frowns at me, then agrees that it is a test.

Everything changes when we get home.

Everything changes for ever.

At first we don't notice anything different. Home just looks like it always does: quite a bit messy, which makes me think about Elizabeth's first rule: Tidy up.

Then we see smashed things: and I know at once it isn't just mess.

Funny how some things you can't know all at once. It takes maybe the third or fourth try. It's maybe even my fifth look that tells me things went very bad.

Elizabeth goes and sits on the floor. There's a dirty mess on my bed. Heaps of stones and dirt from the garden. A teddy covered in blue paint. This isn't so terrible. But my pencils: snapped. My pillow: jam spilt on it.

This is enough to make me sad – but then I see that Elizabeth is staring at something else. For the first time, for me, a bit of good news. They got my bed, but *the wrong* bedside cabinet. Alex must've left his book – there it is, *Dr Dog* – on my cabinet. Thinking wrongly, they tipped up and smashed all the stuff in his instead.

Me: 'It's better news for me.'

'Shut *up*,' Elizabeth hisses. 'Shut your face *up*.'

This shocks me: she never talks like this. I want to tell her how sad she makes me feel by saying that, but she's just staring at the floor beside Alex's cabinet.

'There's red on the floor,' I say, taking my chance to talk again. 'It's a very bad thing to spill the food dye for our water, isn't it?'

Elizabeth: 'You know what this is? On the floor, over here?'

Me: 'No.'

Elizabeth: 'It's Alex's insulin.'

Me: 'But what's it doing down over there?'

Elizabeth: 'It's *smashed* that's what!'

Me: 'Well . . . but did you not keep it in the cool box?'

Elizabeth: 'I *did*. But that was before I brought it here for safe keeping.'

She doesn't want to hear me say he might be all right without it. She isn't interested when I act brave and start to clean my pillow. Instead, Elizabeth looks furious.

'Of course he needs it,' she says. 'This is bad, this is very bad . . . Have you any idea why they'd do this?'

'I – no.'

'So here's something you *should* know. There's only one vial left. That's in his pen, and that's only quarter full. You know how long a quarter lasts?'

'Twenty days?'

'Two days.'

Alex is standing by the door. He looks at the mess. More than that, he looks at the glass. Elizabeth hurriedly kneels down on the floor to try and hide it, but he sees and understands completely.

'Someone has done a bad thing,' he says.

We find them at the big ferry pier. They've tipped out a pot of white paint on the tarmac. Both of them are cycling their bikes through it, making bendy lines like a cartoon road or planes flying circles in the sky.

Calum Ian stops short of Elizabeth. At first he thinks she's going at him for making a mess with paint: then his face changes. Duncan stops, too. He has spots of white all up the back of his trousers, on his hands, on his face. It makes his scarred bits look even stranger.

'Why?' Elizabeth asks.

When they don't answer she says, 'Know something? Right now I hate your bloody guts.'

Calum Ian starts to say that it's just a bit of jam, that it was just a bit of food dye.

He stops when she tells him about the insulin.

Duncan begins to shake and tries to brush all the white dots from his jeans, but they only smudge into fingerprint-lines.

'He made me do it,' he says.

The first thing we do is go to the hospital. We go back to the room with the broken white cupboards. Calum Ian checks inside the fridge, even though it stinks. Then Elizabeth goes through every single drawer and cupboard – twice. Me and Alex do all the cupboards in a room called The Sluice. We don't find anything.

Next door is the nursing home. Nobody wants to look in these rooms, but we have to. Their cupboards are empty. Each bed in every room has an old dead person in it.

Alex doesn't want to look, and neither do I, but we can't stop ourselves.

I see one old lady whose face is like rotten bark on a tree. I shut my eyes, try to unsee. Too late.

In the hall of the nursing home there's a big trolley with wheels. Inside the trolley are lots of packets of tablets. Elizabeth makes a *bingo!* sound, but then goes quiet when she doesn't find any kind of injection.

Feeling gloomy we return to the hospital corridor. Elizabeth puts on her perfume-hanky and Calum Ian tears off the ☣ **BIOHAZARD** ☣ tape and clear plastic from the doors.

She goes in quick, checks the bedside cabinets, cupboards, then comes out quick again, before the smell gets onto her, before she has time to take even one breath.

'*Think, think, think,*' she says.

*   *   *

92

We all go outside to sit on the craggy stones at the edge of the car park. It's a place where the wind skirls around. Elizabeth tucks her hair down inside her jumper.

I sit several steps behind her, because it feels like the safest place to be: not too close to anyone who might think to blame me.

Me: 'Why are we waiting?'

Elizabeth: 'Because I don't want to think about what needs to happen next.'

'What needs to happen next?'

'We need to get into the practice.'

This means the doctor's practice: that's all. Big deal! We went in there once before when we were looking for bandages for Alex, after he cut his arm. The practice wasn't too spooky, plus it didn't have a smell. The main doors had been broken open by the adults, and we found bandages in a box in the nurses' room.

When I tell Elizabeth how easy it'll be she hisses, '*Not* easy. This time it's the dispensary we need to get into.'

'We couldn't open that door.'

'*Great* memory.'

She stands with her arms folded, looking between Calum Ian, Duncan and me. I nearly don't recognise her: with her scars gone red, her eyes narrowed.

'There was one door,' Calum Ian says. 'But with three locks. Only we didn't have any key. An adult must've tried to break it – the door was splintered all up one side, remember?'

'So since you have *all* the best ideas, how are we going to get in when the adults couldn't?'

'It was an accident with Alex, I never—'

93

'*I don't care* about anything you say. I wouldn't care if you jumped off a cliff. I only want an answer.'

Calum Ian looks away to the sea: sad then angry then sad again. Finally he puts his head down on his lap for not knowing.

With a too-calm voice Elizabeth says, 'When it happened, Dad wouldn't let anyone in. There were too many people trying to get in: they were all banging on the main door, shouting. So he kept the keys on a chain. And the keys must still be with him.'

Alex chews the neck of his jumper.

'We need to go inside the gym,' she says. 'And I'm sorry, but I'm not doing that. No way. I'm not going in there.'

Nobody wants to go. It would usually be Elizabeth but that chance is broken. We argue about ways of choosing, but all of them are unfair for Alex or me.

'Why does he need insulin anyway?' Calum Ian asks, now looking as big with regret as Elizabeth.

'He can't be healthy without it.'

'Why?'

'He needs it for his sugar to stay normal.'

'Then he shouldn't be eating sugar. No more sweets or treats. What can he have instead?'

Yet Calum Ian sounds tired by his own words, as if he didn't really want to be asking them.

He goes to the rocks, beyond. He's gone for a moment, and I think he's sulking, but then he comes back. He's holding something in his hand.

'We'll draw straws.'

He's got four bits of grass. Reluctantly, Elizabeth takes them from him.

She holds them up in her hand so they all stick up the same way, with the same thickness showing.

We each have a turn. Elizabeth doesn't want Alex to draw at all, but Duncan says he has to.

No surprises then, when Alex chooses the shortest straw straight away.

He starts to cry.

Elizabeth shouts and grabs the straws back and throws them away. 'Stop it, it's not his *fault*.'

Duncan gets up and begins walking alone back on the road to the school.

'I'll do it,' he says, turning around. 'It can be me, right? Nobody else needs to bother about trying.'

Calum Ian points at me.

'No, *she* should. It's her fault. You told them what you did to our house, *Gloic*? Go on then! Tell her what you did to the pictures of our mum!'

Elizabeth doesn't want to look at any of us.

'It was you, you made me do it!' Duncan shouts at Calum Ian from the road. 'I never wanted to do it!'

We all wait on Calum Ian.

Finally, he bends down to pick up the straws.

He throws away the longest, one by one, until he's left holding only the shortest one.

'Me then.'

This time we don't go in between the primary and the big

school. Instead, we go straight through the main entrance, then in by the assembly hall. There's a link corridor, then after that the door to the swimming pool. I remember from when we came before that its cover was left half-on, half-off.

The cover is still the same, only now the water's gone pongy, stringy, grey-green.

From the lifeguard's box Calum Ian borrows goggles. He already has a nose-clip on. He wraps his head and hair in lost property towels, then puts two lots of plastic bags on his feet, rolling elastic bands on top.

Lastly, he ties a perfume-hanky to his face.

'Where are they.'

This is how he says it: not a question. Elizabeth has a firm mouth like she wants to stay calm.

'OK. Go in. Right in, to the end. Dad's in the last row. There's a card to tell who he is. Remember I said about the orange plastic bags with clothes beside? Look inside his. You might get away with just looking there.'

'Fine.'

'I could draw you a map. Of the people. A plan?'

'I'll watch. For names. Where's your mum?'

'She's on a side bed. At the side of the room. She's not . . . in a bag, her clothes are still on. But it might be—'

'I'm not scared. You don't have to warn me about anything, I'm fine.'

'Keep looking mostly at the ground. The flies might get on you so just keep your mouth—'

'Stop bothering, I'm fine, I can do it myself.'

*　　*　　*

96

But truly, he doesn't look fine. Calum Ian checks his nose-clip, then his goggles, at least ten times. After this he fusses with the plastic bags, breaking the elastic bands holding them on and having to put on new ones.

Before going through, Elizabeth gives him flowers to take in.

Then we all stand on the other side of the double doors and say good luck.

There's a very bad smell: then an even worse smell as he passes through the two sets of doors. I don't hear the sound of flies until he opens the second set.

Afterwards, he says it wasn't hard, not really, though he's gulping for air and forgot to leave the flowers.

'That's definitely the way to do it, definitely,' he says. 'If we ever needed, next time. Three plastic bags each foot would be better, remember that. It's a long way to the end. There's so many! I forgot about that man, sitting in the chair, he's weird! Didn't scare me, though! Then I thought someone had moved, but they couldn't actually move, could they? I was only imagining, right?'

The flowers are crushed in his hand. He's twisted them to shreds by holding them too tight. In the end he looks down and remembers what they are, were for.

'Sorry,' he says, to Elizabeth.

He keeps speaking fast: on and on about how crucial it is to keep on the goggles, though he could just as easily have done without. Finally he just sits and won't stand up, not even when Elizabeth tries to help; instead, his eyes go sharp as he tells her to leave him alone.

'You'll want to know,' he says, 'there was a list of all the mums and dads. Saw my mum's name.' He does a so-what shrug. 'Knew that, anyway. Knew she was there. At least Dad isn't. At least Dad escaped, he's out in the world, I know it. *What?* Stop all your bloody staring!'

We go back to the pool to wait.

When he comes out his face is red. Even so, he's trying to smile, trying even harder to laugh.

He empties out a plastic bag at our feet.

Two sets of keys and a purse fall onto the tiles.

He still won't look at me. Not even when I praise him for today's top bravery. He'd usually say something, anything, even if it was just bad, but he doesn't.

Around the front of the doctor's practice there's a lot of swirling dandelion clocks. The metal shutters are broken. Someone forced them up: with maybe a stone, or an axe, or a hammer. There are dents in the shutters where the silver's been jabbed, but no right-through holes made.

Elizabeth stops at the sign by the door. **Drs B & W Schofield**. Her mum and dad, her dad's letter first.

She touches the sign, rubs some of the salt-rust off. I touch the sign on my way past, too, to add my own respect.

I went in to see Elizabeth's mum once, when she was a doctor. It was with a sore ear. She was busy, though not too fussy. Tall, with hair that smelt of perfume. When I saw her dad later for a cough, he showed me how his stethoscope worked. I only pretended to understand his instructions.

The air in the practice got old. Cobwebs stick to our faces

as we walk in. The waiting room has signs, pictures on its walls: *Nutrition in Pregnancy*. SEE OUR NURSE FOR SMOKING CESSATION ADVICE. **What's pneumococcus?** BREAST IS BEST! Our counsellor holds her clinics every Tuesday Evening. STAYING ACTIVE IN OLD AGE.

But then other signs, over the top of these, about what happened. They're mostly in small letters, black and white. The advice in them never mattered. Or it came too late to matter.

The little play area's in the corner. Coloured beads on wire. Train blocks. Books. The play area looks too tiny for anyone. There's a yellow wooden stool, plus a green table, hardly big enough for one baby, let alone two.

The seats are shiny wood all around the walls. I remember sitting here before my injections.

I remember the other time me and Mum came, near the end. But I don't want to remember that right now. It would only worry or upset Alex.

Someone – one of the adults – had tried to break into the dispensary. The wood of it got splintered around next to the lock, but it looks like they didn't get in.

The keys work: first time.

We wait to see if there's a puff of air, or a bad smell, but there isn't.

Calum Ian goes first. There's bits of crumbly wall, from where they tried to break the door. Apart from this, it's like a new tomb in Egypt, with zero mess.

On shelves, lots of boxes of tablets, with strange names. **AMITRIPTYLINE. BISOPROLOL. DETRUSITOL. IMDUR. MICROGYNON. ZOPICLONE.** Alex says they sound like characters from *Star Wars.* For me, it's more like ghosts or spooks from *Howl's Moving Castle.*

We look through the cupboards. Elizabeth goes straight to the fridge. It doesn't have much of a bad smell.

Also, it's empty.

The cupboards have things like soap, or cream, or paper towels, or tubes of medicine or stockings. Everything has a clean smell, though, which is a relief.

'Don't see any,' Elizabeth says.

She sits on a footstool, bent right over, looking down at the floor. Calum Ian kicks at the wall behind her.

'I went in that gym for nothing?'

Her face goes bright red. Already, before anyone else can move, she's next door, opening cupboards.

'None of us are giving up.'

Only we don't find anything. We do find two more fridges. One has an old can of juice in it, which we share out after wiping off any invisible badness. The other fridge is just empty. It doesn't even smell, which is this day's newest mystery, maybe without a solution.

Then Elizabeth has another idea. She decides we should look through all the patient records. When I ask what these are, and where, she says, 'All around us.'

She's telling the truth. There's shelves in a clanking metal cupboard, and on the shelves are hundreds and hundreds of brown folders. Then loads more, in an ordinary cupboard that doesn't move and doesn't clank.

All of the people: families together, with names I forgot until now. There's even the kids from my class, even the teacher, even the priest. I want to think that these bits of paper might bring the people back: but they don't, of course, and so I deliberately don't look for Mum's notes.

Calum Ian grabs a record. He reads the first pages then throws the record away. 'Just scratchy bloody writing,' he says.

I think he's being daft, but when I collect one it's true: I can't read it either.

Elizabeth pulls out a stack, then begins to go through them. Even doing three takes her ages.

'There must be a faster way,' she says. 'This will just take us for ever.'

We make a plan of choosing ten each, doing them carefully. Pretty soon, though, my ten gets mixed up with Alex's ten; plus I get bored after six and want to look around for quicker ways.

Me: 'Make your eyes go special for that word. How do you spell that word?'

Elizabeth spells D-I-A-B-E-T-E-S.

Me: 'Look for it like you're looking for a colour. Then it jumps out. I've done that looking for shiny packets with sweets. It really works, try it.'

We make our eyes go sharp for DIABETES. Except it doesn't work: they go sharp for other words like **FIRE EXIT** and DISPENSARY and **AIR AMBULANCE CALL** and **YOU DON'T HAVE TO BE MAD TO WORK HERE BUT IT HELPS**. Never for DIABETES.

Then Elizabeth has one more idea. She looks for a single record. The records go by alphabet – A, B, C, D – until it gets to M. Then there's a whole wall for Mac, and a shelf for MacNeil.

101

After this, the letters go back to normal, until the end, when there's no X or Z.

She has Alex's notes – Alex MacLeod. Elizabeth turns them over, upside down, inside out. When Calum Ian asks her what she's looking for she says, 'A sign, a label, anything to say his illness.' But there isn't one.

Calum Ian gets fed up. He kicks the footstool Elizabeth sat on, hard enough for it to flip over.

'Looks like you're facing your worst enemy,' I say to him, when he decides to calm down.

With eyes narrowed into slits he looks at me and says, 'So I am.'

Now Elizabeth says she wants to be alone, wants to go to one of the other rooms. Me and Alex are left behind.

We swirl on chairs, play stone-scissors-paper. Alex invents a new category: fingers waving for fire, which burns paper, melts scissors, cracks stone. Fire is the all-time winner.

'You play games,' Calum Ian says, 'while the rest of us have to go through fucking bloody hell.'

We try not to look at him. Alex pays attention instead to the scab he has on his knee. He picks it off, and I watch the red dot grow into a red bead.

Me: 'Does it hurt?'

Alex: 'Not if you're brave. Injections make me brave. It's easy. I used to hate it, but my skin went strong.' His eyes go blurry through thinking then he says, 'Even so, I don't mind not getting my injections.'

Me: 'But you'll get sick.'

Alex: 'Don't care. Then I might get to see my mum and dad. Because I'm not scared. Not any more. Fact, not opinion – when you're dead you're zero.'

I get him in a friendly kind of head-lock.

'Listen,' I say. 'The only obstacle is us. It's better to believe in being alive than what the opposite might be. It's infinity better to believe that.'

Alex: 'So why d'you talk to your mum?'

I didn't think he'd noticed. Now I feel shy about it, not knowing at all what to say.

'Gave your mum a fright once,' he tells me.

'*My mum.* You know about my mum? I want to know all the facts, tell me.'

Alex looks worried, or surprised, like I sounded too keen. Then he says, 'When I was little. Four, maybe three? Your mum was delivering letters. Mum saw her on the path coming. It was very funny.'

'Keep going, keep going!'

'We waited by the door. Just before she got there I shoved my whole hand through the letterbox.'

'What did she say!'

'Em . . . My mum, it was her that told me to do it. She wanted to give your mum a letter to post. Your mum took letters as well as bringing them, didn't she?'

'*Anybody* knows that! She was a postwoman.'

'Well, so I gave it to her. Said, Hullo! She took it and gave me hers. I heard her go away laughing.'

Because it's about Mum I can't find it normal like any other story, or even boring: I'm instead hungry to know every last detail.

'Didn't see her,' Alex admits, in the end. 'But she was laughing. She took my letter and she went.'

It's when he says this that I get my best idea.

Elizabeth is on her own, in her mum's old doctoring room. Her eyes look red like she's been crying, but that's impossible, because Elizabeth is way strong and never cries.

'Go away,' she says.

I hide behind the door – nearly leaving, wondering if I barged in, wondering if she's in a crabby mind.

In the end she calls me back – makes me stand straight at the desk in front of her like a soldier.

'Only wanted a *few* stupid seconds alone,' she says.

I don't know if this means she's already had them: so I count thirty in my head in case she didn't, then begin to tell her about how Mum used to pick up letters from people, even letters without stamps. But then I notice the room around is a mess: too much of a mess for Elizabeth to have made it on her own. Cupboards open, books on the floor. The bin overflowing with plastic aprons, gloves.

She stops me talking. Instead, she shows me a framed picture. Of Elizabeth with her mum and dad.

In the picture she's making her eyes go squint. I didn't know she could do it – make a squint, be funny. She looks daft, happy even.

'Just after we came.' She rubs a smudge from the glass.

104

'We were at the beach, Traigh Eais. This was Mum's favourite because it was early days. Dad had a beard then, see? And I didn't have any scars.'

She puts a finger on her picture-cheek, then on her real cheek, to feel the new hardness there.

'What I don't know is what to do. Usually I think: what would Mum do? What would Dad do?'

'What would they?'

Her voice cracks with – *I don't*—

I start to tell her about my idea. It begins with how Mum didn't just deliver letters, she collected things as well. And one group of things she collected were the squares of paper from old people, or ill people, which she took to the practice and exchanged for white bags of medicine.

'She delivered the drugs,' Elizabeth realises.

'Which makes her important, right? So maybe we should look for the squares of paper?'

'Maybe.'

It takes us a minute to find them. They're in five big bundles done up with elastic bands like money, in a back drawer of the dispensary.

Elizabeth counts through twenty. She lays them out on the desk, then goes and fetches Alex's medicine-pen from her rucksack.

The insulin inside it is called Mixtard.

In another minute we have the names of two people who had the same stuff. Then Elizabeth, after checking a book, writes down some more names.

105

We look through the piles of paper, until we find three more that are definitely a kind of insulin.

'One address – see, it's here in the village, nearby,' she says, 'it's really not far. But after that . . . how are we going to find all these other places?'

Feeling a happy rush of pride I reply: 'I know the answer to that as well!'

I'm thinking of the laminate cards that Mum used for her deliveries: the ones she gave for people who were doing the post round and didn't know the island as well as her. And I think I know where they are.

Back Bay

When you're alone mist and rain only makes it feel worse. You can't see where the sky stops and the sea starts.

Every house, every postbox could be the shadow of someone standing still.

It gets me nervous: so I pull the curtains and go into my sleeping bag and begin to count from where I left off—

Seven thousand and one . . . two, three . . .

I remember how Mum used to take a breath in when she was listening. *The Gael's Breath,* she called it. She did it when other adults were talking: a gasp to say: I'm still paying attention. Like she had to drink as well as hear what they were saying.

Now when I close my eyes she's there.

She's doing her talk to the stand-in postman. I go down deep into my bag, down to the crumbs and sweet wrappers and old socks at the bottom, covering up my ears so I can hear her, only her—

'*You've the name given by the registrar,*' she's saying. 'Likely a Protestant from the mainland, olden days. Mary for Mairi,

James for Seamus and so on. Official letters will bear these names. If the letter's sent local it might have a familiar name – with reference to the father, mother. Seumas Nèill – Neil's James, for example. This helps to distinguish him from all the other Jamie MacNeils.'

Mike, the stand-in postman, is trying to write everything down. He has red hair, brown freckles on his hands which are a blur as he tries to write all she says down exact.

'Just as likely the envelope may bear a nickname. This could relate to appearance, work, habit, even something the person did as a child. For example: I am *Mairi a' Phosst* – Mary the Postwoman. *Ailean Còcaire* – Alan the Cook. My daughter here, *Rona Aonranach* – Rona on her own. Likes her ain company does this one.'

Mike the stand-in chooses one letter from all the bundles yet to be sorted.

'*Doo-tang* MacLeod. What is this word *Doo-tang*?'

Mum wrinkles her nose. 'Unluckily that's not a perfect example. It doesn't mean anything at all.'

'Oh?'

'No, it's a nonsense word.'

Mike, frowning, writes down: nonsense word.

'So, names covered, we will move on to addresses. As everybody knows everyone there are no house numbers. Equally, no house names. There are some streets numbered, sure – but not many. Accordingly, even if you do find numbers they are *often not* in the right order. The sequence might be obscure: order of construction, left or right of that wee stream, even peculiar to that street. Perhaps no one knows why some of the numbers are the way they are. To sum up: it isn't always clear-cut.'

'Of course . . .'

'Also, do not assume that a street exists *in one piece*. Our forbears liked to name things according to the contours of *workable* land. For our purpose this means that a village or street may have two halves – two *strands* – existing either side of a hill or watercourse. You have to imagine following the doors *underground*. Consider the lie of the land and not what the map wishes to tell you.'

'Not the map.'

'Lastly, our letterboxes are often sealed against the wind. In which case you will need a key, available by application from the householder in advance.'

His pen stops moving.

Mum hands over her postbag. 'I should say it took me ten years to fathom the intricacies of all the doors. Sure I imagine you'll have it licked by noon.'

He looks at Mum. Back at his notes. At Mum.

'In case you don't' – she goes into her bag – 'here are some laminate cards that I made giving the names, nicknames, numbers and the lie of all the streets, so you can't go wrong. Each village set out on a new card.'

He shakes Mum's hand.

'I was scared for a minute there.'

Mum does her straight smile. 'By the way, that was also a joke about the letterboxes being sealed.'

'Ah. And a right good one.'

*   *   *

109

Mum: do you remember when I said before that there were two times where the new world was beginning, but I didn't know it yet?

The second time came that afternoon: after we left Mike the stand-in to get on with his work.

We were on a rubbish-collect, working the shore with the adults. It's my last truly normal memory, so we both have to remember it, like Elizabeth always said.

The clouds were way out at sea, not over our island. Tide low on Traigh Mhor. Cockle-pickers, miles out, raking lines for the sea to rub smooth again.

'Spread yourselves; take a bag each.' Mrs Leonard points us into spaces. 'Can we have adult, child, adult, child. Adults: keep the children in order. For the children: remember, it's not all junk. There could also be treasure.'

Mrs Leonard doesn't know it, but there's always treasure, and not only the sweets she hid in tubs.

Crab moults. Smoothed glass. Crab legs. Kelp tangles in the shape of mermaids. Bird skulls. Feathers. Kissing stones. Cowrie shells, rarest shell of all.

We drift apart, together. Mrs McClure has her shoes off – bare feet. She's the old woman who swims every day, even when the big hill has snow on it.

'The island salts itself,' she said to Mum once, pointing at the frost creeping up the hill. 'Which our council takes as an excuse for never gritting the damn road.'

Bad smells along the beach: usually sheep that fell off the dunes, or propeller-cut seals washed up.

This time it's a bird: an oystercatcher.

Seonaid Galbraith tries to lift it up, but she gets warned to stand back.

'*Tch*, it'll have germs child, keep your hands away,' Mrs Grant says. 'Don't want you getting sick.'

Seonaid kneels to look close at the bird. 'Doesn't look like there's any badness on it.'

'Well that's the rule with germs. You can't see them, but they see you fine.'

Where the burns run into the sea the sand and peat get mixed into fish-stripes. The river Taing cuts a big channel with crumbling cliffs of sand either side.

Mrs Grant finds me sidling closer and says: 'Oh here's the lassie on her own. How is your mother, Rona?'

'All right.'

Mrs MacDonald asks to see my collected rubbish so far: one plastic bag, one plastic bottle of sailor's piss, polystyrene block gone round, old glove, glass, glass, bottle-top, float.

'*A 'nighean mar a mathair,*' I hear Mrs Grant saying to Mrs Connolly: 'Like mother, like daughter.'

She takes the bottle of piss from me with her eyes and nose wrinkled up.

'*Ah* why are men such filthy pigs? A whole ocean for their excreta, and still they do it in a bottle.'

She holds up the bottle and shouts across to Mr MacNeil: 'Ho, Roddy? Is this your handiwork?'

Mr MacNeil, Duncan's dad, drifts in. He examines the bottle like it's the rarest treasure.

111

'Certainly mine's more luminous than that.' He holds it up to the light. 'And I've a preference for cola bottles when I'm passing water.'

Mrs Grant dumps the bottle in his bag.

Follow Seamus Cowan. Can smell his sweat, mixed with the sea and oilskin-reek.

'Will take him out, soon as he learns,' Duncan's dad is saying, to Seamus. 'Not before. There's no excuse for the eldest son. Look what happened to my father, eh? So now there's the swim-pool, he has no excuse.'

'But you can be too hard on the boy, no?' Seamus says. 'Young Calum Ian looks right fed up with himself. Getting out, even on the bay, giving him a taste of it, that would pull him along don't you think?'

'I disagree. He needs to learn his swimming first. Then he goes fishing. That's my choice.'

'Sure, but you have your ain mind.'

Mum – even this last normal memory told tales about what would happen. The lack of swimming became important for us later on, as you'll find out.

And I never forgot what Mrs Grant said about germs – *you can't see them but they see you fine* – although understanding this, *really* understanding this was always going to be the one big problem for us.

Eleven days ago

It took us a day to pluck up the courage to leave. With our school lessons, and shopping, and our homes, we'd made a bit of life that felt normal. So now the thought of going away: to the places we don't know, past the safe edge of our village, makes everyone worry for what we'll find now that we're forced to go and see.

We're nearly ready to leave – when Alex goes missing.

I find him hiding under his bed, in the thick of a mess of dusty toys. Only he's not playing: he's just looking up, at the wooden boards holding up the mattress he sleeps on.

'Wonder what it's like to die,' he says.

I try to reach him, but he just shuffles further in.

'Don't know,' I answer. 'Never did it. Not even when every-body else did.'

'I think it's like your DS. When you take out the game, and the screen freezes. It's like that in real life. Your eyes keep seeing their last thing for ever.'

113

It's strange – like another idea of his, that lava is just beneath the pavement. This one sounds half-true.

Me: 'What if you saw a bit of dog shit then you died? You'd see dog shit for ever.'

His eyes warm up to an almost-smile. 'Or if you saw a fat man with a fat arse?'

Me: 'A famous person farting in the bath.'

Alex: 'The Queen?'

Me: 'Good choice. You have to be careful what to see.'

Alex: 'Our mums and dads?'

Me: '*Best* choice. You just have to get the choice right, see? Then everything's OK.'

We bunch together in the gap by the beds. I see the broken rim of Alex's bedside cabinet. There's still a red smudge on his carpet from the spilled food dye.

Alex must be looking at this too, because he says: 'I get unwell without my injections.'

He lets me link my arm in his. 'We're going to get some. We could be at your home by tonight even.'

His eyes go bright when I mention home. But the brightness of them goes out just as quick, so I'm left noticing how dirty around his mouth is.

'Do we have to go to my old house?'

'You don't want to?'

I remind him we need to look for insulin. He gathers up a ball of dust and says, 'Don't think my mum and dad are alive. And you know what else? I worry really about finding them when we get to my old home.'

He comes out, brushing off his trousers. Then he brushes his hands, as if he's showing that we settled the business. Still, he looks unsure.

'What if you stayed seeing a bad thing?'

'You worrying again?'

He kicks the wooden stump of our bunk beds. 'To see a bad thing for ever – that would be the same as going to hell wouldn't it?'

I want to argue against this – but Alex only smiles, the way adults did when they were just pretending to agree – and we have to be leaving anyway.

Mum's van is where it always is. Like every other car there's bird shit and cat shit over it, and the tyres have gone flat.

She must've stopped using the car, because she wouldn't have let standards slip so far. She liked to keep things clean, shipshape.

Mike the stand-in postman left Mum's laminate maps in the van before he left us.

He went back to Oban, so we didn't get to go to Glasgow, and we didn't get shopping for Christmas. At the time I thought this was the worst thing to happen, but now it's become small beside all the other stuff.

The van door's stiff and creaks loud. There's still letters, undelivered. Old elastic bands on the floor. The seat has Mum's smell, sadly gone quiet now. I find a scrunchy on the floor which smells so much of her I can't stand it.

Calum Ian and Elizabeth whistle at the laminate maps as if they're treasure, which I suppose they are.

I try to tell Elizabeth that Alex got sad – but she shushes me. While they get busy puzzling the streets and places I whisper an ask in Elizabeth's ear.

'All right, but be quick about it,' she says.

My home once-upon-a-time already has a **P** sprayed by me on the door. You get to spray your old home, that's the rule. So I sprayed **P** for perfect, because it was my real home in the world before.

Houses are **G** for Good if they don't have a smell or a dead body. **B** for Bad if they do. It lets us know where we've been, and if we have to go back there, what we'll find.

Except for the curly **G** that I sprayed on Calum Ian and Duncan's home. That broke all the rules, even though I wasn't thinking about rules or anything when I did it.

'Hullo?'

Nobody answers.

In the kitchen there's dirty washing in the sink. Sinks can smell, though ours doesn't. Mum's grey pants and bras are on a clothes horse. The tablecloth with those pen marks she scolded me for. Our folding chairs. The bit of wallpaper I used to peel. She scolded me for that, too.

In the living room there's six Christmas cards on the mantelpiece. *Season's Greetings*, says one. Greetings here doesn't mean crying or meeting but Happy Returns.

There's the Christmas tree. Now I remember her putting it up, on our last night together. Plus the broken boxes, including the box for my game, which she flattened then tried to make good again right at the end.

Mum's boots; her spare post office jacket. That smells of wool and oil and being in the rain.

Upstairs, everything got small. My room. Most of all I see the stickers I shouldn't've put on the wall. Left-alone bits of Lego. My Sleeping Beauty costume, my armbands for swimming. Everything with dust on it. There wasn't as much dust last time we came in.

My best CD. Mum bought me *Queen Greatest Hits*. It's only the case, the CD proper is at our new home. It gets ten stars from everyone, apart from Alex who doesn't like the bit where the man sings 'I don't like *Star Wars*'.

The bed feels cold, which is wrong because it's summer. It doesn't feel like my bed. It doesn't feel like my room.

In the cobweb-dirt underneath I find two things: my teddy-chimp called Tom. Then an old plastic sword that Alex could like. I give Tom a cuddle, but his eyes are just stitches crossed so I decide not to save him.

Mum's room. As well, looks smaller. I open the curtains. A seagull flaps off the windowsill.

Just an empty drying green. Bits of torn washing, still up, amazing.

Her case, halfway to being packed. Some perfumes on the bedside cabinet. I spray once then all over. Stings my eyes. Then I get up on the bed.

When I close my eyes the bed sags down beside.

'Do unto others as you would have done unto you,' Mum says. 'You have to be kind.'

Then she says, 'Concentrate and the world is yours.'

I concentrate.

117

'Don't run with bullies.'

'Who would!'

'Hold scissors by the sharp end. Never, ever run with scissors.'

'I would never run with them. Or with bullies.'

'*Tha sin ceart*. Keep in mind, last of all: many hands make light work.'

'We call that teamwork these days, Mum. But don't get stressed, you're only catching up.'

I lie beside her for a bit. But then I catch a smell: which makes me open my eyes, quick, to make sure she isn't actually there.

In the hallway downstairs I notice: one of her letters.

It got crushed against the wall when I shoved the front door open. It's white on one side where the sun paled it.

Not opened.

Her signing-words: *Mo Ivaidh Rona.*

It looks too clean against my clarty fingers.

The truth could be she's been and left it today. For a truth it's a hard one, but nobody could say opposite – that she hasn't. Nobody could say better than me how Mum comes and goes, where she goes between.

Calum Ian is hiding outside when I open the door. He had his ear to the letterbox. Quickly I push Mum's letter down inside my jumper, praying he hasn't noticed.

'Yet another stupid kid holding us up,' he says, poking me in the chest. 'You headed to stab someone?'

I don't know what he means – then I see that I'm holding the plastic sword I picked up for Alex.

'It's a present.'

'You get presents for all the rest of us as well?'

'I forgot.'

'Then what did you put down your jumper? See – it's slipping away free – nearly at the bottom—'

I push the letter back up by folding my arms. But as I go to walk past, Calum Ian catches me. He tries to tickle the letter out, but his fingers are too angry for it to feel funny.

We struggle – I don't want to give up first – so I nip his arm and he pulls away, wincing at the sore bit.

Now I see a new look in his eyes – a look I never saw before, fiercer than the one he gave earlier about his camera.

'Keep it close, *Gloic*,' he shouts at the back of me. '*Real* close. I'm not finished with you.'

Calum Ian has a very heavy backpack. He won't show us what's inside it, which is bothering Elizabeth, maybe because she's nosy enough to want to know everything, though not enough yet to force him to show.

'You'll find out later,' is all he'll say.

We don't take the bikes, because Alex never learned to ride. And we don't need Mum's maps to get to the first house, because it's still in the village: at the end of the single-track road that begins with the broken-roof church.

The doormat says **NOT YOU AGAIN**. This is just the kind of dumb joke adults like. Me and Alex take an edge each, throw the mat over a wall.

Calum Ian and Duncan have been here before. They sprayed the door – not **G** or **B**, but **L** for Locked. I try the handle but they got it right: it is locked.

It's an old house, with an upstairs bit, and a mossy garden. We search around its edges. There's brown board on the front windows – shutters? And on the side windows. Elizabeth thinks it's cardboard, Calum Ian doesn't.

We circle the house to see if there's a trick way in or an easy way, but there isn't. I want to give up – then Elizabeth notices the bathroom window. It's got frosted glass, but doesn't look like it's blocked over inside.

'Stand back,' Calum Ian says.

He finds a good-sized stone and throws it.

It's maybe the tenth or ninth throw that smashes the glass in. After this, he uses a slate from the path to knock the broken edges away.

'Is it me who's got to be brave again?'

Everyone finds the best bit of their shoes to look at. Calum Ian nods, makes a sound in his throat like he knew we'd be too shitting it anyway. Then he gets Duncan to punt him up through the hole – and he's gone.

It feels like a year before we hear the kitchen door further along being scraped open. Then he comes out.

'I'm not doing this on my own,' he says, glaring at us. 'For why? Because there's a stink.'

When Alex hears this he won't come in. I feel the same: and want to tell them all to turn around, yet I'd rather not show my fear, or make them think I'm just a kid made the same as Alex, so I don't say anything.

The kitchen's half-bright. There are pans filled with water in plastic bags, on the table, on the floor. Whoever the person was they used clear plastic bags, which meant that their water inside went slimy. It's a mistake many people made, but we're far wiser now.

On one wall there's a map of the world. In the map are lots of red and blue and green pins, mostly around Asia, but with some around America, Europe. Alongside the map are cut-outs from newspapers. It's all to do with what happened. There's a heap of cut papers on a chair, maybe the ones this person never got around to sticking up.

'Should've spent time reading up on water instead,' Calum Ian says. He picks up the papers and begins to read them out with a posh adult voice—

'Chief Medical Officer confirms WHO report on Guangdong Virus.

'As feared it seems to have an extended incubation.

'Aerosol spread from shopping malls: bogus oxygen bars. Ban on reporting this story finally lifted.

'UN security council: no consensus.

'Those in urban centres advised to stay at home. Those in rural areas under no current restrictions.'

He laughs at this, then angrily raps the page: 'Did you not see what happened to us, then? Did ye not? You got it right for everybody else, so why not us?'

And he begins to tear the pages, into smaller and smaller pieces – then looks up at us looking at him.

'Get a *move on*,' he orders – like we were the ones keeping him back.

He makes us pull all the kitchen drawers. We don't find any medicine for Alex, but we do find: tins of Carnation milk, garibaldi biscuits, croutons, brown sugar, raisins, treacle, flour.

121

I'm keen to start taking things home but Elizabeth says no, we've our job to do first.

The living room's dark. Strings of sun around the boards. The smell worse here. Calum Ian goes to the window and finds that Elizabeth was correct: the boards are just cardboard.

He tears a strip, the sun comes in.

There's a tile fireplace, plus a couch, chair the murk colour of pond but hanging with lace. On the floor, lots of bottles of water: pans, jars, tubs, covered, laid out just anywhere. On the couch, a scrunch of sheets looking like a human with bad dreams got twisted up in them.

I walk between the bottles, pans. Duncan knocks one over – we all hiss at him to be careful.

From the hall Calum Ian shouts – 'Dead person!'

The body's on the stair.

It's a man – curled up, at the corner of a bigger turn-step. He has plasters to keep the skin on his face. The proper skin behind these went black, which makes him look all in bits, like patchwork.

There's a carton of milk-yuck at his hand. Plus a box of the pills we've seen in lots of houses.

The smell of him is bad, but not the worst, maybe because he's in the dark.

Elizabeth puts on her perfume-hanky and goes as close as she dares to see if there's any insulin on the ground beside him. There isn't.

We do the rest of our search, quick. In the second bedroom, in a cabinet, Elizabeth finds a box with an insulin pen, and one glass vial.

122

But it's empty.

'It's only the first house,' she says. 'At least we found some-thing, which is a good sign.'

On the way out we stand to pay our respects.

Elizabeth shows me a framed picture she found upstairs: of an old man, smiling beside the school gates. Now we know who it is: Mr Roseberry, the retired headmaster who used to be the teacher for Mum at the big school.

Everyone tries to remember at least one nice thing about him. Duncan goes first: says Mr Roseberry was one of the people who used to tut if you were noisy in the shop.

I remember him as an old man pushing a trolley, buying meat and eggs.

Elizabeth thinks of his eyes being blue.

Calum Ian, though, doesn't have a memory. Instead, he starts unpacking his rucksack.

Now he's holding up – what?

A plastic water gun. I recognise it from the Co-op, from a display of toys nobody needs now.

He holds it up – then begins to *wet* the body of Mr Roseberry. It's so strange that I nearly want to laugh.

Elizabeth: 'What are—?'

'Fucking shut up; keep your eyes peeled for once. This is one way we'll survive, just you watch.'

'Is that – *petrol*?'

Calum Ian is holding a packet of matches. With the gun he sprays a line on the floor between us and the headmaster.

'Who wants to light?'

Elizabeth can't seem to talk, or move – but then she

remembers how and tugs at my jumper, pushing Duncan, who's behind her, back towards the door.

'Go. Out, *quick.*'

So we're pushed back through the living room: her hand jabbing at our backs, until we're on the step again, still expecting a flare or a flash from behind, running in case the heat of a fire swallows us up.

In the end there's no fire. Did he use the spray for show, or just to worry us? Now we're back on the road.

Calum Ian is showing us the rest of what's in his backpack.

He unwraps a square of blue tarpaulin. He's taped it at the edges – making pockets on the inside, from which we can see handles poking out.

The handles are of knives. He slides one out. It's the sort that Mum used in her kitchen. On the handle of the first knife he's put a sticker: of the devil, grinning.

There's another knife: very long and all-silver. This one has a tiny skull-and-crossbones sticker.

Elizabeth stands quite deliberately ahead of me and Alex, blocking us from going too near.

'The sticker ones are poison-tipped,' Calum Ian says, sounding casual like it's normal for knives to be poisoned.

'What should I say?'

'Say you're impressed.'

'What kind of poison?'

'Homemade. Stuck them in dirty water I created. If you

want to know how to make the water dirty – just look at what the dogs leave on the road.'

Elizabeth stares at him, as if it were opposite-day from how she felt yesterday – when he helped at the surgery, when he went into the gym.

Then she says: 'I want you to put those away. I want you to wrap them up and get rid of them. Now.'

Calum Ian looks at her with the same hard face, then doesn't do as she says. Instead, he goes inside another pocket and hands something to Alex and Duncan.

'Found *these* in the pub. Darts. Keep them in their wallets till you need. Practise with them, much as you need. For when the time comes.'

Looking at me he says, 'You're not to be trusted. So you're not getting anything.'

I make a rude sign at him, then fold my arms for not caring.

After this he puts away the wrap.

Elizabeth lifts, shrugs on her rucksack: but slowly, still keeping an eye out for what Calum Ian will do next.

'Are you scared of something?' she asks.

'What me, scared? Ha! I'm not scared of anything.'

'Then let me give you a different question. Why do we need weapons?'

Now he doesn't answer: instead he looks ahead, to where we're going, to the road going up over the hill and beyond.

He says, 'Just dogs. They could've gone wild.'

'We live beside them here. They don't bother us, not even the ones that kill the cats, chase the sheep.'

'Only trying to be safe.'

But even I can see – maybe even Alex can see – that he's only telling half of what's worrying him.

Past the signpost at the end of town we look back. The cats are dust, the dogs just specks. When I hold up a finger to cover the rubbish on the beach, and the wrecked trawler, everything could be back to normal.

Soon we've passed the furthest anyone went on their own. Elizabeth's furthest mark is a toppled rainbow of fish crates; Calum Ian's, a rusted van.

We go quick at first but then everything slows down. The bigger kids want to walk at different speeds. Elizabeth goes way out in front, from where she calls on us, pulling Alex's hand to help him go faster. Calum Ian, meanwhile, is the opposite: he stalks in the fields alongside, calling on Duncan if there's anything he's suspicious of or doesn't understand.

This is why he slows so much at all the dead sheep. One, then another, then another. He thinks it's too many to be a coincidence – and so he shouts on Elizabeth, who's forced to come back and look at the nearest: a ram with its neck stuck through a fence.

After dying it turned into a head with no eyes, and straggles of skin and wool behind.

'There wasn't a farmer to set it free,' she explains. 'After a while it died. End of story.'

She asks him to look at her then says: 'There's something you're not telling us. Right?'

Calum Ian won't keep looking. Instead, he goes back over the fence, and crouches there, waiting until she moves on before starting up his stalking again.

It takes us all day. Calum Ian holds back, holds back. It gets in me that he's waiting by the roadside to see if we'll get into trouble first. Which is not very nice.

At least ten times Elizabeth comes back and shouts on him to speed up, but he won't: won't walk the road or walk beside us, even when there's rocks he has to climb, or lines of fences.

'We set off too late,' Elizabeth says. 'It's late.'

I forgot how big the world was. Forgot how the west beaches had big waves. Forgot how the sun could be shiny on the sea. Forgot that sand blew in drifts on the road.

And we all forgot the roadblock.

Nobody wants to see it, be reminded. Yet here it is. It truly did happen.

Maybe fifty, maybe a hundred cars jammed together on the uphill beside a cliff. It looks eerie: like all the people of the island were here all along, waiting until we plucked up the courage to come and find them.

For safety we throw stones at the back of the nearest cars for a while. When nothing serious happens, we get close enough to touch the one that's nearest.

Its tyres went flat, like Mum's van at home. There's salt-swirls, dust, bird shit covering the windows.

Up ahead are five big metal baskets, filled with stones and boulders. The baskets are way bigger than us. They're spread out, right across the road, with the spaces between them only big enough for side-on walking.

'I saw them put the baskets in here,' Duncan says. 'We got stuck on the other side. It was when Mum was trying to get Flora to hospital. It felt like all day.'

'It *was* all bloody day,' Calum Ian says. 'Then they came and took her anyway. And left us on the bad side.' Grinning not for fun at Elizabeth he adds: 'Bet *you* were on the good side. 'Course you were, being the *doctor's* daughter. Only the best for you.'

Elizabeth doesn't bother to reply.

We pluck up our courage to walk between them. Further in the cars are jammed so close that they're nearly touching. I guessed that they were all empty – but then figure my guess was wrong when Alex calls out and begins to cry and Elizabeth shouts, 'Don't look in the windows!'

Too late: he already did.

Once again, Calum Ian comes last. Elizabeth watches him – while he watches us, bending down between cars, ready with his gun and matches and knives.

'What is *wrong* with your brother?' she shouts at Duncan. 'Why is he being like this?'

Duncan only finds a hole in his jeans to widen. If he does know, he won't say.

We're tired out when we get to the second house. I'm ready for it to have a smell – after the last place it seems likely somehow, and I'm ready, even though I never slept one night in a bad house – but the smell is clean.

We don't find any insulin. We even don't find the things a person might have along with insulin, which is a mystery nobody supposes on. What we do find, though, is that the bath is plugged, covered, and full of water – so we have enough to drink, after Elizabeth drops in a sterilising tablet. Plus there's OK food in the kitchen: although microwave popcorn feels like a joke done by the devil.

For dinner we have tinned ham with pineapple juice, which nobody wants much of. After this, we spend ages trying to puff up the popcorn using a lighter, which only makes it go black, even though the smell starts off true.

We make camp in the living room. When Calum Ian joins us, everybody goes quiet. He puts his rucksack, with the weapons inside, by the room's fireplace.

The petrol smell of it is there: also strong on his clothes, his jacket.

Darkness comes around us. Duncan opens up his own rucksack, and takes out his portable DVD player and battery pack. He puts on *Jungle Book*, mainly because Alex doesn't want to see anything that isn't a cartoon.

It's good, though these days Mowgli gets on everyone's nerves: all he had to do was get through a jungle of mostly friendly animals and he was with his people.

By the end of it Alex sighs and says, 'You forgot my insulin.'

This is a surprise: mainly because Elizabeth never forgets. She will even wake him up, or go looking for him as far as the other side of the village just so he isn't even five minutes late.

Then I understand better – when she opens up the tub of injection things and says, 'Possibly we should save . . . if I had

129

a better idea from someone . . . I mean it's difficult, can't truly tell . . .'

'What?'

'There's only one shot left.'

We all gather to look at the pen. She clicks out the glass vial to show us: it's at the end.

Still, Alex looks easiest of all about it. He tells us to wind up our smiles, then says: 'I can feel a luckier time coming. Seriously! So you might as well just give. See, my home got saved. It's got lots of cupboards for keeping medicine in. You'll see.'

But then he looks less sure, and begins to curl a finger in his hair until it snaps. It sounds sore, but he doesn't seem to notice: and I just know he's thinking worst-case: about what – and who – we'll find when we get there.

Then he says, 'I made Mum a sandwich with jam. Only she didn't want it. She said to me don't come too close. Which is hard when you're only five.'

Elizabeth takes out her swabs, cleaning stuff. She rubs the skin of his stomach, puts the needle in.

'Done,' she says.

Done, which here means: there's none left.

After a long gap of quiet Calum Ian says: 'Supposing he can do without it for a bit?'

I expect Elizabeth to disagree – instead, she unties her rucksack and takes out one of her mum and dad's books, and begins to read with her finger.

'Might not be serious,' he whispers, trying to keep out

Alex. 'Mean to say, maybe it's like when you get your jabs? For measles and stuff. In the old days – before? You need them, but it isn't like you *die* if you don't get them. I bet it's like that.'

Elizabeth writes in her notebook. She reads and reads with her finger. Then says, 'Don't know. I've read it all. It's not like it tells you how things go if you don't give. It just says you have to give. Maybe that's clear?'

Her voice has gone loud. Calum Ian mumbles something. Then he takes some of the popcorn from the packet. He puts it in a spoon and uses his lighter to try and burn it bigger.

'For God's sake,' Elizabeth says. 'You're stinking of petrol. Can't you just *stop* using the lighter in here.'

Calum Ian puts his lighter away. He clicks his torch on and off instead.

Out of the silence of many minutes I hear Elizabeth say, 'So we're your guinea pigs. True? You're letting us go ahead of you on the walk. True?'

'Not true.'

'Because you're scared of what we'll find. You're scared about the stuff we haven't seen yet.'

'Why didn't you want to go past *your* house? It's on the other island road. Not far. Answer me that.'

'You think you're a tough boy – actually you don't help the group. You're not a team player.'

'Cos teamwork is the *dreamwork*,' Calum Ian spits, making the last word sound like poison.

Elizabeth answers: 'Bad-sounding word? You hate it? So you know what I hate? Cowards.'

131

He bites his lip: an angry bite, the kind that leaves your mouth bleeding after.

'I'm not a coward,' he says. 'That's never going to be true. Who went inside the gym? Who went into the old man's house? The same answer. Me.'

'And who let us walk ahead all day? Holding us up, so we only checked two houses? Same answer.'

'Who couldn't help herself for the first month? Who had to be fed with a spoon cos she forgot how to eat? Who heard voices of people that weren't there? Know what the answer is for that?'

Elizabeth, rather than saying back, just stares at the wall, at the photos of the family who once lived here. Of course it was her. But then she came around, and we need her now.

I shine the torch – at my own face, showing Calum Ian with an ugly look what I think of him.

'And don't *you* think you're so great,' he says. 'Heard you talking to yourself earlier as well.'

When I say that I didn't, Calum Ian answers that he heard me talking – back at my house this morning.

'Wasn't to myself.'

'Who, then? Tooth fairy? Easter bunny, Santa? Sorry to say, they don't exist and wouldn't care if they did.'

'None of your business.'

'Who?'

I wait for him to forget about it. But he doesn't – and instead asks me again and again, until the real answer is too much to keep inside: 'It was with my mum. All right?'

Calum Ian nearly starts to laugh: then his face changes,

132

becomes more serious. He asks, 'How do you know it wasn't your dad?'

I wait until I'm sure he's being genuine about knowing – that it isn't just another trap of his – then I say, 'I know because it was her voice. She comes out with her sayings, that can only be her. And anyway – Mum and Dad didn't live together. They lived apart. He lived on the mainland.'

'So they split up. Was it a big fight?'

'No, come on.' I'm wanting to sound like it's easy to speak about. 'There wasn't any fight. Mum told me it was because they couldn't agree on baby names.'

Calum Ian *does* laugh now. He tries to hold it in, but the sound of this only makes it worse.

'Shut up!'

'*Gloic* – that's just what she *told* you!'

Elizabeth turns on her torch. I see her giving Calum Ian a furious stare.

'My mum never lied,' I say. 'It's true.'

'Don't be dull, *Gloic*. Mums and dads don't break up over baby names. There has to be other stuff. Y'know, like fights, arguments. Over money, dishes.'

My face feels red hot. Even in the dark it seems like everyone's looking at me, staring.

'What about yours? Your dad's probably dead.'

Calum Ian grabs the torch and shines it right in my face. '*You* fuck off! *Bheir mi dhut sgailc!* He told us: all we had to do was wait – at home. He said sit tight, collect water, save our food, keep strong, he'd come back. And if it wasn't for you we'd still be there waiting for him!'

133

'You don't collect food; you *steal* ours.'

'*You* did worse to us. If you hadn't've done it then none of this would've happened. You *killed* the pictures we had of Mum. Of our sister Flora.'

'Your teeth are brown and stinky.' Now I try to think of the worst possible thing I could ever say: and knowing how angry he got already about it, this is it: 'Hope your dad's dead.'

In the torchlight I see his eyes go tight.

The next bit happens too quick, or too slow for me to understand all at once.

I see him reaching for his rucksack. Hear the zip of the top of it opening, fast.

Then Elizabeth lunging forward: she calls out, half a scream, half a shout. Her torch is knocked to the floor.

Then she's crying.

'You stupid, stupid boy,' she's saying. 'Stupid, stupid. How will we keep going like this?'

Duncan and Alex come to see what happened. Duncan shines his torch on her leg: and we see where the dart he tried to stab me with jabbed into her instead.

A few drops of blood running down.

Calum Ian makes a sad sound – why should he also be the one to cry? Then grabs his rucksack and goes off to sleep in one of the other rooms next door.

I have to go out, get away. Out to the back green, where I throw stones at a wooden fence, imagining Calum Ian's face being smashed into a thousand tiny pieces.

My breath comes back; my anger goes down. I look around.

134

I recognise Mrs Barron's house, just up the road. There's rubbish snagged in her fence, under the washing line where Mum stood, once.

I touch her letter, hidden still in the fold of my jumper. The paper of it warming my stomach.

Mum sits on the fence, five posts along. I try and bounce her up. She doesn't bounce back.

'You should've been here to stand up for me,' I say in a huff.

'Been here loads.'

'Well you could help, you could help a bit more . . . Did you post this letter earlier on today?'

'For me to know.'

I look to the sky, back again. She's still there.

'If you're going to stay, I'll tell you – today's news is: Calum Ian is my enemy. He makes weapons. He's just hurt Elizabeth. Plus he says you and Dad didn't fall out over any baby names.'

'You keep a good hand to that letter. It's the early bird that catches the worm.'

'Alex is always picking up worms.'

'*Tch,* dirty boy.'

'I'm going to get back at Calum Ian. I know what his weak spot is now. It's his Dad.'

'Top marks, *mo a ghraidh*! But I can't always be minding you. Stay away from bullies. Never—'

'—run with knives. You said that the last time, Mum. Can you not say something different this time?'

Mum turns into only air.

I close my eye and catch her in the tear it makes.

135

Back Bay

To the edge of the dunes, God. Layers of the world.

Sometimes bones stick out: of sheep, rabbits.

Don MacPhail put cars in the sand dunes to stop the island from blowing away.

'Come see my traffic jam,' he said to me once, when I met him with Mum on the beach.

He surprised us with steering wheels, engines, seats in sand. His collie dog ran ahead, tail circling the wind.

The island – always moving, he said. Like a giant that hasn't decided yet where it wants to be.

And now, from up here, I can see most of it.

The hill gets me sweating. The grass gone-yellow, tough so it scratches my legs. Bits of bog-cotton wafting. Then, keeping away, small birds, not seagulls, with wings so thin they might be made of paper.

I look away out to sea. No boats. Just islands, black with shadows on one side, gold the other.

There's the tanker, or trawler. It's too square-long to be an island, too brown. I don't like to look at it for very long in case there's ghosts on deck.

Then I think I see something that's not an island.

My arms know it first. My arms are moving, even before my heart or my head catch up. It's a boat. Not an island, or a wreck, it's too white. Surely it's a boat with the sun on it, with the shine of sun coming and going?

I shout, shout until my voice gives up. The paper-wing birds go up, circle me high in the sky.

Then the shine tells me something different.

It's only a buoy. Guarding the entrance to the bay. And worse: I've seen it before. It did the same thing to me before.

Mum, back to this memory: You keep me in the van. You don't go to the doors as you do your round. There's other stuff for delivery, but not as many letters as usual. You're smoking, which you said you'd stopped for ever. It makes the van stink. When I tell you not to you don't even notice I said anything.

'Why'd he go?' I ask.

You don't hear until I shout, then I have to tell who I'm meaning: Mike, the stand-in postman. He never even made a single delivery. Plus he left all of your laminate cards on the floor of the van, just to keep reminding us about his going away and leaving us.

'Had family,' you say.

Then you turn up the radio. As we go around the side of the island to the north end it loses signal. You switch around stations until you get it back.

'Hush – trying to hear.'

But I wasn't saying anything, not for ages.

On the ribbon road there's two lorries from the fish factory. You flash your lights and roll down the window at the passing place, to indicate you want to talk.

'The tankers get in?'

The driver in the red overalls shakes his head. He talks about diesel, something else I don't understand. Then you talk about the bank, the ferry, most of it in whispers. When I turn down the radio to hear a bit better you turn it up again and get out of the car.

Some other cars come; you wave them past.

It starts to rain when we're driving again. You keep turning the radio to get any kind of signal.

'Will Dad come?'

You light another cigarette with the car's red glow button. Then say, 'He'll be looking after himself.'

'Why are the ferries cancelled?'

'It's temporary.'

'But there isn't a storm. Or even any fog.'

'I know.'

'Did the ferry engine break like it did last summer?'

'No.'

'So why, then?'

You pull the car into a passing place, then turn around to speak to me. Sometimes when it's raining your face gets dirty from the ink on the letters. Like today.

'To stop people coming in.'

*   *   *

138

The shadow of Beinn Tangabhal gets long. It grows like the tongue of a giant over our village.

I climbed over the counter at the post office. In a dusty cupboard I found cartridges of ink.

I cracked a black one open, then used the ink to make my cheeks smudged, like Mum's.

But with only halfway light in the mirror at home it looked stupid. Like a girl with scars had decided to draw all over her face, pretending she had a beard.

'Like you're facing your worst enemy,' I say to the girl.

She only just beat me to it this time.

Ten days ago

Next morning, for the first time, Alex misses his insulin. We watch as he eats his favourite breakfast – wafer biscuits with jam, dried apricots with juice – to see if he'll start to become unwell or act strange.

All that happens is he gets fed up of all our staring, and takes his food off to a different room.

Nobody talks about what Calum Ian did with the dart. When it's time to go he packs quiet and separate from the rest of us, talking only to Duncan and Alex.

His rucksack looks as heavy as it did before; and the smell on it is still strong with petrol.

When we start off on the road again he's exactly the same as yesterday: holding back, always being last, watching. But now Elizabeth has slowed, too: though for why, to annoy him or to outdo him, I can't tell.

Alex's house is a mile up the road. It has a red roof, a garden around. There's a trampoline blown on its side, jammed under

140

a fence. His old bike is there, but rusted so much that we can't turn the wheels or the steering.

We spray our perfume-hankies. Alex stays at the gate, nervously chewing his sleeve.

'Please don't be spraying petrol,' he says, putting his hands together in prayer in front of Calum Ian.

Calum Ian just waves him away.

The house – has no smell. Calum Ian goes right in, takes off his hanky. He breathes deep. Then he comes back and claps Alex on the back like he's a competition winner.

'It's all right.'

After this, ahead of schedule, Duncan takes out his spray-paint and sprays a gold **G** on the door.

'I'm the luckiest kid,' Alex says.

In the hallway it only smells of coldness. His house reminds me of my old home, with its stairs, shoe rack, curtains. There's a pair of Highland dancing shoes with red laces on the floor, which Alex says belonged to his big sister, Clare. I forgot or never knew in the first place he had a big sister. He was only ever Alex to me.

The living room has black leather chairs. There's a scrunched yellow duvet on the longest sofa. On the floor, a mess of plastic aprons, masks, towels. Some of the towels have dirty bits on them, which seems to get Alex ashamed, because he kicks them into a corner.

We get on guard for finding something bad, but Alex says it was like this before: the same mess.

'The masks were dumb,' he says. 'They made my face go hot and my nose itchy.'

141

'What – you prefer being dead?' Duncan asks.

'Lots of dead people are still wearing them,' Alex answers.

There's a pile of Alex's old DVDs on the floor. He looks through them, though we've found most of his favourites in other people's homes. Elizabeth, meanwhile, looks in the kitchen for injection things. She opens the drawers as softly and as kindly as she can, for respect.

In one drawer, in a plastic box, she finds bandages, antiseptic creams. In another: tissues, candles, kids' plasters with brave faces on them.

No insulin.

I stay in the living room beside Alex. He stares at the sofa, at the scrunched duvet. Then says, 'This was where Mum was sick.' He pulls back the duvet and calls out in surprise. 'See I just found it, look! There's her plate with the jam sandwich I made her!'

Duncan goes ahead to look. The sandwich isn't a sandwich. It's a shrivelled crisp of green-grey mould.

'She never ate it,' Alex says.

'No wonder,' Duncan laughs, trying a joke, then seeing that the not-eating is a subject Alex is sad about.

'If only I'd made a better job,' he says. 'She might've had it and got her strength. She might've got better.'

Duncan forgets his joke. He puts an arm over Alex's back instead. Alex says, 'Auntie Jane was crying about us being in here, but she was too strict, wasn't she?'

'Strict? For what?'

'For going away. When the men came they wouldn't let me

go with Mum. I told them I wouldn't get sick, that I didn't have a cold all summer. I said "Cross my heart, hope to die; stick a needle in my eye." I even kicked the edge of the rug, but it was no use.'

'They took your mum . . .'

'So I stayed with Auntie Jane. Only she was too scared to inject me. After that I don't remember.'

We cover the sandwich up. Alex pats the duvet like it's a favourite friend, then frowns, calls himself *eejit*.

His sister Clare's room is the first one upstairs. She has a sign Sellotaped to her door: PLEASE KNOCK BEFORE ENTERING and if I am not here GO AND LOOK FOR ME. The OOs of LOOK have dots to turn them into accusing eyes.

There's a bookcase, striped carpet, bed, wardrobe. She has a silver CD player. The CD inside is by Lady Gaga. Her bedsheets are pink. So's the carpet.

We wait for Alex to decide what to do. For once he's the boss; even Calum Ian waits.

After thinking about it, Alex goes to Clare's bookcase to look through her books. He spends a long time there, then picks up something from the floor.

It's a girl's shoe: shiny black. Alex puts it back on the floor next to his own foot for measurement.

'Her feet went less of a size,' he says. 'I never realised my big sister would go that way.'

Next along is his mum and dad's bedroom. The duvet's missing – it's downstairs. The wardrobes emptied, with a lot of

143

plastic bags of clothes on the floor. The bedside lamp, broken. Perfumes on a dressing table.

We follow him to his old room. There's a sign on the door made of red card and gold tinsel which says *Santa Stop Here*. He has a small bed, and the wardrobe's small too. There's a teddy bear temperature-reader on a chest of drawers, which right now says **COLD**.

He opens his toybox. There are a lot of things inside for a boy. I want him to have a party of it, but he just stares at the contents. Then closes the box.

'So this is my house,' he says, circling his hands. 'I hope you like it. It's quite dark. Also, it feels lonelier than it did. But it's a good house, and I'm proud of it.'

He sits on the toybox. All of a sudden the fun seems to melt away from his face, and he says, 'What if they won't understand? What if we've changed how we speak so much that when adults come to find us we'll be talking a different language?'

Everybody goes quiet – maybe because there isn't any way of proving that it *couldn't* happen, other than it not being long enough for time.

'*We'd* know,' Calum Ian says. 'I'd tell you straight if you started talking rubbish. We'd give you a clap on the head to get you normal again.'

Alex doesn't answer back. He gets up from the toybox and goes out to the hall.

We follow, and he stops on the stairs.

Still being in charge he points at Duncan like he's the smaller kid then says: 'You can be the one to put on my DVD.'

Duncan says, 'You want a film?'

'Not a film. Something else. It's part of the worst. I'm not scared if you're here. It's downstairs.'

'What worst—'

'Downstairs.'

We follow him to the living room. After a time of chewing his sleeve Alex points to the DVD player then says, 'Inside that.'

Duncan takes a metal ruler out of his rucksack. He uses it to break the lid of the DVD player.

There's a disc inside: just silver, no film name. He hands it to Alex. Alex doesn't want to touch it.

Duncan looks at us, puzzled, then goes back into his rucksack and takes out his portable DVD player. He connects the battery-pack, puts in the disc.

We try to bunch together by sitting on the floor and on the chair behind.

When the screen gets broken into choices we press **PLAY**.

The first is an *advert*! Everyone cheers, it's amazing! There's a bathroom being cleaned with blue stuff. A lady with shining blonde hair smiling at her clean toilet. Adverts only happen when the world is going OK!

Then it's the news. Alex hides his eyes.

It's an early news. They didn't know yet. There's a foggy picture of a night-time street. Then a lady reporter, wearing a mask and lifting it up to talk to the man in a blue suit beside her.

We press return for **MAIN MENU**. Elizabeth reads the dates of the clips with her finger. Her shoulders drop and she makes a sad groan in her throat.

November, December.

'Who did these? All these recordings?'

'Dad.'

Next: a newsman beside a fence. Behind him is a plane. This one and lots of other planes have been told not to leave. But the people can't get off either.

They're waiting for days. The steps to get people down are forbidden. Some of them jumped.

Food gets passed up, after dead people start to land on the runways. Flat trucks come and take them away.

Elizabeth goes to **MAIN MENU**. More adverts. More news. She doesn't want to press the button to start – but then Calum Ian presses it for her.

It's cold in the news, because the people talking have smoke on their breaths, plus they're wearing scarves.

'He's the one that frightens me,' Alex says.

'Him?'

'No, the next one. He's the one that made me scared of seeing zombies.'

It's a film we've seen before. Someone being chased by police. The picture freezing into dots, like when storms used to shake the satellite dish. Then, when the picture comes back, the running man has fallen asleep beside some stairs. Black paint is coming out of his shoulder.

'Shot,' Duncan says.

Elizabeth holds her head like it's sore. Calum Ian covers his ears from the film's shouting, though it's crackly and it isn't even that loud.

'He was only ill,' Elizabeth says.

146

Calum Ian chooses another one. It's a film of someone talking: a man with a sweaty face. He looks at the camera and smiles and talks patiently, so you'd think he'd be a good teacher. There are two people sitting beside him. They both look strict, or bored. Or fed up. These two don't look like nice teachers, and they don't look at the camera.

The man talks about growth. He uses words we don't understand. He mumbles, then talks too fast, calls growth a cancer that has to be stopped. There's a light that's too bright for his face. He might be patient, but still, he looks like he's in a hurry. We all agree that even though he's smiling it's probably not a true smile.

'Can't understand him,' Alex says. 'It's like he's talking in sore tooth language.' On other days this might make us laugh, but right now, here, it doesn't.

The man goes on and on. I get bored with him, which is fine because then the clip changes. And then I want to be bored again, because it's a man Elizabeth recognises as the Prime Minister.

'I am appealing for calm,' he says. 'I want you all to know we are doing the best we can. Please put your trust in the efforts of our emergency services—'

The clip cuts off – then there's a film of people camping or working inside a sports stadium.

Elizabeth rubs her eyes with her sleeve. She's shaking like she's been outside for too long and got cold.

We watch the rest. I don't even remember the one about the man running from the shopping place. I feel sorry for him, because he's left behind his box of stuff. It's all tipped onto the shiny floor beside a Christmas tree.

The DVD stops. It goes to blue screen, and we know we've come to where the electricity stopped.

The big kids should be in the lead, but they're not.

Alex: 'What was that man doing?'

Elizabeth puts on a smile. 'In the very last clip? I know, actually. Mum and Dad used the same thing to help people.'

'What?'

'He had a mask. Called a nebuliser. Doctors and nurses use them to help people: maybe if they have asthma or lung problems, for their breathing.'

'But the mask didn't help the people who died.'

'No. The bad man used it to hurt them.'

'How?'

'He used it to send bits of sickness in the air.'

'Is the sickness still in the air?'

'I don't know.'

Alex goes quiet for a bit. After this he frowns and says, 'If the people didn't have asthma, or lung things, why did they want to put the masks on?'

'Because he told them a shitty lie. He said it was oxygen. To give them energy, for shopping. He told them it was extra healthy, that it would give them extra strength for their Christmas shopping.'

As we leave the house the last person still sitting is Calum Ian: staring and staring at the blue screen of the player until Duncan has to wake him up, ask for the player back, tell him to get going.

Calum Ian clicks out the DVD – then he takes it outside and sprays it with petrol.

He throws a match, and we all watch as the silver top of the DVD bubbles and melts and goes black.

Alex keeps turning to have one last look at his house: watching to see if there will be any change, maybe hoping for some sign of life at the windows or door.

Then we're back, walking the road.

Up in the north, where the wind blows hardest, some of the telephone wires got knocked down. Rubbish, plastic bags and fishing nets all snagged in a line along the fences. Tin cans, plastic tubs buried down in the sand drifts that the wind has built at the corners of the road.

It's when we come to an abandoned car that Calum Ian, still walking behind, whistles for us to stop.

The car has been spray-painted.

There are red and blue swirls on the doors. Also on the front window.

No names, no letters or messages, no drawings: just swirls of spray.

We look inside. Calum Ian stays by the grass verge. There's empty crisp packets and juice cartons and tins bashed but not opened on the front not-driver's seat.

We look around, but there's nothing: just some blank houses, the rubbish-snagged fences, the empty hill.

Duncan whistles on his brother, who doesn't come but instead hunkers deeper in the grass.

We open the car door. It creaks bad, plus the inside smells old: old like the sun dried the air in it for weeks.

'Nobody recent,' Duncan says.

Still though: he looks at the hill and the nearest house in case there's a trap we didn't see.

When nothing bad happens Calum Ian comes over to us. I notice he's got one of the knives out: tucked in the side of his belt so the end of it points backwards.

He takes out his tarpaulin and rolls it out on the road: offering us weapons, if we want. Then says, 'Duncan saw smoke. Three month back. It was coming from the other side of the big hill. From the side we're on now.'

Nobody speaks.

He must see something in how we're all looking because he adds in a hurry, 'Listen: it was hard to know if it was really smoke or just more clouds.'

Elizabeth gets him to slowly repeat what he said, and to give more details: about the exact date, about how long since, about whether the smoke was black or white.

'Why didn't you *tell*?'

Even though the question is aimed direct at Calum Ian it's Duncan who finally answers: 'He ordered me not to.'

Calum Ian looks caught. But then he gets his confidence back and says, 'Tell me then: why didn't they come and help? If it was truly friendly adults, they would've come. If it was my dad, he would've come. But nobody did. So you work out if a person doesn't come – maybe that means they're *watching* and not wanting to be found.' Pointing to the rubbish inside of the car he says: 'An enemy.'

Elizabeth looks at him like she can't believe.

She stares at the weapons, back at him.

150

Then she nods, only not for agreement, but more for realising the worst in somebody.

She goes to fold the tarpaulin roll, then seems too disgusted to let her hands even touch it.

'You and your stupid weapons.' Then: 'What if there was a search party? What if that was our only chance and we missed it? What if we missed our last ever chance of being saved? Did you *think* about that?'

'What if they were bad bastards. Did *you* think about that?'

She hitches her bag up, then starts on the path, going quick like we're in an even bigger hurry.

'You don't know what you're walking into,' shouts Calum Ian after her. 'I was just trying to defend us. To keep the team safe. You're the one that's always going on about teamwork. That's what it was.'

'Protect us: from who? It's you who wants to poison people. Maybe it's *you* we've to worry about.'

Now he's made Elizabeth nervous. I see her move from the middle of the road to the side – trailing the fence, then kneeling, like his words had some effect after all.

It gets us all nervous – so when we see the wind turbine moving – just before the houses of Bagh a Tuath – there might as well be a hundred folk on it, waving.

Calum Ian orders us to wait in the grass, where we hide and watch for a bit: listening for strangeness in the sound it makes as it chops air.

Alex thinks it's a sign that adults are still alive. Elizabeth

151

doesn't agree. She says it turns all by itself until the day it gets rusted and stops.

Our third house has a ramp going around and up to its front door. There are two gates, both with stiff bolts. We take it in turns to climb over. There's a door-knocker with a nameplate which says: E. R. KERR.

As soon as we open the door there's a smell. Not the worst smell, but a definite one.

The hallway's narrow, middle-bright. There's a tipped-over walking frame on the floor. It's got an empty string bag tied to the front of it, plus a long stick with pincers for picking stuff up. Old person things.

Because of the smell Alex won't come in.

He waits on the step outside, and begins to count aloud to tell us how long we've taken—

'Stopping at two hundred. One, two, three—'

We tie on our perfume-hankies, which is the best thing to have done, because when we go into the kitchen we discover that there's an old woman dead in a chair.

She's not alive. It's easy to see. She's fallen to her side, all twisted up like the trees by the north shore.

Her skin went black.

We search the rest of the kitchen, trying not to look at her. In the end Calum Ian puts a towel over her head.

I worry that it's disrespectful, but truthfully, it's better not to see.

We open the kitchen drawers. The fridge stinks, plus it's empty. We look in the bathroom cabinets, the bedroom, then every cupboard in the kitchen again.

At the end of this Elizabeth just sits on the hall floor.

'Nothing.'

Calum Ian bangs his hand on the doorframe.

'Who tells Alex?'

It's just then, when we're trying to pluck up the courage to go out and tell him, that Alex begins to shout.

Something scared him proper: because now he comes *into* the house to get us.

He's shaking, won't stop.

Calum Ian gets to him first. He puts Alex's hands at his sides for attention then asks him what he's playing at.

'Was no—not—'

I remember now how his words got broken up, after it happened. So does Elizabeth: she kneels down and speaks to Alex quietly, trying to unmess his thoughts.

'Remember, one at a time. Slowly.'

'N—n—'

'*Think* of all your words. Separately, like you did before. Go on. A big breath, it's easy.'

'Th—there. Was.'

'OK . . . there was what?'

'A thing.'

Calum Ian straightens up right away: and looks at all of us, making a told-you-so noise. He asks: 'What *kind*? A man, right? He must've been hiding, I bloody knew it! Did he look bad? Was he like the bad man in the DVD?'

Alex presses his hands to his cheeks.

'I can't believe it was real! It wasn't a dream!'

153

Elizabeth gets his attention by clicking her fingers in front of his face. She speaks sharper now.

'Describe for us.'

'Ran away . . . it had eyes and a face.'

'So it was a dog, or a cat.'

'No. It was running up on its two legs like a person.'

'*Alex.* You can't be making stuff up.'

'Cross my heart, hope to die.'

Now when Calum Ian takes his roll of knives out of his rucksack we don't say a thing.

He chooses the all-silver one: checking the sharpness of it by jabbing it into the wood of the floor.

For now we let him be in charge. He tries to look angry, like a man could be, but still, I can see he's scared.

I wait for Elizabeth to tell him to put down the knife; this time she doesn't. Nor does she tell him to stop when he hands out darts and knives to the rest of us.

I don't know how to hold a knife for proper defence. Neither does Duncan, who drops his.

'You grab – always – with two hands,' Calum Ian whispers fiercely. 'So go for the guts. Or the throat, and you attack first. Always first. We come in from three or four sides, that puts up our strength, right?'

He forces us down in the grass.

'*Listen.*'

For ages there's only birdsong, and the *whurry-whurry* of the wind turbine.

Then there's barking – we see three dogs.

They see us as well, and they come close, tails wagging and their ears backwards for friendship.

One tries to get close to Duncan who holds up the shaking end of his knife.

'And we were afraid!' laughs Calum Ian, with a rise in his voice for relief, that it was maybe only dogs, after all.

But these dogs are strange.

It gets in me that they've been painted. They have blue stripes along their sides.

One of them has a blue face. Blue-tipped whiskers.

'So they tried to drink paint,' Calum Ian says, though he doesn't sound convinced by himself.

It's when I look at Elizabeth to see what she thinks about the dogs that I notice she's looking in a different direction: with her eyes fixed, just staring.

When I follow where her eyes are going, I see.

A little girl.

We stand to show ourselves and the girl runs away.

Seeing an animal that isn't a dog or cat looks so strange that nobody can even react.

But then Elizabeth does – 'Wait!' she shouts, but the girl nips between two hedges and is gone.

We close in around on both sides – and she jumps out again, running fast.

It's hard to follow her, she's so quick: running around the back of the circle of houses, crawling behind and between bins, rubbish-piles, gas canisters.

'She went in at the end!'

The end-house has a load of rubbish in its front garden. Black bags, tarpaulin, held with fishing rope, lines all twisted in an untidy heap. The garden smells. I see lots of shit on the grass, which I hope is from dogs.

Alex and Duncan are posted to the back door. Me and Elizabeth and Calum Ian stay around the front.

By the doorstep there's a shivery cat, with five rag-doll kittens taking milk. It's lying on a pair of jeans inside an old tyre. The cat meows, hisses at us.

We ring the doorbell. It's not working.

There's a strong smell when we open the door. The smell is of many things: rotten food, damp, shit, pee, dogs. It's hard to tell if there's a dead person's smell there too. Calum Ian says there is. Elizabeth says there isn't.

It's cold. Straight ahead: a kitchen with one fluttering torn curtain. We see Alex and Duncan out the back, through the window. They don't see us inside.

All the shelves are pulled out. The kitchen floor has a broken centre. Mostly it's a mess: dried-dirty plates, tins, crisp packets. There are hundreds of small empty cans of something called *Indian Tonic Water.* Then up on the kitchen table, lots and lots of tins of dog food.

There's teddies, sitting on the seats around the table. Then at the middle of the table there's a framed picture – of a man, a lady, a boy, with plastic flowers beside it.

Calum Ian points at the boy in the picture with the sharp edge of his knife.

'Knew him,' he says. 'His name was Rory.'

There's a camping stove on the floor. It's gone black. Maybe it went on fire? The wall beside is also black, but that's different, the black is from spots of mould.

We go through the kitchen. In the hallway Calum Ian shushes us – then Elizabeth calls, 'Hullo? We want to help. To become friends.' Then: 'Are you very hungry?'

There's the smallest sound.

'Door – there.'

We open the door. It creaks loud.

The room's dark. The curtains are hanging off their rails. The mess here is worse than in the kitchen: hills and forests of rubbish. A part of the corner of the ceiling has the paper peeling.

Our eyes get used to the dark. There's a stick-tree in one corner. As my eyes get stronger I see that it's a Christmas tree gone down to bare branches.

In another corner there's a nest. Only it's not for a bird, it's for a person. The nest is made of duvets, dressing gowns, sleeping bags, clothes, and even, I think, a big blue flag. It all looks filthy. On the floor around are thousands of sweet wrappers and bits of silver foil.

There's a face: very dirty, with white eyes. Watching us, from a hole in the side of the nest.

Calum Ian doesn't know what to do. I don't know what to do. Elizabeth gets us to kneel down, to get ourselves small. Then she holds out her hand. The dirty face goes further into the nest. Then reappears.

'You're all right,' Elizabeth says. 'You're all right to be feeling curious. What's your name?'

157

The dirty face just stares.

'Mine's Elizabeth,' says Elizabeth, and she gives the rest of our names. 'Is anybody with you? Maybe your mum or dad? It would be a very big help if you could tell us if there's adults. We definitely need to find adults.'

The dirty face just looks.

'You on our side?' Calum Ian demands. 'You should be, and now you've got to talk, so give us your name.'

The dirty face disappears. Elizabeth puts her hand up to Calum Ian's mouth. Slowly the face comes back.

From deep in the nest she's found something.

She throws it. Calum Ian falls away, annoyed, or scared.

But it's nothing. It's only small: a key fob.

Elizabeth picks it up. The key fob is pink, blue, with a smiling cartoon girl's face. **Mairi**, it says underneath.

Now we remember her. She did have a big brother called Rory. Both of them had dark hair, dark eyes. She liked to show off, I remember, by dancing in the playground.

'Come on to hell,' Calum Ian says. 'Rory's little sister never looked like *that*.'

We look at Mairi. She's more of a dirty broken toy than a girl, thinner than the thinnest of us, which is Alex or Duncan. I think I remember her being in P2. If it isn't Mairi, then it's hard to imagine who else she could be.

'Where's your brother?' Calum Ian asks, then he spells out the letters, first in words then using his fingers to write in the air. 'BROTHER? *Tha?* Yes? Did he get sent AWAY? Did he get put in the Community Centre?'

Mairi stares at us like we've come from space.

158

'Where is he? *A bheil Gàidhlig agaibh?* Or English? *A bheil an t-acras ort?*'

After a bit she points at the door we've come through.

'Outside?'

She shakes her head.

'*A-staigh?* In the house?'

She nods.

'Up the stair?'

She shakes her head.

'Downstairs? That other room next door?'

She nods.

Next door is also dark. It has the worst smell. It's another living room: only instead of a coffee table in the middle there's a mound. Elizabeth opens the curtains. We see that the mound is a pile of clothes and cushions. The mound is topped with fairylights all in a spiral.

At the very top, on a pink pillow, there's a face drawn on paper. It has shells for eyes, tinsel for hair.

'Like our Last Adult,' says Elizabeth, of the mound.

Around the edges are things which Elizabeth calls mementos, though they're really only toys. There's an Action Man and a green teddy-snake. There's some food: cornflakes on a plate. The flakes look mouldy.

Mairi has now come out of her nest. She's in the hall, still too timid to come close to us. Calum Ian stands the same distance apart from her, nervous as well.

'Your brother under there?' he asks. 'You bury him?'

Mairi doesn't seem to hear. But then she nods.

159

'When did he die?'

Mairi doesn't nod or shake her head.

'Same time as everybody else? Later, then? You lived together for a while? He survived beside you?'

Mairi nods – a tiny nod, but definite.

'He died *after*. What happened?'

At first I think she doesn't understand. Then she points to her mouth.

'He was hungry. No, he was sick. OK. What got him to be sick? Did he get toothache? His mouth? Did he eat something that made him sick?'

Mairi doesn't look sure. Instead she points to the mound, and keeps pointing until we get to the bit that's warm in the warmer-colder game.

'The box?'

She nods very strongly.

The thing she means is a shoebox.

We open it, and inside there's purple silk material and Christmas decorations. Also, a drawing – of Mairi, in a dress, with individual fingers drawn like flowers.

Her brother is in the drawing as well. He's standing along-side, but with his eyes closed.

Also in the box is a mountain-picture calendar. The days gone past are marked with crosses. Except that the last day crossed goes all the way back to March 5th.

'Can't have died *then*. That's not possible.'

Mairi moves her lips without talking. The hushed word she's saying is: Yes.

'That was *three months* ago . . . that's too long. You can't have survived on your own for *that* long.'

Mairi looks like she doesn't care if we believe or not.

It's strange to see another home owned by kids. Mairi's home is far, far messier than ours. And also darker – they didn't collect batteries for light-ups. Also, there's no radios, no room full of clocks. It looks like they didn't have as good routines.

It looks like they didn't have so many good ideas.

Duncan comes in, and looks shocked by Mairi, in fact he can't stop looking. Alex must still be outside.

'She doesn't talk English, or Gaelic,' says Calum Ian.

Mairi has finished three packets of our crisps. She goes out of the room then comes back with something from her nest. It's a naked doll.

She creeps in behind Elizabeth's feet on the floor and curls up to stroke the doll.

'She stinks,' Duncan says.

She doesn't hear the rudeness of it: but instead, still lying on the floor, she puts a hand forward and begins to play with the lace of Elizabeth's shoe.

Elizabeth tries to lift her up, but Mairi won't allow it. She fast-crawls back to the door and watches us from there. Her eyes dart to see us all.

With her patient voice Elizabeth says, 'You have to come home with us Mairi, because we've got a better place. You'll be safe and sound there. We've got toys. We've got films. Have you a favourite?'

161

Outside, Alex is noisily counting. Mairi stares and stares until we get uneasy about her.

'This could be a trap,' Calum Ian says.

Elizabeth gives him a look which means *Shut up*.

'Listen,' she says, 'We're in a bit of a hurry. It can be a big help, in a group. You'll get teamwork. It's crucial to be helping together. It'll be your best ever decision.'

Mairi starts to creep back. She's keen to play with Elizabeth's school badges. She points at the one that says **BANKER**, then points like she wants it.

Elizabeth gives her both badges.

'You haven't seen Alex yet,' she says, with a hurry to her voice. 'I'll tell you one big issue, Mairi. He needs medicine. If he doesn't get any he'll become sick. So for that reason we've got to go back. It's our mission.'

Elizabeth pins the badges to Mairi's T-shirt. All the smudged dirt makes the gold and green shine.

Elizabeth takes out a wet wipe from her rucksack and begins to wipe clean Mairi's cheeks.

'So we start to see you.'

Mairi looks very solemn. Her face comes in like a window being cleaned. Her skin's the colour of clouds. Or even whiter – it's the colour of snow.

Elizabeth's hand stops moving. Then Calum Ian makes a mad sound I never wanted to hear.

Elizabeth quickly cleans all the way down to Mairi's neck and ears.

With her mouth sagging she says – 'Show me your stomach.'

Mairi shakes her head, so Calum Ian gets behind her and grabs her arms. She kicks, but she's too small.

He pulls up her jumper. After this he turns her around to look at her back.

'She's got none. None at all.'

I don't know why, but Calum Ian pushes us away from Mairi. And for once Elizabeth doesn't disagree.

When we get back outside Alex is writing with dirt on the path. His face goes amazed like Duncan's did when Mairi appears. She keeps hiding at the door, as if Alex was the bad person we were hiding from her.

It's Elizabeth's face I don't understand. She looks like something awful happened – which can't be true.

Alex holds out his hand, to shake. Mairi doesn't reach for it. 'You want water?' he asks. When he holds up our bottle of red sterilised Calum Ian stops him from getting too close.

'Don't think about touching her,' he says.

I ask what's wrong. I ask it ten times or more and then I get angry because they don't want to tell and it makes me feel like a dumb kid who doesn't understand.

In the end Calum Ian says, 'It should be obvious. Just look at her face.'

I look at Mairi's face. It's mostly hopeful, like she wants to be friendly. Plus it's more clean. I mention both.

'*And* she doesn't have scars.'

I see that he's right: she has true skin like from an old photo or DVD: not broken around her nose and cheeks like all of us.

163

'So she got lucky,' Duncan says.

'But none of *us* got lucky. We all got ill.'

'Then she's still lucky.'

'*Not* if we give it to her. Then we make her sick. Then she might die.'

Everybody now looks at Elizabeth: all at once, as if we need her to tell that it couldn't happen.

She just looks away to the big hill, the turbine.

Mairi begins to touch her own face: a sign that she understands what's being said. Maybe she's only waiting for her best chance to speak?

'But none of us are ill now,' Alex points out. 'Apart from Duncan's face, but that got better. Apart from the insulin with me. Maybe that makes it OK to be friendly?'

'How do you know we're not still infected? How do you know *we* can't make her sick? All the adults who got sick died. All the other kids as well.'

I try to think of another person with no scars. I can't think of even one. All of the babies we saw, all of the dead adults. Every person in every house.

It doesn't feel right. I hate to think I still have some sickness in me. I want it gone. I want us to be healthy.

We end up standing in two groups: her and us. We throw food, we throw water. Duncan makes a line of stones on the road for not crossing.

Yet the longer we wait, the more it gives us of worry: even more when Calum Ian takes out his petrolgun and begins to talk about hiding again.

'Something's not right here.' He curls his finger on the

164

trigger of the gun. 'How can she be the only lucky kid? I think she's not talking because she's not telling.' He sprays one spot of petrol on the road, looking deliberately at Elizabeth, as if challenging her to stop him.

'I vote we leave her,' he says.

Elizabeth rubs and rubs at the sides of her head.

'Can't do that.'

'We could feed her, put down some food. Aye? Then we come back later and check she didn't get ill.'

'No!'

'So *you* bloody take her. But make sure she keeps herself apart. Maybe fifty feet? Till we know it's safe. I'm taking Duncan back with me.'

'When will we know? When can any of us know for sure that it's safe?'

'I don't know – you're the expert! You're the expert-girl, doctor's girl! *An e dotair a th'annad?* You're the one who knows it all! The one whose mam and dad knew so much they couldn't even save themselves!'

When he shouts this Mairi sags her head. I want to put the dirt back on her cheeks so no one knows the truth.

He goes to the edge of the stones, stares at Mairi, then begins to rearrange his rucksack, for going.

When a paint-swirled dog comes to make friends with him he kicks it.

We watch him stuff Duncan's rucksack with the blankets we carried. Then he throws clothes belonging to me and Alex onto the ground between us.

*　　*　　*

I pick up my clothes, pack them safe beside Mum's letter.

And we watch the MacNeil brothers walk away.

Mairi comes nearer. She looks worried, as if we'll kick her like Calum Ian already kicked the dog.

Elizabeth puts a hand up to say *Stop*; but the hand trembles like it got too heavy to hold.

'Don't come past there,' she says. 'We need to think about you, all right? Decide if you're safe.'

Mairi stares and stares at the stones, like the only thing she wants now is to be part of the team.

Back Bay

How does an alone kid keep alive? I think this when I think of Mairi. For starters, she kept her count of days. For second, she knew the idea of having friends: dolls to stand in for real people. She even painted the dogs, maybe because that was like giving them clothes, and clothes equals human.

But still: alone, she forgot how to talk. Which is why I've started to say aloud all the adverts and films I could ever remember.

It gave us trouble, in the end, Mairi not talking.

The other question: how does an alone kid keep safe? She was the best at that. Now I want to shake her hand and tell her how well she did.

Today, I made it a theme for the 'Plans and Activities' jotter I started—

ACTIONS
I have no one else to blame for my actions. There's only me who did it. Everyone else can't be blamed.

167

MESS

It's the same with mess. Try to blame Alex? But my mind knows that can't be true.

Now that I'm at risk, I could never hit anything. Even the snails. Or flies. They are like spiders, only more innocent.

STAYING SAFE

Be careful with the edges of chairs. You can hurt yourself on the top of the edge. DON'T swing.

Glass is bad. Plastic cups don't break. If you get glass in your foot then infection gets in.

Chew until there's no hard bits. You never want to choke, the dogs can't help.

Whether I am the last of the island kind, or last of the world kind, it's the same for safety.

FEAR

Fear of heights keeps you safe. Use it.

Fear of the dark is because there used to be wolves. Dogs should be safer.

Monsters: remember you were scared of a monster in the plughole? Never existed. So the new monsters don't exist, either.

Fear of being alone is

I can't find more inspiration. Asking the blank page never works, so I put my jotter away.

There's only a short memory, today. I get to the bottom of

the sleeping bag to find it: deep down, back beside the biscuit crumbs and empty wrappers.

To the time when we definitely began to know that the world would for ever be different.

We're at the supermarket. And the big strangeness is that everyone's wearing a mask: all the shoppers, the lady on the till, even the man minding the door, letting one person in at a time, for one going out.

And the lights are off – apart from the light in one bit of the freezer section. There's the sound and the stink of a generator – set up in the car park, with cables coming in just to keep that one freezer working.

I want to go to the playpark by the store and play with the other kids, but Mum tells me to stick close by her.

When it's our turn to go in I hear Mum swear: 'Fuck; they emptied the place.'

There is one long queue of people, going from the fridges, past the freezers, back to us.

The man on the till is only letting shoppers buy ten pounds' worth. The people keep arguing with him for more, but he won't allow it.

But it might not matter for us, because the shelves of the store are nearly all empty anyway.

Mum jangles her keys. She keeps looking around at the door, then the people taking food in front of us.

For shopping the rules have changed: you're only allowed to take when you reach twenty places from the front of the queue. And that's miles.

It's strange how dirty shelves are when you see the back of

them. I want to go and play there, in behind, but Mum holds my hand tight like I got a row.

Suddenly in front, someone shouts. Another person at the front – an old lady – has tripped over. Or did she fall? She kneels then starts to shake. This part is frightening and strange: but stranger still is what the adults do.

They begin to shout, scream. They hold their masks tight to their faces. And rather than helping, they move away from the woman, leaving her alone on the floor.

'Out, out of here,' Mum says.

She pulls me back to the car, even though I saw things we could've bought, even though we queued for ages.

We drive around to the other stores, but the queues are just the same, so we head home.

It's on the west road that we see the ambulance, parked up in a sandy lay-by.

There's white tape flapping in the wind, tied around spikes to make a square you can't go into: just like when they found that rare orchid two summers ago.

But there's no orchid this time.

Just a man lying flat.

Mum drives slow. She goes to roll her window down: but the ambulance-man waves her past, waving like he got furious at us for being nosy.

I come back up for air. So it was no use as a memory. It didn't help – and now I'm thinking of what happened anyway. Not then, but nine days ago: in the hours after we found Mairi.

170

'The Lord giveth; the Lord taketh away.' Father Boyd, the visiting priest, said that once, when he came to talk to us in the school about the meaning of Easter.

Except I think that the Lord shouldn't take people when they're only trying to help: that isn't fair.

He should give first, then afterwards not be greedy or cruel with what he takes away.

Nine days ago

My eyes get used to seeing Mairi, which makes me remember bits of who she was. She was a flower at the Easter concert: growing big when the teacher fed her sunbeams from a torch. She was fidgety and busy at dancing. I saw her once shouting on her brother.

Now she has this new life; the same life as us. Where it's being alive that counts, and where nobody makes concerts or holds classes for learning to dance.

And where it's more normal to have scars on your face than not.

We wait on Elizabeth, to see what she'll do, but she doesn't act clever. She tries all types of knowing how a person might be safe: using her books, talking out the problem, asking the sky. Asking us.

It's Alex who comes up with the idea of asking about her brother, so Elizabeth does that.

Mairi rubs the dirt on the palms of her hands into black strings, then wipes it free. After this she reaches in her pocket and takes out a crumpled drawstring purse.

She empties it on our barrier line of stones.

There's five shells, some glass beads. Another key fob. Feathers. Plus a picture of her brother.

The colour in it got faded, the picture criss-crossed where she folded it too many times.

'That's from before,' Elizabeth says. 'Mairi, it's great you've got a picture from before. But we need to know what he looked like after.'

Mairi doesn't make a sign of hearing: instead just puts the collection back in her purse, all except the feather, which she watches for the way the wind ruffles it.

Me: 'We could dig her brother out.'

'*Sure.* We dig him out, look at the skin on his face. Because it's easy to spot the scars on the rotten bony skeletons we see in houses. Great idea! The best yet. Well *you* can be the one to do that.'

Her voice goes hard, much harder than true kindness. I pretend not to notice. But anyway, Elizabeth is looking instead to see if Mairi heard, or got sad by hearing her brother called a skeleton, but she didn't seem to.

'The right thing is sometimes the wrong thing,' Elizabeth says. 'Like when you wanted to be near someone at the end. That was wrong, even though your heart said right.'

When she says this I wonder: will we be leaving Mairi behind? But then she shows another idea.

173

She takes out a ball of string from her rucksack and begins to unroll it. Then she walks on so that it trails and dangles behind her.

When it reaches the length of about five kids she beckons Mairi.

'Stay that far away,' she says. 'Until we know better.'

We follow the shore road. We have to be strict with the string – though Elizabeth has now turned slowcoach, she's walking funny, and Mairi keeps nearly bumping into the back of us.

'Why are you walking so slow?' I ask Elizabeth. 'Is there something wrong?'

'Forget about it,' she says.

A long road, the North Bay ahead. One abandoned lorry, one dead sheep stuck in a fence.

Then we see the MacNeil brothers. But they're not going away – instead they're running towards us fast, so fast that Elizabeth stands in the road with her body in defence, ready for an argument. Then we hear Calum Ian shout—

'Our dad's here!'

We heard him the first time, but still: nobody can truly take this in. His whole body's shaking and when he says again his voice goes as high as Alex's, still higher when we make him say once more to be sure.

'Your *dad*?'

'You've got to come and see!'

For now the string-length gets forgotten. We follow him: to the church, to the community hall. There's Our Lady – the

174

statue of Mary – on its island in the bay. Another wind turbine, a broken or switched-off one this time.

The tide sitting slack. There's a boat stabbed in mud on its keel. Another, on its side, half-broken, fallen onto the pier wall.

I see now that we imagined too much, or he got us ready *for* too much.

It *is* his dad's boat. But just not his dad.

Mr MacNeil's boat is in the bay, at the furthest end of the pier, roped at the outside of three others.

Duncan is there, shouting at us to come on, come *on,* shouting so his voice screams and cracks.

'Remember his green ladder, look!' Calum Ian says.

'He bloody got back safe!' Duncan shouts back at him. 'We just have to find where he went!'

The boat's been here a while. We can tell. It's all dried up in mud. I feel let down – maybe Elizabeth does too – but we don't say anything because that would spoil their time of getting to be excited.

'Dad,' Calum Ian says, his voice gone flatter.

The boat's made of wood, metal. There's a small house, which Calum Ian calls the cabin, with windows like a lighthouse, plus a metal frame at the back which he calls the winch. Then on the side, between lines of blue paint, a name, written in wavy black letters: Mary Anne.

The wires from the winches of the other boats are tangled up. With the tide out there's maybe ten feet to fall onto sand and stone. Even so, Calum Ian wants us all to climb across: all except Mairi, who keeps her own distance this time, waiting

175

for us on a bump of grass beside the pier wall, chin on her knees.

Alex comes as well. He has to stretch hard to reach from one boat to the other. The furthest boat is Mr MacNeil's. It stinks of mould and dried-out seaweed. At the back of it are lots of slippery green nets, piled in tangles.

In the middle of the boat there's an open cardboard box, with lots of smaller boxes in cellophane inside.

The smaller boxes have gone damp – especially near the edges where there was no shelter from the cabin.

'So he did bring back supplies,' Calum Ian says. 'He did his job; he did it right. He was a hero! Then all he had to do – it wasn't a big deal – all he had to do was come and find us. Rescue us.'

He frees one of the small boxes. The paper of it flakes into powder. It only takes a rub with his fingers and the whole side of the box crumbles away.

'Medicines.'

We knew, already. It's the same medicine we've seen when New Shopping in people's houses; same as beside the Last Adult. The medicine that Mum delivered.

Boxes and boxes of it.

'No one got any,' I say.

'They argued before he left,' Calum Ian says. 'Mum and Dad, all night. Dad said he was going on a mercy trip. Mum said, "Whose mercy? We can keep the fish you get for us." But see, it wasn't only fish. It was more important than that. He was trying to save the whole people, not just us.'

We scrape open some more of the boxes, but they're all

the same kind. After this, we search the cabin. Nothing: apart from a dream-catcher hanging from a radio with a curly cord, and one of Duncan's old drawings, of a man on a motorbike jumping through a ring of fire. Duncan says it was his dad's favourite.

Calum Ian clicks the radio switch, but it's not working. After this he puts his hands softly on the boat's steering wheel.

'The view he had.'

In the cupboards we find tea, sugar and a cup which says **WORLD'S GREATEST CATCH**. There's a pair of blue overalls, very oily, then an orange waterproof suit, which reeks of sea-mould.

Calum Ian starts to look through all the cupboards again: and for a dumb second I think they're actually looking for their dad *inside* the cupboards – but then Elizabeth says: 'I might know where he went.'

Which makes me realise that they're only opening cupboard doors because they don't want to start looking properly.

It's not hard to work out where all the people in this village ended up. Around the Community Centre there's too many cars. They're parked in a jam, just like the roadblock we found back on the coast road.

The door of the centre is taped shut with criss-crossed ☣ **BIOHAZARD** ☣ tape. At the top of the jam of cars there's an ambulance, with its back doors open, so that the inside of it got filthy with bird shit and leaves and sand.

Mairi follows us again, but now doesn't want to come anywhere near the Community Centre. She waits just outside the gates – curled up, but still watching, not looking away for one second.

Calum Ian looks at Mairi, then at me and Elizabeth.

'You decide to keep her?'

I see that Elizabeth doesn't want to talk about it – or doesn't want to tell what she decided. And for once, Calum Ian doesn't turn it into an argument.

Duncan is sitting on the steps leading to the Centre door. As I get close I hear him whisper, 'Why didn't you come for us, Dad?'

Calum Ian goes to stand beside him. He takes out our bottle of red sterilised and drinks, afterwards wiping his mouth on his sleeve.

'Anyway,' he offers Duncan some, 'Dad should've kept to his side of the bargain. And now, what: do we have to find him because he didn't come and find us?'

He stares at the taped-up door. Some birds fly over. We watch them as if there was nothing else to watch.

'I'll go inside,' Elizabeth says.

Calum Ian just keeps on looking up at the birds.

She adds, 'Mainly because you did it for me. Not because I think you've been a good friend, because you haven't always. But because you did it for me.'

Calum Ian swirls the water until there's a whirlpool.

'I'm not going to ask you to do it.'

But Elizabeth doesn't answer: instead, she just starts to get ready.

She opens up her rucksack, takes out her perfume-hanky, sprays it twice. Then she puts spare plastic bags on her feet and on her hands.

After this Calum Ian stands in front of her, to put his goggles over her head. He sprays her perfume-hanky on the outside – five times for luck – while Elizabeth holds it firmly over her mouth.

'Did I leave any gaps? I could tape it around twice? Do I look stupid? Or scared?'

'Never scared.'

Mairi, still on the road, now seems to realise what we're doing. She waves her hands crazily, but doesn't try and come any closer than she is.

Me and Alex and Duncan say we're going to try and calm her down, so we begin to walk back. For me it's really a trick to get further away. I feel mean to be doing it, but I don't want to stay near that door.

Elizabeth cuts the tape with her big scissors. Then she gives the thumbs-up, and opens it.

We look the other way when the flies start to come.

She's inside for six minutes. When she comes back out again she kicks the plastic bags off her feet, pulls down her perfume-hanky. She crouches by the door. I think she's going be sick, then I see that she's crying.

Calum Ian tries to encourage her. But it isn't easy because Elizabeth is bent down too much, so in the end he kneels beside her, puts a hand on her neck.

We creep nearer. Elizabeth has stopped crying. I didn't like the sound of it and I'm glad she's stopped.

She hands over a yellow bag. Calum Ian rips open the top of it. Inside – his dad's wallet, keys, phone. There's also a note,

179

which Elizabeth says was pinned to the outside of a bag which contained his jacket and shoes.

We gather in close to read:

Roderick MacNeil 23/05/70 – 9/12. Wife Mary Anne MacNeil 3/08/72. Deps: Calum Ian, Duncan, Flora. Children? at crisis accom. Mother deceased 5/12, school mort. NOK?

We read the note, then read it again, until the words lose their sense, turn strange.

After this Duncan just goes back to sitting on the step. Calum Ian folds the letter up, smaller and smaller until he can't fold it any more.

We wait for him to tell us it's bad, or sad. But he doesn't. He's trying to work his mouth to say something: then instead of that he kicks the metal railings leading up to the door: over and over again.

Then he sits down – but not by bending his knees, more by forgetting how to keep the strength in them.

His dad's phone has a cracked screen. The wallet has fifteen pounds plus plastic cards in it.

Duncan lays out all the cards on the step. There's one with his dad's picture. He and Calum Ian look at it – even though it's just small, even though the colours in it went to grey.

'This could be your mum and dad's fault.'

Calum Ian is saying this – to Elizabeth.

He continues: 'Dad tried – every night, every day to get

180

through to that hospital. Because Flora was sick. She was the first out of our family to get sick. We didn't know what to do, she wouldn't wake up that morning. Not even when we put her in the bath. He tried and tried phoning, but nobody ever answered.'

Elizabeth doesn't look ready to talk. But she does anyway when she says, 'I never even saw mine.'

'Flora couldn't get help when she needed it. You understand?'

'And *I* never saw my parents. Not for the whole of the last week. I never saw them, except for once, when Dad talked to me from the other side of a door. At least you saw your mum. At least you *had* your mum.'

It sounds like an argument where both people win – or at least, agree not to lose.

Alex shifts along, bit by bit, until he's sitting between the MacNeil brothers.

He says, 'Your dad was a hero. He was going to bring us all medicines.'

He rummages inside his backpack and takes out some lemon biscuits. No one wants any, they're too soft.

'Everyone has their weakness,' Alex says. 'My weakness is bad men. Zombies. Also, having diabetes. Yours is finding your dad not alive. Only it's not your fault it came true. It's not your fault, or anybody else's.'

'Get lost, Bonus Features.' Calum Ian points to the hill, to the sea. 'Go on, get away from me.'

Alex zips up his bag.

'It was just a thing I thought could help.'

181

I get uneasy. I want to help Duncan, and Calum Ian, but all the same I don't. I want to tell Calum Ian to be kinder to Alex, but it isn't always easy to make someone be a good listener, especially if they're sad.

He lies on the paving stone, without using his jacket for softness. To be a help I lie facing him and say: 'Sorry your dad died.'

Calum Ian blinks as if to mean: *Heard you.*

'You know how you said about your dad coming to find you? Just before? Well, when my mum stops hiding, she can come and look after all of us. All right?'

Calum Ian doesn't blink.

'She's got lots of sayings. She's wise for that kind of thing. Here's one: "Concentrate and the world is yours." It works for lots of other choices – like Smile, or Laugh. I forgot to ask her how many. She could help us find the other adults. Or help Alex. The whole lot.'

Calum Ian sits up. Tiny stones from the ground have stuck to his cheek. He brushes them off.

'*Gloic.* Remember, back in the class, when we talked about facts and opinions?'

'OK.'

'So your mum isn't a fact. She's dead.'

He turns away from me so I can't read his eyes. I say, 'She likes it when—'

'—she likes nothing. She's fucking dead, all right?'

'If—'

'You hear? Can you even listen?'

'It's bad you're sad, but you should never get the right to hurt people's feelings. By telling tales.'

182

'It's not a fucking tale, it's true! You want to know how I *know* that?'

'*Stop it,* stop right now,' Elizabeth warns him.

'—I know it because she's in the gym. Which I had to go into because of fucking *you*. I saw her.'

'She—'

'*Calum*—'

'Know what? I'm fed up not telling her. She needs to bloody learn the truth. So *Gloic*: I – saw – your – mum. When I went in the school gym to get the keys. She's in a bag. To the left side of the room. Dead.'

'*If— wh—*'

'Her clothes. She was the postwoman, right? Her jacket, the red and blue one? It's in an orange bag. I saw it. And her name. On the list of dead. Dead.'

I try to push him away – but he steps back.

'So she won't be looking after us. She won't be looking after anyone. So stop saying she'll take my dad's place. Because she won't!'

My words stop. It takes me ages, ages. Duncan and Alex and Elizabeth are waiting. They look ashamed to see me making such a mess of speaking.

Then I'm back at the gate. I've gone right past the jammed-in cars – and not even noticed.

Mairi is beside me; she's looking at me. I don't want to be nice to her or talk to her or smile at her.

I pick up Calum Ian's rucksack.

Then I tip it up, emptying everything from inside onto the dirt.

He starts to come over, so I unroll his knife-wrap, take out the big silver knife – and point it at his neck.

He stops. Duncan comes out from where he was hiding and stands beside his brother.

Calum Ian does the *Come on* sign with his fingers.

'Do it.'

'I bloody fucking will!'

'Go on, then. Or are you a coward?'

The knife wobbles in my hand. I nearly want to harm him, or harm me, but I can't.

Instead I go away, keep going, throwing the knife away after I pass the gate, away.

It's the opposite road of the island, going home. I look back, look back, nobody's following.

It starts to rain, light then heavy. My feet get wet. All the cuts I have on my knees, my elbows, have started to hurt, because there's no distraction.

At the end of the village I find a kid's bike. The pedals don't move from rust, but the wheels do.

I let the bike take me down to the lowest bit of road, then I leave it.

My jacket gets wet. There are lambs and a ewe on the road. How did the dogs miss them? The lambs jump like they didn't know they were going to. One of the lambs is black. I remember asking Mum once where the black ones went before they grew into proper sheep. She just laughed, drew a smile across her neck.

I pass the forest of fifteen trees, then the postbox with the

184

spray of black graffiti that Mum used to moan about.

After this, the rain turns to mist. There are some houses getting lost in cloud. My knees get tired, and I remember the snack that Elizabeth gave us for emergencies: custard creams, ginger snaps.

I know where I'm going. But I don't want to think about where that place is. What that place is.

I stop at someone's house for water. There's a white bucket in the garden. The rainwater looks clean, so I drink it, and don't care if it's a broken rule.

In the garden, a red plastic ball. It's gone flat. I imagine that it's Calum Ian's face and kick it hard, hard.

'Don't be mean,' says the ball.

I remember years ago I had a thinking book at school. I didn't know how to draw sad, so I drew a cloud. But the teacher didn't understand: she thought I was being moany because the weather outside had been sunny for weeks.

I think I see a boat, but it's only an island.

Someone was building a house. They were living in a caravan beside. There's a blue ship's container with a painting on it of flowers, a smiling family.

I open the house door. The windows have labels on them. It looks new, apart from having no carpets: but there's a bad smell. Which makes sense: if you'd just built your new home you wouldn't want to leave it.

Mum said the new house would blow down in the next winter gale. But it didn't: winter's already been.

They should let me wind back to the moment where I

pointed that knife. Where I deleted the pictures of Duncan and Calum Ian's family.

They should let me do that.

I look up at the sky to ask God.

For an answer he just sends mist-rain in my mouth and eyes.

Mum finds me on the last hill. She starts out by copying my steps, which is odd and very frightening.

'You're scaring me,' I tell her.

'Don't mind me, *mo luaidh.*'

'He's a liar. He's not my friend, Calum Ian.'

'Sounds like a tall story.'

'No – honest.'

'You're in deep blue water trouble, my girl.'

'I didn't do anything wrong!'

'Use a fork! You're not an animal. Well OK, if you say so. You're a cat in Chinese Years.'

'*Mum.* I don't need a fork, and I'm not even eating. You're scaring me. Why can't you speak normally?'

'Finish up your plate.'

Then she's ahead. I think she's waving. I try not to follow but it's like the opposite of the story of the hare and the turtle: we're always in the same place.

It's now I search for her letter.

Gone.

I even take my jumper off in case it stuck to my skin. But it's not stuck to my skin. I must've dropped it.

186

The road goes into mist, behind. I try to look up and scream at God, but my voice only works for screaming if I look down at the wet dark road.

There's another roadblock. More cars. I think I remember these ones. They're on the top side of the big hill, before our village. I climb over a fence so I don't go near. There are lots of seagulls on the cars; some of them go up and squawk when the fence does its noise.

I walk around the edges, staying in the field, so I don't get close enough to see bad things.

Some of the dogs have come to say hello. I tell them about the places we went: to the headmaster's, to the family house where we stayed, to Alex's, to the old woman's house. I tell them about Mairi, the boat.

The dogs don't notice when I miss out the bit about Calum Ian and the knife. Dogs are good listeners that way.

Sometimes they're not friendly when you're alone. There's a bigger dog: brown, with black spots. It doesn't wag its tail like the rest, but only watches me.

When the dogs follow me into the village I pick up a clam shell and throw it, to remind them who's boss.

They run off: then watch me from a distance, apart from the big dog. I have to throw a stone to be rid of him.

My goggles are pink. Even though I'm not a girly-girl. The bag on my left foot is green with gold writing. It says *Harrods*. The other one is for the Co-op.

'You can't stop yourself crying if you're peeling onions. It's an example of something that's not optional. We learnt about optional at school.'

This is what Elizabeth said, once. At the same time she gave us another example: 'Staying alive is not optional.'

Calum Ian said she got it the wrong way around: that it sounded like staying alive was something we *couldn't* do. But I knew what she meant.

With a bit of practice you can stop yourself from crying with sadness. That's because it's optional. You can turn sadness into other things: like quiet-voice, or cold-alive, or worst-ever anger, just by thinking.

Anger works best. So I'm angry at the side door. Angry at its rubbed-off paint, at the glass with criss-cross wire.

At the school's not-turning turbine. At the playground with all its lines for basketball, netball.

Elizabeth used to put wet paper up her nose for the smell. I can't find my nose-clip, so that's what I'll use.

At the Sports Stars Fresco in the gallery above the gym, with its reminder of all our superheroes. I rip a corner, then tear the whole thing off the wall.

Mr Mollison of the butcher's shop used to say, 'You been behaving yourself, Rona?' It gave me a guilty sensation. For superstition you had to tell him how good you'd been, other-wise he'd know the truth.

At the piles of dried-out flowers we left, just here.

At the smell. The fly-noise.

On a very stormy day once I heard Mr Mollison tell a fisher-man: 'Sea doesn't need you today.'

188

When your fingers shake they become smaller. Or maybe the world gives them more room?

Alex and I used to practise fainting. We'd lie down, stay still. Alex would get a cushion first to be comfortable for his faint.

I never, ever want to faint here.

I'm careful to be angry. If you cry with goggles on they fill up. It's the opposite of swimming.

Trails of black stuff on the floor. Mouse shit, maybe rat shit? Duncan's best at telling the difference.

There's a waiting place. It's piled with tins, plus cartons of soup, powdered milk. There's a door which says **PRESS BUZZER + WAIT FOR ACCESS.**

I don't wait, or press the buzzer.

The longest I've ever held my breath for is thirty-six seconds. You can't cheat by inhaling quietly, you're just cheating yourself.

I feel the stink on my face. The world got filled up with stink. Wind flutters in. It's like a ghost checking things are all right, as if ghosts had their worries as well.

The flies are buzzing. They blast from one side of the room to the other. I'm worried that one of them will touch me, so I pull my jumper up so there's no spare face.

I have to rub the goggles, they're steamed. Now I see – tables from the big school. Scrunched blankets, plastic aprons, more dirty stuff on the floor. There's a table with hand-sprays and an orange bag stuffed with gloves.

A man sitting on a chair.

I run back to the waiting place. Can't breathe.

Then I remember: Calum Ian, he spoke about him.

He told us about that man – that man who was sitting, even though he was dead.

Like the old dead lady. She was sitting upright. And she wasn't too scary, or not the worst anyway. So I warn myself: some people just die on seats. You'd never read about it in books, but it truly happens.

In the waiting area I get my breath back. Then I sing, 'Made you look, made you stare, even though you weren't there.' Even though he *was* there. I do it over and over until my heart falls back to normal.

If you keep moving it makes the hall less scary.

Plastic, hanging in long walls on metal poles. It makes lots of long narrow tunnels of the hall. More tables in rows, and yuck on the floor. Someone's slippers.

Curled-up Rona wants to cry. Coward-girl. She has to stop herself crying, cry-baby.

Some of the people are in bags. Some of the people are not in bags. There's baskets, like washing baskets to put clothes in. One person has no clothes.

The plastic screen has fallen down, here. I have to breathe. The wet paper in my nose stinks, it's stopped working.

There is a new tunnel. Part of me wants to train my eyes for dark blue. Another part of me doesn't. But it's no use, once you've had the thought it happens anyway.

Look Mum: your blue jacket. The one with the red lining. Why didn't you tell me? There's your work shoes. I never realised how scuffed they were.

Were you trying to tell me something? Your mouth, open wide. Perhaps it was one last yawn.

I'm not angry, not any more, I'm crying. Maybe optional means something else now.

Now I can't think, can't believe about it. That there: the person who got me born, brought me up as a baby, cared all the time she could. Who got me presents, made things fun at Christmas. Who laughed so loud it got me embarrassed. Who made jam on toast on Saturdays.

The person who did all of that: is that thing there. Could reach out, touch it. But it's not her.

How right can it be that she can't hold back my hand?

I'm in bed, with a knife from our kitchen drawer beside me, when they come home.

I clasp the knife tight – get ready to use it to defend myself – then I see it's just Alex and Elizabeth.

'Thank God you're safe,' she says.

Mairi comes in behind them. There isn't the five-kid distance between her and them any more.

Somehow, when I didn't notice, Elizabeth has taken the knife from me, put it somewhere else.

It takes me a while to pluck up my courage to get up, but in the end I find the MacNeil brothers have not come to our home. The others are sitting on cushions on the floor.

I want to tell them where I've been, but it's too much to think of right now, so I don't.

Mairi is wearing a pair of Alex's trousers, plus Elizabeth's old school jumper. She looks too small for the clothes, even though Alex is still small.

'You decided she was safe?' I ask.

Elizabeth fills my blue plastic bowl with rice pudding, then hands it over.

'Decided we were all in the same struggle,' she answers. Then she looks across at Mairi. 'Decided we just had to take the chance. Decided we couldn't leave her.'

I watch Mairi: with her clear, clean face, scooping rice with her fingers. So she's the one that breaks Elizabeth's rules. Maybe that's what she tells us in the end.

'Where are the MacNeil brothers?'

'Gone to their house.'

'It wasn't my fault. Calum Ian should've used his inner voice, not his outside one.'

Elizabeth doesn't agree, or disagree. Instead she says, 'We had another house to check. Remember?'

She and Alex take it in turns to tell me about the last house. How it was at the end of a road going to the ferry terminal. How it had windows with torn curtains, and a boat in the garden filled with orange flowers.

How it didn't have any smell, not even in the room where they found dead rabbits in a cage.

Then, last of all, she tells me how it had insulin. But not in a fridge: in a plastic box in a bathroom cabinet.

I get up to dance on the bed for them. They smile but don't want to join in too much.

Elizabeth takes out the insulin for us to look at. It's called

INSULATARD. Then she fetches her books to solve whether or not it's the right kind.

'We decided on the way back that there was good news and bad news,' Alex says.

'The good news first, please.'

'The insulin!'

'OK . . . so then what's the bad news?'

He chews his sleeve and looks away, like they left the bad news in another room.

Then he admits: 'We only got a single glass. Plus: it's gone cloudy.'

He holds up the glass to show me.

The water inside it looks full of cobwebs.

I look at Elizabeth, but she's gone back to reading her books.

When I ask Alex if he's had any yet, he rolls up the front of his jumper, and points to a swollen red spot just beneath his belly-button.

'She gave me a test.'

The test has gone sore. When I try to press it Alex pulls back. He tugs his jumper down again.

'Was only a first test.'

I ask if Elizabeth is planning to give him more, but she won't tell me or talk about it.

Mairi has been put back on the other side of a divide – a skipping rope on the floor – only this time, she's just one kid distant. For the illness we had it might work, though nobody really knows for sure.

I ask if she still hasn't said anything, and Alex says no. He tells me that she followed them home, and would only allow Elizabeth to get close – nobody else – and that sometimes she would start to miss her old house and would try to get them all to turn around.

'Calum Ian was strange,' he says.

'How?'

'He didn't want her. Mairi. And he was talking funny. He was—'

Elizabeth holds up her hand for Alex to be quiet.

They both keep looking at the door, like they're worried someone might come through it.

'He thought we were too slow,' Alex says.

Now he goes and sits on the couch beside Elizabeth.

When I think about it, I'm surprised by the look of her – she looks worn, or tired-looking, maybe even sick.

Alex asks her, 'Did your leg get worse?'

She pulls a face, then takes off her sock and shoe, and rolls up her trouser leg.

Her right leg above the knee went swollen. Just like Duncan's face did. Just like the spot on Alex's stomach.

But this redness is much bigger. Much darker.

We stare at it, wondering what it means.

Alex: 'Is it healing yet?'

Elizabeth laughs but with sarcasm and says, ''Course, *sure*. I only had to walk on it all day to make it better.' But then she adds, 'Don't worry, I've been checking it. Drew around the edges. You're meant to do that, to watch in case it gets bigger.'

'Sorry.'

'It isn't your fault. It was Calum Ian and his stupid dart.'

194

I remember about it: when he stabbed her leg, back when he was trying to get me.

We watch as she puts on cream, then a brown plaster. This last bit hurts and she has to bite the skin of her arm until the leg is wrapped up again.

'Better now,' she says, blinking tears.

She puts her sock back on. It's crusty and smelly from where the redness has started to make liquid. Maybe she's going to wash that later?

'Sometimes I don't think I can—' she stops – looks quick at all of us, seeing if we heard her or not.

Nobody asks what she was going to say – because nobody wants to know the things Elizabeth can't do.

To make her feel better I tell her about my memory of her mum and dad.

It was at the end: after I was put in the Cròileagan.

My window looked out on the school; I tell her I peeled back the plastic cover, and saw them.

'What were they doing?' she asks.

'They were meeting the ambulance, the police. Your dad kept giving out white cards, and the people would go in one way or the other. I remember that.'

'How did they look?'

It feels like something I have to get right. I try to think of all the names for the ways a person can be.

'Helpful?'

She smiles at this. I notice how puffy and dirty her hands got.

'Lastly, I saw your dad. But it was from the side, so I didn't see if he was happy or sad. He was helping your mum to walk.

I thought they were having a hug first, but not in the street, surely? Sorry I saw that.'

Now her lips have gone dry like crinkled paper.

'Don't be sorry,' she says. 'You've given me something to remember. It's a help.'

She gets up, and tries to walk with her sore leg, holding our beds to turn a circle on the floor.

'One day this is all going to be better,' she says. 'We just need to get through the hard bit first.'

I don't understand what she means about there being a hard bit. But I don't want to ask her, either, in case I find out sooner than I want.

Before bed Alex gets one more test.

Elizabeth chooses a faraway part of his stomach from the last, while I distract him with juice.

But again – it hurts.

The redness this time begins almost at once, and gets sore enough to make Alex cry out.

'Don't want any more tests.' He tucks his jumper firmly down inside his trousers. 'Let's find some other houses to check instead, all right?'

Elizabeth just packs away his injection kit.

We don't get to sleep until late. It takes Mairi an age to get satisfied about bed. First she wants our type of bed: then she wants to make a nest for herself, like in her old home: using a box and blankets and last of all pulling a pillow over the door to seal herself in.

196

Elizabeth stays up. I hear her on our radio: going through the stations, listening for anything but static.

When I ask her again what Alex meant about Calum Ian being strange she tells me to forget it.

Back Bay

There was the day when Calum Ian and me talked about fate. That was back in spring, back when we were still working out how to stay alive.

It was just the two of us, at Message Rock. He'd thrown in a bottle – he still believed in sea-mail back then. I was on a rock, higher up. It was my job to spot the way it drifted, in case it came back into the bay.

He asked if I believed in fate. When I said I didn't know (because I didn't know what fate was) he said, 'Dad said there was nothing you could do about it. Like it had to happen, no matter what.'

'Like going asleep?'

He shivered at the sea-wind. 'Listen: Gran met Grandpa because she was late for her bus. Fate. Aunt Clare fell down the stairs and broke her leg, then the man who pushed her in the chair at the hospital, he ended up becoming Uncle Frank. That's fate.'

I tried to know fate from these two examples.

'When a mistake leads to marriage?'

Calum Ian clicked his tongue. 'More than that. Like I said: it's got to happen. It could be something good, like meeting Uncle Frank, or bad, like this.'

He circled his arms to mean: all the world. The island we were on. The sea keeping us on it.

He threw a stone in the direction of his bottle then said, 'Keep wondering how it could've turned out differently. What I could've done to change things. Only what if the stuff we did never made a difference?'

I gathered up pebbles for thinking. 'You mean we shouldn't bother sending messages?'

'We could try. But maybe it's the same, in the end?' He held his head for thinking, then said, 'You can't change the end of a film.'

I let him go ahead on our way back to the village: so far ahead that he was just another brown dot, just another rock under the headland.

I didn't like the thought of being part of a film. Not being able to change it. But I didn't argue against, because I knew by then that Calum Ian had to have all the right answers.

It's just that now I think I could've said more. Because a person can't always come up with the right answers.

Especially when that person is in a hurry.

I'm about to tell you about my last good night at home with you, Mum, so listen up: because this is the memory that keeps me wanting to be alive.

In this other life you arrive home. I run at you when you open the door.

'The electricity went off!' I say.

You find me in the pitch-black. I expect to be rescued, for you to notice my bravery, but you don't.

You're wearing a clear plastic suit. I stare up at you as you rip it off, stuff it in the bin.

You find a torch, then light some candles, then go to the sink and scrub your hands for a very long time.

I feel ignored, so I can't stop myself from moaning.

'You don't care,' I say.

You make a face then pull me close.

'You not eat yet? Huh? *A bheil an t-acras ort?* Let's get something in us right this instant.'

With the gas fire on and after some food it's better. We find the old radio in the cupboard, and listen to the local Gaelic station, then to an English BBC station on long wave.

'Is it true people got sick?'

'Yes.'

'Will I get sick?'

'No. You're well and I'll keep you well. We can look after one another.'

'Will you get sick?'

'Rona: nobody in here is sick. OK? We're doing just fine. We just need to sit tight and stay indoors.'

I curl up in a ball for you, so that I'm sitting tight. You don't notice, or if you do then you're not in your usual playful mood.

You plug in our power-cut telephone, the one that doesn't need electricity to work, then you sit in the hall and phone people.

Your voice stays quiet, like you don't want me to hear.

I look out of the window and realise there that are no lights on in the village.

I want to go outside and look, but when I ask about it you say no, we need to get some sleep, you're bushed.

You let me sleep in beside. Neither of us can get to sleep, so I ask you to tell about when I was born.

'You were late,' you begin. 'Ten days. Everybody ready but you. Happy where you were, curled up inside, safe and warm. Liked your own company right from the start. *Rona Aonranach.*'

'How did I get born?'

'They induced me. Oh, but then . . . Then you were coming! Your dad was in and out. He fell asleep in the canteen, nearly missed you. Not that I could bloody sleep.'

'Tell about my eyes.'

'They were open right away. So I thought: Here's a lively one, keeps her eyes open. Knows how to look after herself.'

'What did I do?'

'You didn't do anything. I mean to say, you didn't cry. Just looked at me with those big wide eyes, as much as to say: Is this it? Getting the measure of the world.'

'Was it because I came that Dad left and went to the mainland?'

'No, Rona. You should never think that.'

The wind moans in the phone lines outside. There's the noise of sand crackling on the skylight, above. Outside, a car drives past quick, then another.

'Mum?'

'What?'

'Has Dad phoned?'

201

You're reading a book by a small torch – still, I can tell by the sharpness of your shoulder, by the way you hold your breath, that you aren't really reading.

'Rona, he's one of the people who got sick.'

'But he'll get better, won't he?'

'I'm sure he will. I'm praying for him.'

This makes me want to pray as well; I put my hands together between your shoulder blades and pray, so the magic of it goes through you too.

Another car goes past, sounding very fast.

Then a siren-noise, which I think is the ambulance, but which turns out to be the police.

'Happening,' you say, from the window.

Eight days ago

Alex's bed is wet next morning. He stays late so he can hide the dampness of it. When Elizabeth finally stands him up he wobbles like he's still inside a dream.

Alex: 'It's only sweat . . .'

Elizabeth: 'Look, it doesn't matter. It was an accident.'

Alex: 'I *said* it was sweat.'

Elizabeth: 'Here's a flannel, OK? I got you some fresh clothes. Want a drink?'

'I get sweaty, thirsty if I don't get my injections.'

'I know.'

He drinks and drinks, caving in the plastic bottle of red sterilised as he tips it high and finishes it.

The water dribbles down his chin, settling in beads on the mucky front of his T-shirt. He begins to change his clothes and we see that Alex now has three red lumps on his stomach. One is the same size as his hand in a fist.

He tries to scratch this but it hurts, so he presses around the edges of it instead.

Covering up his stomach again he says, 'Know what my dream told me last night?'

Me: 'Say it.'

'It told me I didn't have any weakness. That I wasn't scared of zombies, or bad men. Or dogs. And even though I had diabetes, it didn't count.'

Alex looks at us confident – so confident that we can't argue back, to say that it *does* count, that a person can't just dream away their weaknesses.

Still, he maybe sees that we're unsure, because he gets the same doubt in his eyes that I feel and says, 'When you die you have worms up your nose. Sad to say, I haven't lost my weakness for that.'

As I don't have an answer he just sags his body and adds, 'The injections aren't working.'

'You should ask Elizabeth. She's the boss.'

He looks across at Elizabeth, who's now gone to the window and is peeping out through the blinds.

'I did. She won't tell. But I know. I'm not a very stupid boy, I know already.'

'They're coming,' Elizabeth interrupts, coming over to shake Mairi from her nest-bed. 'Alex, be beside me. I want the two of you out of sight.'

I go to hunker down in the dusty back corner of our bunk beds. Mairi kneels under the table. In a minute we hear voices outside. Then inside. I put a finger to my mouth to warn Mairi to be quiet, in case there's a war, but Calum Ian doesn't even come looking for us.

Instead, I hear him talking to Elizabeth. She doesn't tell about her leg. I think the telling might be about me, yet when I listen at the door I realise it's about Alex.

Calum Ian: 'Think we should just give him some, *seadh*? What else is there? You're too scared of taking chances, if that's all—'

Elizabeth: 'It's gone bad. It's giving him sores in his skin. And there was only half a vial, anyway. The stuff inside is worse than useless – we can't use it.'

'What about the radio?'

'I listened all night. I'm fed up listening. We listen and listen and for what!'

Arm by arm I let myself creep out. Mairi stays crouching in her place, watching to see what happens.

Elizabeth is bent down, with Calum Ian standing over her. She's holding Alex. Her body is shaking.

Something about the look of her – some oldness in her eyes – reminds me of the last time I saw her mum.

'Is there something wrong with you?' he's asking.

'No. It's nothing.'

Calum Ian keeps himself close to the door. I can smell him: he stinks of petrol again. His white T-shirt and trousers are grey-smudged from smoke.

'Now look at *her*.' He's pointing at me. 'You were the one said we had to stick together. And what did *this* one do? Back when I got the worst news ever of my life? Pulled a knife on me then ran away.'

'Leave her alone.'

I look for the knife he tucked in his belt yesterday, but can't see it. The brothers have on their backpacks. It's not hard to guess what's inside his.

'She's keeping secrets from the rest of us. Aren't you? And where's the other one? Miracle-girl with no scars. How many worlds would that be the chance in? You hiding her back somewhere, she scared?'

'Leave them both alone.'

'So she's not going to die then. Maybe it doesn't matter for her that she doesn't have scars. But what about us? What about her making *us* sick? Did you think about that? Did you not even think she might be a trap?'

Elizabeth holds her ears. Her hair hangs down in long wet threads, falling onto her lap.

'Stop it. *Stop.*'

This word she says over and over. She won't cry, she'll never cry. But her body is shaking.

I look at Calum Ian: and begin to see him as the type of person who's strong when someone is sad, or weak, which I think could be the worst kind.

I'm getting ready to find the best way to throw all my anger back at him when Duncan says: 'We've got a boat.'

This makes Calum Ian stop. This makes him look less like he owns us, owns all of the room.

He looks at Calum Ian and says: 'You were going to tell, weren't you? You just lost your temper there. Weren't you Calum? You never meant it. We – him as well – we came to tell, for helping.'

Right away Calum Ian is furious at Duncan: 'Come away *out*,' he says.

They go out. We watch from the window. We can see them arguing. Duncan seems smaller, much smaller, maybe more scared than we feel here.

When Calum Ian comes back again his voice sounds sent to how it was when we found his dad.

'You better follow me,' he says. 'But I want to say that it was *his* idea. I want to get that told right now.'

We follow him through the village: to the shops, to the House of Cats, to the church, to the pier.

Elizabeth is slowest of all, so that I wonder if she woke up the wrong way, without her energy.

Two boats got tipped over in winter. Another two stayed the right way. They're all tied to the big ferry pier. Their nets got snagged, and the mast of one boat fell on top of another. The first one sank, and in the shallow water the bottom of it sticks up like a whale's back.

Past these turned-over boats, in the sheltered space above the beach, are the boat sheds.

The door of one shed has been broken open. It smells inside of oil, rotted seaweed, mud.

Calum Ian turns on his torch to show us around.

There's an orange boat: not big-sized, made of rubber. It has boards to sit on, plus two paddles, which look snapped, but are in true fact folded. The engine motor is grey: Duncan calls it an outboard.

'Uncle Frank's rib boat,' he says. 'Went out loads with him

– and Dad – checking the creels. We had to work it, made sure we could – on our own, find the way. It's ready to go, petrol in as well. Checked it the other week. Isn't that right, Calum Ian, didn't we check?'

Calum Ian doesn't say.

'So . . . so we can use it. To leave the island, right? We get medicine for the wee man, we can use it.' Duncan shows us how to fix the paddles, how to make them straight.

Elizabeth puts a hand down on the rubber rim of the boat. Then says, 'Why didn't you tell us? About *this*?'

It isn't Duncan she's asking – but his brother.

Calum Ian scrapes the broken door open: all the way to the edge until the hinge of it groans.

'Have a closer look then,' he says. 'Go on. You'll see. You get cracking, drag it out and see.'

He doesn't help us when we take hold of the rope going around the edges and pull. We drag one way, then the other, until the boat sucks, scrapes, comes unstuck.

When we get the boat outside we see that the bottom of it is dirty with mould and grey water. There's a plastic milk carton cut in half on a piece of thin rope, which Duncan says is for bailing out.

We stand staring for a minute. Then Alex asks, 'How do we get it bigger?'

It's a question that sounds small-kid, or wrongly put, until we realise that it's not.

The boat lost its air. The sides of it get blown up – and they've gone halfway to being flat.

When Elizabeth says it needs inflated Calum Ian barks:

'You think we didn't *know*? Anyhow, we tried already. There isn't a place to blow it up: not on the side, or on the top or underneath.'

'You use a pump?'

'No, we used our breath . . . *'course* we used a pump.'

'Was just wondering—'

'You find one then, you're the leader! You're the doctor's daughter, who knows everything there is to know.'

Elizabeth holds up her hands for not needing a fight.

'Let's float it. Let's float it and see.'

We clear a path through the rubbish on the shore, then together drag the boat to the water.

It folds with the first wave, but only a little. Otherwise it sits high enough for a person to get in, maybe even two.

Duncan climbs inside. We steady the boat for him, then he warns us away and stands at the back as he tries to turn the engine on.

His third shot makes the propellers roar.

Birds go up. The noise, the smell of engine: it's like the adults came back, just to this *here*. It feels like victory: we left the island already, we are the winners!

While we cheer, Duncan turns the engine's handle, so that the boat spins, makes waves, churns, roars.

Calum Ian runs in to give him orders: '*Go easy, don't rev it on the bloody sand! You'll wreck the propellers, stop ya eejit!*'

After twenty seconds of revving Duncan turns off the engine. Nobody talks: we're still amazed by the churn, by the petrol smell – which reminds me so much of adults that I want it turned on again right away.

Duncan jumps out and wades over to us, then grabs Calum Ian by the neck and rubs his head, then goes around to shake all our hands, including mine and Mairi's, even though Mairi tries to hide.

'It's going to work,' he says. 'It's bloody well going to work, it is!'

Then Calum Ian comes back from the shed with two orange bundles.

'Life vests. We've only two. Which is all we should use because we tried the boat already. Result: it took me fine. It took Duncan fine. But it took me and Duncan together: not so fine.'

He takes off his backpack, then ties on one of the life vests. ''Course we never tried with three or four or five.' He throws the other life vest at Alex. 'I bet you any money that it doesn't work.'

To prove him wrong we begin to try right away.

Duncan gets in first, then Alex. They steady the boat, then Calum Ian gets in as well.

Elizabeth goes to sit inside too: but she's too much. So we go back to Alex, with just the MacNeil brothers alongside.

The boat sags in the middle, though not very bad. It folds when a wave comes past, but stays high.

Calum Ian pulls the string for the motor. He pushes the boat off with his unfolded paddle, then they go out a short way, just as far as the start of the pier and back.

He shuts off the engine as the boat returns. The fold is there in the boat's middle.

Alex climbs out as soon as he's near the shallows.

210

He looks frightened, relieved to be back on land.

Calum Ian looks around for the eye of everyone like he won the argument.

'Any more proof? Two's the most that can go.'

Nobody gets a surprise when he next makes his claim for who the two should be.

'We're the only ones who know. Me and Duncan. We've got fishing in the family, in the blood, me and my brother. Has anyone else got fishing in the blood? Thought not. So it has to be us.'

'It isn't just about fishing,' Alex says. 'It's also that you want to leave on your own – and leave us all behind.'

Calum Ian stands close to him, looking down.

'*Can a-rithist sin?* Do any of you know how to sail? No. Did you go out with Uncle Frank? No. Anybody know how to steer or go up over waves? No.'

'You want to leave. Now that you know your dad isn't coming. That's why.'

'*Shut your face*, Bonus Features – don't you ever talk bad on my dad's name, ever.'

'You're forcing. You can't force. We can be free to make any of our own choices. That's the rule of freedom.'

'And I said *shut it*. Unless you want some of what that one there deserves: keep your trap buttoned.'

He's pointing at me: like I'm the one deserving.

Elizabeth doesn't seem to want to use her age or better argument to stand up for us. But instead she just asks, 'Will you leave from here?'

Calum Ian finds a stick to draw a map on the sand: putting an X for our village, a circle for the nearest island.

'Except the closest place to leave from our island is Ard Mhor,' she tells him. 'And that's back next to Mairi's village. Back on the north shore.'

'So we keep it short. Short as possible. Duncan and me go around the island first with the rib. It'll take us: an hour? We'll stick close to shore. Then on the other side we'll meet you – here.' He scratches boxes for houses, then another X in the sand. 'The ferry slip, Ard Mhor. We fill up, do the main journey. Maybe two at a time?'

Elizabeth counts us up.

'We'd have to go back, come back. It would take how many—? Four, five turns?'

'Give me a bloody better idea.'

'I don't *have* a better idea. It seems to be you with all the better ideas, all of the time.'

'That's because I've got the brains. Brains are better than teamwork in any situation you can think of.'

Calum Ian waits for her to disagree with his saying. When she doesn't, he goes on, 'So you fed up with me taking the lead? Someone has to. Or is it something to do with that pair – the one who doesn't talk and the one who pulls knives—'

'I will need to go in the boat.'

He never expected Elizabeth to say that.

Neither did we.

Elizabeth now points at the fat wrap of bandaging she has put around her ankle.

'I can't walk. Or I can: but not very far.'

His mouth drops into an O when she undoes the wrapping to show what's underneath.

'How did—'

'You did it. With the dart.'

Now bits of her skin are broken. Drops of yellow are coming from blisters. Her leg went fat, swollen.

He looks long at what she's got, like he's working out what to do, what it changes. What he did.

'You can stay here.'

'You bloody well *owe* me. There was poison put on the dart, wasn't there? *Wasn't there?* Don't you even try to say there wasn't.'

He looks for the right saying back in the smoke-dirt on his T-shirt, without finding any.

'You could wait . . . Wait here. We take Alex. You could wait here with—'

'*I* – need – medicine. I don't want to die. You've made me ill, so now you bloody owe me.'

Her face falls, crumples. It's the worst ever to see Elizabeth look this way: worse than anything, because I need her to be the one who's strong.

Calum Ian stands at the edge of the water beside the boat. He presses both hands on it, testing the air inside. Maybe hoping it'll turn out to be fuller than he thought.

'It's tough, but I need to go with my brother,' he finally says. 'We're a team, the both of us. We were brought up to be a team.' Then he looks again at her leg: and thinking once more says: 'I could do you a favour.'

'Don't talk to me about favours. You *owe* me.'

'A deal, then.'

'The deal is: you take me.'

'Or the deal is: one of us takes you. Then at the other side it's me and Duncan. We leave together, and go to the next island to find help, fast as we can, for Alex.'

'The deal is everyone sticks together.'

'Then you and Alex get sick. Because we can't all leave. Somebody has to stay, the boat won't take everyone. And it needs a strong person to go looking for help – and a strong person to sail it back. Are you strong?'

Elizabeth can't think of an answer. I notice her hair is damp, with sweat coming off her forehead.

'Then at the other side we look for medicine.' Calum Ian holds his hand out. 'We already know there's none here. Deal?'

She doesn't say if it is or not. She just shrugs, which Calum Ian takes for a yes.

'So Duncan can sail with you.' Now he turns to us. 'Which makes it me and the kids. Isn't that right, kids?'

Now *he* has surprised us. Nobody shows a sign of agreeing. I look at Elizabeth for guidance, for what she thinks, but she doesn't seem to want to make any more arguments.

'Why do you want us?' Alex asks.

'It isn't that I want you, not one bit. It's that you've got *me*. Duncan gets his shot with the boat first: fine. He goes first. But then it's me for the main crossing. That's what *you're* getting.'

More on purpose he puts out his hand, and gets Elizabeth to shake it: 'I take the kids. OK? End of story.'

Then to us: 'We'll go as a team. Isn't that right, kids? Who wants to walk with me? With their Uncle Calum Ian?'

We don't say: Yes please.

'*Nach thu tna toilichte?*' he does thumbs-up. 'That's right! We'll all get there first, we'll beat them. All of us the one big friendly team. What's going to work?'

Nobody says teamwork.

We get our rucksacks, and pack clothes, water, small toys. Calum Ian shouts instructions at everyone: saying we have to try harder because Elizabeth is sick.

She sits on the sand, looking away for trying to forget, until Calum Ian orders Duncan to the swimming pool to look for floats or armbands for the passengers.

When he's not watching, Elizabeth pulls me close and whispers fierce and quiet: 'Go after him. Go where Duncan goes.'

'Why?'

'You need to get him to walk with you. Instead of his brother. Go after him, go now.'

I don't need to ask why. And then I can't ask anyway, or find out if even she's scared to be in the boat with him, because Calum Ian is there with us, taking out the heavy things he says we shouldn't've packed.

Duncan goes too far ahead. I run to catch him up – and just spy him going through the big school doors.

Inside, there are three ways to go: to the library, to the assembly hall, to the rest of the school.

The swimming pool's empty. Floats, goggles on the floor from the last time we came. He didn't come here.

The sign over the assembly hall door says **TRIAGE**; that one over the school door says **QUARANTINE**. Only the library door says what it truly is: **LIBRARY**.

215

It's dark in the library, because there's only skylights, no windows.

'Hullo? Anybody in?' The room doesn't answer, just stays smelling of old stale air.

When I go between the shelves of **Space** and **Explorers** I find Duncan.

He's crouched down, hiding, like he didn't want me to find him. My heart goes fast with fright.

'Thought you were a creature,' I say.

He's got books on the floor which he's covering up. I think he's going to be angry, just like his brother, so I get ready to defend myself, or run away – but instead he just gathers what he has and goes to sit at one of the tables.

'Humans *are* creatures,' he says.

There's a gap on the shelf next to where he was crouched.

The name for this shelf is: **Seafaring**.

He puts the books on his lap and tries to read the topmost one with his arm still covering.

Pretending not to notice I go and look around the shelves. In the **Science** section, next to **Volcanoes**, I find a book we looked at before, when it was dark and cold in winter. The title is *Electricity: Turn it on!*

For a peace offering I show it to Duncan.

'Sure, that one was useless,' he says, keeping a watch on me. 'Loads of crap about how electricity makes your hair stand on end. Nothing about how to get it back.'

We stare at one another. Duncan's scars look deep in the dark. I suppose mine must do as well.

'You followed me here.'

'That's true.'

'Why?'

'Because I wanted to ask if you'd come with us on the walk, instead of . . .'

He knows why. Right away he knows why I'm asking: and for the look he gives me it feels unloyal.

'My brother is not as bad as you think.'

'I wasn't—'

'His bark's worse than his bite. Truly. I should know, I live beside him. That's what brothers are for.'

'If Calum Ian would burn a body – like in the headmaster's house – could that not mean he could do it to other people? If he made a mistake, I mean. Or got a wrong idea in his head.'

'Like the wrong idea *you* had – of dirtying our house, of killing the pictures of our family? Are you meaning that sort of mistake?'

But Duncan doesn't really want to rub in the bad of what I did: because he adds in a kinder voice, 'I don't know why he did what he did. I wasn't expecting it, either. But if you need the truth: he's on our side. He's not as bad as you imagine, so you shouldn't be bothered or even scared. Want to know how I know you shouldn't worry?'

He unzips the front pocket of his rucksack and takes out an envelope.

I know what this is right away; I try to grab it.

He makes me take it nice.

The letter inside is dirty, and it's been torn into lots of pieces. I look at Duncan, unsure if this is a trick.

217

'You dropped it on the road,' he says. 'Beside the fifteen tree forest. It got torn up . . . by me.'

I put the pieces back inside the envelope. Then I take a book from one of the nearby shelves and unpeel its plastic cover, to keep the envelope safe inside.

'Go on. Why don't you put the pieces back together?'

'It might not go . . .'

'You won't know if you don't try.'

I hold it: ready to show him that I could: but then I can't. I'm too scared to find out what Mum wrote.

He doesn't push to know.

'Calum Ian saw the letter. Saw your name on it. It was me that tore it up. Because you took the knife out on him. So you know what he did? He picked up the pieces. Made me promise I would give them all back to you. He said: She's sad . . . You can cheer her up with it later. Just don't tell her I said so.'

Duncan gives me a thumbs-up.

'See? My brother's not bad, he's all right. You just have to give him the benefit and not the doubt.'

We both look down at the book he's hiding.

It's called *More Scottish Fishing Craft*.

Duncan frowns at me like he's worried I'll say something.

'I just want to do my best, for the boat trip.' He reaches for my hand and makes me shake.

'So don't tell. Specially not Calum Ian. Because he's my big brother. He knows I can do it. You never want to let the big ones down. You've got to be a winner.'

I promise not to say anything.

*   *   *

218

'I made Mairi a bag of clothes plus toys,' Alex is saying. 'She had to begin hers from the start.'

When I get back Elizabeth gives me a keen look: asking if I managed to persuade Duncan.

'It's all right,' I tell her. 'He convinced me it's all right. You shouldn't be worrying so much.'

She nods, mouth pressed firm: then holds out her hands for a hug, which I give her, and which she uses to whisper in my ear: 'Keep your eyes peeled. If anything bad happens: run. Head towards the sea and wave your hands. Get the others to run in different directions if it comes to it. I'll get Duncan to follow the shore around.'

Then she's hugging Alex, still looking at me.

We pull the boat down to the water's edge, until it starts to float. Then Elizabeth and Duncan get in.

They stand at both ends to get the balance right, then we put their bags in – only already there's a problem. The weight of everything makes the boat sag through its middle so much it's like it got cut in half.

'Lighten your bags,' Calum Ian orders, pulling jumpers and clothes out of Duncan's. 'Less weight the better.'

Duncan's fiddle and family pictures are left on the pier. Elizabeth, still in the boat, begins to ask a lot of questions: about the tides, what if it rains, what if it gets dark, what if the outboard stops working. She even asks about whales or sharks. Duncan tells her not to be so dumb.

'I'm the son of a sailor, I can *do* it,' he says.

For the last packing he takes an extra plastic milk carton of petrol for the engine, plus a spare canister.

Finally, he ties on Elizabeth's lifejacket, then Calum Ian ties up Duncan's. We put a packed lunch for both of them under the seat: chocolate mints, baby cans of tonic water.

'Wave to the captain!' Duncan shouts.

He turns the engine on, and we cheer loud as it roars.

For a moment the boat moves like a see-saw: but soon they get the balance right, and it flattens out.

'You lot better get ready to run,' Calum Ian hisses.

The boat makes smoke. We take it in turns to watch them with binoculars, and it's still my turn when they go around the headland past Message Rock. For a second the east shore has white waves, then we see an edge of ripples and smoke on the water, then they've gone past.

After this he pushes us hard. We shove the prams while he acts as slave-driver. Mairi has a pram as well, though it's getting most of the way to being her size.

When we get to the steep road going up the big hill she can't push it: her strength is not enough.

Calum Ian just watches, as she huffs, digs down her head, slides her feet away on the loose stones.

'Useless. Ach, give it to me.'

He takes some big steps ahead, turning often to check we're being as strong and going as fast as him.

At about quarter-way up Alex's legs have gotten sore. I give him some chocolate buttons in case it's lowness of sugar, but he doesn't much want them. Instead, he wants juice: as much as he can be allowed of our journey-supply, until he's had lots more than his fair share.

220

At halfway up Mairi tries to help him. She takes one side of Alex's pram and pushes.

Right away me and Alex step back – holding up our hands, drawing back to how far we agreed for safety.

'Why're you stopping?'

'She came too close. It's for her health.'

'Just let her bloody help.'

'But it's bad for her safety. We don't want to make her sick.'

Calum Ian drops his rucksack between roadside stones.

He comes back.

Spitting on his hands he wipes them on Mairi's face: making sure that some of the spit goes on her nose, and in her mouth.

Then he rubs his hands off on her jumper.

'Now it doesn't matter how close she gets. So let her do it. Or this'll take us all day.'

Mairi's left looking at the spit-smear on her jumper.

I bite my tongue and touch the letter Duncan handed over; try to keep in mind what he said, try to remember the good side he mentioned.

Alex stops again and again to look at boring things: sticks, rusted cans, a bird skeleton. He stops to pee and takes ages to catch us up, even though we're bored waiting.

He stops by the forest of seven trees, twice. It would seem ridiculous, only Elizabeth already told us that going to the toilet lots is what happens with diabetes – so the only ridiculous thing is how Calum Ian never gives him a proper rest for doing it.

I hold onto my anger. I hold onto my shout. It's nearly too much, but I manage.

Calum Ian keeps looking with his binoculars, stopping almost as often as Alex does, trying to stay high on the hill for as long as he can for the widest view.

'Don't see them yet,' he says, standing on a fence for a longer look. '*Seadh*, they must've got ahead.'

We come to the first forest, then the sheep-wash, then the village called Breivig.

Where Alex stops and says he needs more water.

'No – you've had enough.' Calum Ian upends an empty bottle. 'You had all your share, plus half of mine as well. That's your bloody lot. No more.'

'But I feel bones when I do this.' Alex sucks in his stomach. 'You can't be not giving me it.'

'Bonus Features, you're only showing your ribs, see? It doesn't mean anything. Doesn't mean you need more.'

But Alex pushes away his pram. His bag was hung over the handle of it, so when he pushes it, it topples backwards.

'Not going any further.'

Calum Ian throws away the empty bottle. Now Alex is sitting on the ground in protest.

'Get up.'

'I need another drink first.'

'I said you already had your share. A big greedy share. Get up.'

'My legs are sore and my arms are sore and my—'

Calum Ian grabs him by the neck of his T-shirt, which rips when he tries to haul Alex up.

'Look what you did! This was the last T-shirt Mum ever put on me!'

'Quit your fucking whining – it was old anyway. It stank. You wear it too much, that's why it ripped.'

Alex, wishing to disobey even more, now lies on the road, holding the torn edges of his T-shirt together.

'Shoot me then,' he says. 'If I'm so slow. Go on, I know you've got your stupid petrol gun. I saw it sticking up. Burn me with it – you big bully.'

Calum Ian's mouth is thin-lined for anger.

'If you could do it to a dead person, then you could do it to an alive person. On you go, you're the bad man: it's you. Go and burn me for being slow.'

Calum Ian looks uncertain. But then sure.

He unclips the top of his rucksack, takes out the plastic bag in which he keeps his water gun.

He unwraps and holds the gun up, then goes to stand five feet from Alex, and points it.

'Final warning.'

Alex trembles and screws up his eyes and doesn't move.

'Go on.'

'Last warning.'

'Put a flame on me, you big bully!'

He aims the gun.

Presses.

The spray reaches the cracked end of Alex's shoe.

Now I pull Alex away, away from the edge of the petrol drops. And Calum Ian shivers: seems to wake up to what he's just done.

He doesn't spray more – not even when Alex juts out his chin, calls him *bully, coward, bad person.*

Calum Ian just looks sad: to be him, to be standing here beside us.

I get myself between them. Now I can't hold onto all the good that Duncan told me about: it's forgotten.

'What would your hero dad say, now? Not a lot of good about you. He wouldn't like you at all. He would not be proud of you. No sir. He wouldn't, he'd be sick, sick of the sight. You and your bad bullying.'

Calum Ian waves at me to go away.

'And he's not coming back. Because he's all rotten and dead. Like you said to me. Dead, dead, dead.'

Now he moves. Croak-voiced: '*Gloic*, at least I don't imagine – like a baby – seeing my mum all over the place.'

'I don't do that, not any more. Want to know why? Because I went to the gym. After you said. To check, I saw her. Saw where she was. So now I'm no baby. All right? Now I know she did die – all right?'

This makes Calum Ian's eyes close, as if I'd sprayed some of his own petrol back into them.

'You went there? On your own?'

To prove it I tell him about the man in the chair. About the screen walls. About the signs and the flies and the shoes and clothes left in piles.

About Mum's blue jacket.

He looks at Mairi, then me. Then Alex.

Then he passes his last full bottle of yellow sterilised to Alex.

'Have it all,' he says.

Then he gets up and starts to push the pram Alex was pushing: only this time slow enough for us to keep alongside.

'So this wasn't a trap?' I shout after him. 'You weren't going to burn us? Or harm us like Elizabeth thought?'

He doesn't even answer this.

Ard Mhor goes in and out of sun. Birds go scattering, the noise of them tells you where the dogs are.

The ferry waiting room is middle-sized, on the rocky point, wood walls with their paint peeling.

The car park, beside, has about ten cars in it. Their tyres got flat, and all the windscreens are streaked.

Calum Ian walks to the nearest, then around the rest. One of them got burnt, so the tarmac is black in a square beneath.

'Don't look inside this one,' he warns us, pointing to a white car on its own. This car has yellow ☣ **BIOHAZARD** ☣ tape swirled all around its doors and windows. Alex hurries past to stop himself from looking by mistake.

The land sticks out, meaning the sea is all around. We see oystercatchers on the black rocks. There's so much rubbish and junk along the shore that the birds have to hop up and down to get past it.

'We got here first,' Calum Ian says, checking his watch, then looking out to sea. I notice his voice going up at the end, though I can't work out if the sound of this is surprise.

'Guess that means we're the winners.'

We follow him to where the road goes to the sea – then to the slip, then to the jetty, where he takes out and uncaps his binoculars.

'The bad news is their boat might be very slow,' Alex says. 'But we've got lots of time for journeys.'

Nobody agrees. We just keep watching.

Big clouds come, with red and gold edges for getting on to night. Alex says they're as high as mountains, but I know clouds go higher.

He keeps drinking, going to the toilet, drinking. It gets annoying but I'm not allowed to tell him.

Instead we get out Duncan's violin from his trove and try to play it, even though we sound rubbish. In fact I am the worst – so bad that it makes a sheep in the field nearby run for the hills, after dropping its shit first.

Calum Ian doesn't get the fun of this. He looks and looks at the water, then serves us cold beans and pineapple juice in faded cartons. The juice tastes sour and fizzy.

'Never thought my tastebuds would miss the food of adults,' Alex says. 'Now they do.'

To make the beans taste better Calum Ian adds two small packets of sugar: but not to Alex's, who moans so much that in the end he gives him some after all.

I lose the moment when Calum Ian understands.

We had just started making a den for Mairi out of blankets, and the pram, when he shouts: 'You don't get it, do you?'

It's confusing – because we weren't even talking to him, not a word, not about anything.

'I want to go up that hill,' he says determined, throwing our jackets at us to put on right away. 'We need to look. No arguments about it – *now*. Come on.'

Alex grumbles, but the look that Calum Ian gives us tells him that going up the hill is not optional.

Halfway up, Alex lies down, and I think he's protesting again – but instead he says his legs are too heavy.

Calum Ian lifts him up on his back, which means I'm the winner, I get there first.

Me: 'I see the orange boat!'

Calum Ian drops Alex at once.

He runs to me, I never knew he was so desperate. He even pushes me back, though there's lots of room on the hill for hundreds of kids.

His binoculars take a while to find the orange thing on the sea. Then he wants to steady them – so we follow orders and find a forked stick to rest them on.

He stops looking.

The binoculars are not being used: they're just hanging loose around his neck.

Without thinking of anyone else's turn he drops down on the grass.

'Me, give me a shot,' says Alex.

But Calum Ian isn't even hearing.

When I get the binoculars I can't use them. Then I see that the glass windows got dirty, because Calum Ian dropped them on the ground – which was careless of him – so I have to clean them hard with my sleeve first.

When I finally get to see the boat – it looks wrong.

It takes a lot of looking to know why.

At first it seems far away: but the wrongness of that is that the boat is actually quite near. It's just too small, gone flat in the water. And there's nobody inside it, not even lying down.

Alex knows the answer. He doesn't need to take his turn to understand.

'The boat got filled with water,' he says.

It gets too cold for us on the hill, so we go back to the ferry waiting room.

Inside, Calum Ian makes up four beds on the wooden benches. There's a toilet, though it lost its water and smells as bad as a shut fridge.

'Wait here,' he says, with a dead voice.

'But they had lifejackets,' Alex says, over and over. 'You can't hurt yourself if you're wearing a lifejacket, sure you can't?'

When he begins to cry I have to turn away, because to cry would make the bad become real.

We lie still while Calum Ian goes out to the car park.

After a long time he comes back with a red mouth and a plastic tub half-full of petrol. Alex asks why he went to suck petrol, but he doesn't reply.

At first we don't know what he's doing: then he begins to tear one of his old vests into strips, and winds the strips around and around a stick.

Finally, he dips the end of the stick into the petrol tub and I realise he's making a torch.

He goes back outside to walk the shore.

The torch burns big at first, then yellow, then blue.

After this we see him dip it again: and the bigness and the bright colours start over.

For hours we hear him shouting – and shining up and along, up and along, like a lighthouse that hasn't ever found its boat.

But he does find them. We don't want to look. He kneels beside what must be Duncan. Pokes him with a stick, shakes his shoulders to see if that will be enough to wake him up.

We don't see Elizabeth's body until the sky begins to brighten. It's on the far away beach, around the point.

The tide has gone out, leaving her face down, sand in her hair and in her mouth.

Back Bay

I can't think too much about Elizabeth or Duncan. If I do then all I want is the world to stop. But the only way to stop the world is to stop myself. And if I do that, I might as well stop caring about finding the others.

It's dark. The dark feels damp on my skin. There was orange in the sky when the sun went down. I couldn't stop looking at the colour of it.

It's the same with buoys, or orange pens, or oilskins, or straws. Everything: reminding me of that last smudge of orange we saw at sea.

The same colour as Mum's jacket.

Since they died I've been searching my memory for all the last things. Did we say the right stuff? Did we say please, and keep good manners? Did I tell them how much strength they had, or praise their bravery? Tell how much I was hoping we'd stay friends?

Most of the time I can't remember. Sometimes I remember real bits, and it seems we were in a hurry.

Yesterday I had a memory where everyone took time to tell each other their good points: that one was false.

Earlier on I went shopping. Not Old: but New Shopping. And I did it all on my own.

I discovered that having a bad memory, having the worst memory, stops the worst fear.

Even so, I'm not sure this is a good strength to have.

There was a sign at the coastguard's office which said: *Who's afraid of getting their feet wet? Not us!*

I found a message written in dust on the silver ledge of a window at the pub: *JOHN ♡ ANNE-MARIE.*

I found words written on a dirty van: **ALSO AVAILABLE IN WHITE**. Then underneath: If only my wife was as dirty as this.

I found a pair of slippers, waiting.

I found a house with four people all fallen over each other, beside a note saying who they loved.

I found lots of Bibles in people's hands. I found some on the floor beside their hands.

I found a mess of things I didn't understand, beside a dead cat. Then a mess of fur and bones.

On a school jotter someone had written: *I'm going to draw you a map with no pictures on it.*

I found a game called 'Beat the Parents'. I stomped on it until the box was broken.

One house had all its furniture covered in sheets, like ghosts. It took me ages to realise it was a holiday home.

A house with tins and tins of dog food.

One man dead at his computer.

One of the firemen from the station at home, on his couch, still in his uniform.

Then I found something: alive. I thought it was a dried-out fishtank. But when I looked close I saw there was a lizard inside. I couldn't believe it.

It had a frilly neck, like there was too much skin. Its eyes were closed. It wasn't moving.

I put in biscuits. Then I got a stick like you see people doing with snakes. The lizard moved, once.

I used a bag, and lifted it out. It felt cold, but not cold the way dead people are cold.

We went out to the road. I found some long yellow grass. I made sure the dogs didn't see it, or the cats. Then I found a bit of sunlight, because I knew from school that reptiles recharge their batteries with sun.

I wanted to say hello. But the lizard just moved off into long grass, slow, slow, then gone.

Now I wonder how the lizard is doing. Did he recharge his batteries fully? Is he looking for other lizards?

Does he see them in bits of grass, or old sticks, or even clouds, like the way I see people?

Seven days ago

The sun came up. My blanket got cold on its edges. I can hear the wind going around the walls outside, can see the grass being pushed and pulled by it.

Calum Ian is sitting at the window, alone. I wonder if he's been outside again. He's wearing his sleeping bag. I've decided that sleeping bags don't work if it's too cold.

'They've not moved,' he says.

His scars look the worst ever. There are two dirty marks going down his cheeks from his eyes.

Mairi's on the bench at the head of me, curled up so tight she's nearly gone. There's just one tuft of her hair. Alex is a bit further up, also buried. The bottle of pink water on the floor beside him is caved-in, finished.

'You think there's other people?' I ask.

Calum Ian keeps looking out of the window, and I almost don't hear when he answers, 'Somewhere.'

'Why haven't they come?'

233

'If they're getting things fixed. Like the electricity. Like radios. How the fuck would I know?'

I rub cold from my legs, sit up. Outside the sun is making a long yellow waterfall of the sea.

Me: 'Do you think they'll be kind?'

'Kind?'

'The people. What if they don't want to look after children who don't belong? We'll maybe have to fend for ourselves.'

Calum Ian doesn't answer. I notice the stink of him: the smell of smoke from his fire-torch.

He's not looking out at the world now – he's looking in the way, at us.

'So I lost my family,' he says. 'That should be the worst, but – you—' He looks away, back. 'You got an idea why you don't—? *Family.* I can't have my brother. Now you want to talk about fending for *ourselves*?'

I stare at the dirt worked in under my nails. The dirt on my skin, on the knees of my jeans.

'He was going to be the best fiddle-player,' he says. 'Practised every bloody day. *Oh*, I gave him a big row – for collecting books for the fiddle, and not food.'

Calum Ian holds the sides of his head like there's the loudest noise. He bumps into the bench then kicks it – then keeps kicking until I know it must be hurting his foot.

Then he looks at us and says, 'Was probably her fault.'

It's not the sort of talk for saying back to. And I don't know if he means Elizabeth, or me. Safer not to look at him in case it's me. He says, 'It should've been me with him on the rib. I'd have kept it close to shore. He'd have survived,

234

would be a certainty. With his brother – for sure, and maybe she would've, too . . . well she'd be here, with you, *she'd* be all right. Except now he's – not. I've got nobody left in the world.'

'You have us.'

'It's not the same. You're not my family.'

We just get the wind-noise around the walls. Now-and-then crackle of rain. Alex sniffing.

'At least you *had* somebody. Alex – he always knew his mum and dad were gone away. So did Elizabeth. At least you *had* someone for a while.'

Calum Ian turns to statue. I'm moving the most, Alex maybe second most. Mairi isn't even as still as Calum Ian.

He comes over, sits beside me.

'Go back to lying down like you were before,' he says.

I go back to lying down. Calum Ian has almost a sweet face, or a kind face. Then he puts his hands on my neck. Either side.

He presses, presses. Like he's trying to choke me.

He lets go, then presses again.

I want to remain calm. Like Elizabeth's mum said on choking when she came to visit our class – but his hands are too hard. Instead, I try to twist free from one side.

I hear someone crying – Alex.

His hands are bigger, stronger than mine. His eyes don't look like his eyes – they're angry and scared, but all at the same time, which is the worst thing.

Then Mairi is there. She's tugging on his T-shirt. Waving a hand in front of his face.

When he turns and sees her, she waves again.

235

He lets go. Lets go. Lets go.

He rubs on my neck. 'Made a red bit,' he says.

I get away to the window. My legs don't want to stand me up, they're shaking too much.

Calum Ian curls himself up in the blanket I just left. His face pressed to the wood of the seat.

The noise he makes isn't crying – it's more like a man's sound, like a man gasping, drowned.

'I tried, tried. It didn't come out right . . . If I could get back – to *before* . . . this. I'd be going on that boat. No question. What if it did sink – could it? If it did then I'd just hold onto him – we'd get on with it fine.'

He looks at the ceiling. There's just cobwebs, one cracked tile by the striplight.

'You said, you said Dad – learn to swim first. Then I'll let you on the boat. Let you get sailing. So you were right. The proof's in the pudding, so I turned out to be a big fat coward after all – are you happy with that?'

He says this last word as loud as he can, so that the racket of it seems to stay even after.

'Don't shout, please,' says Alex. 'It makes me cold and shivery when you shout.'

For a long time then, there's just his gasping-breath sound.

The sun comes out: one ray in the edge of the room. It finds Mairi's foot: she moves to be more in the warm of it.

'Nothing else I need to try for.'

'What about us?' asks Alex.

'What about you?'

*　　*　　*

When we look up again Calum Ian has gone back outside, back to search the shore.

I hide the nearest island by covering it behind one finger. That's how little it is for being far away.

Swirl of birds: going up like one bird's wing. Coming down like one wing down.

Mairi has opened her eyes. So has Alex. His breath smells stinky, which makes me remember: we need to give him water – so I pour my ration out for him.

'Boats are coming,' he says.

I look behind. There's just a grey wall, the toilet door, the drawn silver shutters from the waiting-room café.

Me: 'There's no boats.'

Alex: 'I can hear them – they're coming now.'

Me: 'I'm looking. There's none.'

Alex: '*Told* you there was ghost ships.'

That is a bad thought. Can Alex see ghost ships that I can't? I don't even want to see Mum's ghost any more.

He says, 'Did he scare you?'

And I know it's not ships he's talking about. But I don't know my best way to answer. I have to be like Elizabeth, now that she's not here. But what kind of thing would she say? To make things better?

'He's having second thoughts.' Then: 'We should have a minute's silence.' Then: 'Teamwork *will* work.'

Alex nods, like I got it realistic.

I notice he's breathing fast, so I count his breaths like I saw Elizabeth doing once.

My count gets up to twenty – but then I don't know how fast twenty is, so have to stop.

Looking out of the window, we see plastic bags on the slipway outside. I only realise they're the bags containing Elizabeth and Duncan's clothes when I see Duncan's fiddle set alongside.

Alex drinks more of my water, then after this I help him to the toilet because his legs got wobbly. I get him to change the clothes he wet in the night. He does it in private behind the toilet door, even though he wants to keep holding my hand on the other side.

'A picture of God's house,' he says. 'Only there's a cracked bit. On the cloud, at the front.'

Back on the bench I tuck him in, with a fresh blanket. Mairi comes closer to both of us. She pushes something across the wooden seats towards me.

It's one of the drawings she did yesterday. The one she scrumpled. Now it's flattened out proper, like she had second thoughts about destroying it.

Her eyes are keen. I think she wants praise for it, so I give her encouragement, but she keeps pointing.

She points at the drawing – then at Alex. I look at the picture, trying to understand.

Her finger is keeping close to the wrong yellow sun: the one she drew in her picture-garden.

'Alex? What?'

Now she points closer, at Alex's mouth. But there isn't a good enough clue for me to understand.

In the end she takes her drawing back. She finds a blue pen

and begins to add to it: first a flag, then a stick under the flag. Then a box underneath. Then some other flags.

'It's a boat.'

She nods strongly – then points back at the yellow shape she drew in her garden.

'You've got a boat in your garden.'

When I say this she gets up and draws a tick in the air.

It's an effort to get the courage to tell Calum Ian.

We find him outside, sitting on the stone pier, eyes red-circled from staring too long with the binoculars.

'Show me,' he says.

Mairi is first to get to the garden of her old home. She goes and stands beside the rubbish we saw two days before: the hump of tarpaulin twisted with fishing rope.

This time Calum Ian unties and untangles the rope, and pulls off the tarpaulin.

Underneath is a long, thin red boat. Calum Ian, with a flat voice, calls it a kayak.

I remember now that we always saw people going around our island in these. One of the teachers at the school had one, too. There was even a kayak-hire.

The boat has the white-foam stuff from fish crates tied around its edges, plus two orange buoys, wrapped in green nets at both sides of the back of it. There's bubblewrap in spirals along the sides, stuck down with tape, and tinsel in wavy lines along the front.

'Your brother had an escape plan,' Calum Ian says.

Mairi nods.

239

He feels along the boat. Then he looks inside the seat part in the middle. Then he tries to tip the kayak over, to check the underneath of it.

Finally, he taps on the edge of it to listen to the hollow plastic noise it makes.

'My class went out on these, at the school,' he says. 'Last year. But it was only the once. And I didn't go. Dad wouldn't let me. Because I couldn't—' He screws up his eyes, maybe for concentration.

I think he's going to cover the boat back up again, but then he says determined: 'I need to practise.'

Our first problem is: how do we get from Mairi's house to the sea? Because the nearest bay is over the hill.

First we think of shopping trolleys: there's a garden across the street which has two. But it would be too hard to lift the boat up so high as that.

We search the other gardens. In one I find a doll's pram; in another, a real pram. But they're too weak. Then we decide that anything with wheels could be good, so I get a rusty bike, and Mairi gets a kid's walking trolley for bricks from her own home.

But it's the same problem as before: the bike is too high up, the boat too heavy for us to lift. And the walking trolley: too little to fit.

Alex sits on the grass, watching. His face is sweaty. Even though he's not helping he's breathing like it's hard work. I think he's joking, but when I complain Calum Ian tells me to stop, to shut up about it.

We get fed up, so we lie down. Alex drinks all of the pink water. Then Calum Ian clicks his fingers at me and Mairi and says, 'We're all going to drag it.'

He orders both of us – not Alex – to the garden. Then he starts to pull. The boat has a handle on its very point, so Calum Ian pulls that. Then he ties three bits of washing line to the sides, so we can all pull together.

The boat scrapes, turns, scrapes.

It begins to slide. We pull it ten, twenty feet.

I want to cheer, but then I remember about Elizabeth and Duncan – my heart goes cold.

We pull it into the street. Calum Ian keeps wanting to check we haven't scraped a hole in the bottom. Then he goes and gets the tarpaulin and we pull the boat across that, and it's faster, but only until we get to the edge of it, then we have to start again, and again.

We find a gap in the fence and pull it through. In the grassy field beyond the boat slithers rather than scrapes. It's hard work. We do it by tarpaulin, grass, counting each new turn. We get bored, stop and start again.

At the top of the hill we wait. We can see the shore, the sea, some islands. Calum Ian shields his eyes from the sun and looks and looks. I know who he's looking for.

In the end, on the downhill, we go fast. The boat runs ahead of us, scrapes on the last bit of rock.

Then it's in. Then it goes too far – we almost lose hold so Calum Ian falls to grab the washing lines.

He orders us to pull the boat back to the edge – then

241

towards the pier, and the ferry slip. It's the worst hard work, but we manage. Then he shouts at me for dragging it too far and nearly losing everything.

'Always *you*! You're the blame of everything! Why couldn't *you* have been on the boat?'

I cover my ears, which has the best effect, because he stops. Then when I uncover them he's forgotten – or is trying not to remember what he just said.

After this, we sit on the grass. Alex has come to join us from the house. He's in the sun, just breathing, watching. The way he pants reminds me of a dog. But I've learnt from telling Duncan he looked like a pig that you don't tell people when they remind you of animals.

'Try to stay awake,' Calum Ian says, rubbing Alex's hair hard, punching him gentle on the shoulder.

Alex shivers. 'I'm tired.'

'Just – don't shut your eyes, OK?'

We go back to Mairi's house and find a box of kit that her brother put together: armbands, plastic bags, two lifejackets, a float, plus two smelly black spongy suits, which Calum Ian says are called wetsuits.

He tries one on. It's way big. His arms and legs look fat, crinkled. Mairi tries on the boots and gloves.

'OK – right. Don't think too much,' Calum Ian says, to himself, talking fast. 'Use yer guts – not yer brain, Dad said. Also, remember he told you – don't be stupid lad. Forget the fear. Quit being a scaredy-cat.'

Me and Mairi hold the boat so he can get in. It seems very

242

wobbly – especially when his body begins to shake – then Mairi remembers.

She goes to her house and comes back with a brown plastic bag. In the bag are rubber rings.

She points to the sides of the boat; Calum Ian shrugs.

We spend a lot of time blowing up the rubber rings. I see stars from blowing too much. Calum Ian keeps checking his watch. Finally he tucks them in the sides, underneath the green net holding the buoys.

'I'm going to do it,' he says.

He pushes the boat off; I help. The boat wobbles, he cries out, then uses the paddle for steadying. In a minute the net snags on a rock – it comes undone, and the buoys and arm-bands float free. Calum Ian tries to tie them back on, but it's too hard to paddle with lots of extra junk, so in the end he just throws them away.

In the small shelter beside the slipway he practises: going forwards, back, forwards. If he paddles on one side he turns that way; the other, it's the opposite.

'Watch if I need help, all right?' he says.

I sit beside Alex and wrap a sleeping bag around his legs, then Mairi's. All the islands have white beaches, green hills. They look too far across the water.

Calum Ian goes way out, then turns again. It takes him longer to pull himself around on the way back, which I think must be due to having tired arms.

I help him drag the boat onto the slipway.

'It's bloody tough,' he says, getting out. 'You couldn't do it. The waves are bumpy coming back. We won't be coming that direction, maybe that's all right, then? Help me out. Get me the map. How long to the next island?'

We put out our map with the orange cover on the ground. Calum Ian measures with his finger, following the wavy line the ferry takes. Two-and-a-half fingers.

'How far d'you go just now?'

He looks at the map: then points to the end of his finger. Then I see that it's not even his finger he's pointing at, but his finger*nail*.

'More practice,' he says. But he looks at Alex: who's lying down, sleeping again. We can see his breathing, the blanket going up and down.

'Help me load the boat,' Calum Ian says.

In the front store of the kayak we put my things, plus Mairi's things. In the back, Alex's and Calum Ian's.

Then it's time. Calum Ian goes in first, then Mairi, crouched between his legs.

But then there isn't room for me *and* Alex: not even if we go deep within, down past Calum Ian's feet, which is anyway too scary.

Calum Ian gets out, sits in a crumple. His hands are shaking – so I get out and look in our rations, find a sweet. He eats it, looking up at me, slowly chewing.

'Thanks,' he says.

He orders us out of the kayak. Then he unpacks the front store, leaving the store's rubber hat off. He puts a lifejacket on Mairi – and asks her to sit inside.

Mairi does it, but only very slowly. I have to sit in the back one. It's a squash, but we manage.

244

Finally Calum Ian helps Alex to fit inside the main hole, just in front of his own seat.

We push off – but nearly straight away the boat sinks low. Calum Ian can't steer it – it turns in a circle then tips, too far – then we're in the water.

I'm stuck – the water pushes around my middle – but then I come back up. Mairi has already come out: I drag her back onto the stone slip, she's crying, choking.

Calum Ian is shouting desperately: he's trying to find Alex, who's still underneath.

We pull the boat all the way onto the stone. It seems to take too long – then Calum Ian's got Alex, he's out, coughing, dark with being wet.

Calum Ian just sits. He stares at the faraway islands. Stares like they're the very end of the world.

We unzip the sleeping bag. Calum Ian wraps it across all of our shoulders.

'Dad used to say – if a thing wasn't difficult, then it wasn't worth doing,' he tells us.

Everyone thinks about this. Then Alex answers, 'Difficult things are not much fun.'

'No.' Calum Ian hands around his packet of sweets. 'You'll get your fun again soon, Bonus Boy.'

He stares at the sea. I want to tell him I realised the sea is like fire: if you stare at it too long it stops making sense. But I think he already knows it doesn't make sense.

'Never saw Elizabeth's house,' I say. 'We went to everyone else's, but never hers.'

Calum Ian squeezes water from his trouser leg. Then he takes off his shoes, squeezes water from his socks. He looks at me for once without being angry, or annoyed.

'We walked past her house,' he says.

'Why didn't she say? We could've gone in.'

He looks at my neck. I see him make a sad face at the bruises he left there.

'First time, she was worried about you. You'd gone off alone. Remember? Then the second time – that was just yesterday. When we were pushing the prams. We didn't stop because she told me not to.'

'She didn't want to stop?'

'Alex is more important, she said.'

It's a lot to understand. No human being could resist going to their own home – no kid, especially. I ask where, and Calum Ian says that her house is beside the big hill, Cuialachmore, after the first village with a forest.

When I get my courage I ask him, 'Did you like Elizabeth?'

He takes off Alex's shoes, wrings his socks out. Then he does the same with mine, then Mairi's.

'More than I wanted to tell her.' He goes back to the ruck-sack: says, 'If I see her again – I'll tell her.'

I am given a pair of Duncan's old trousers to wear. Alex and Mairi are given dry T-shirts.

I start to feel warmer again. Calum Ian dries off his own T-shirt by laying it on a rock.

'I used to think all the grown-ups had died,' I say. 'But maybe you're the very last.'

He looks pleased that I've said this, but then not much.

It's like when the sun goes behind a cloud.

I look at the clouds, out over the sea. They go blue as it gets further. I train my eyes for an orange boat, but I know that it's impossible. They're dead.

Calum Ian scratches a stone on the ground, throws it away. 'Now I don't know what to do.'

I press his shoulder in a friendly way.

'You'll figure it out.'

This doesn't make him look happy.

'This time,' he says, 'this time I don't want to make the decision. I'd rather there was a bigger person. Then it won't be me to blame if it all goes wrong. I'm sick of being in charge.'

We all go quiet, then I say: 'So I'll be in charge. Tell me what needs deciding.'

It's a very long time before he answers: 'We can't all go in the boat.'

His voice sounds flat, small-kid to me. That's what happens when you say you'll go in charge: everybody else sounds smaller compared to you.

I think about it carefully.

'Firstly.' I click my fingers for an idea. 'If we can't *all* go in, maybe some of us should go *outside*.'

Answers sound smart when you say them. But Calum Ian doesn't answer. It takes me a while to realise that by not answering he's not deciding.

'Right – OK, not safe,' I say. 'Maybe someone has to swim. With armbands, we could tie a rope, drag them behind?'

Nothing.

'OK. The water's too dark, plus too cold. Bad idea.'

We all look at the islands. I try to bring them closer with my eyes – it's called reeling in. Then I close my eyes to bring them closer by concentration. It doesn't work.

'You think Elizabeth and Duncan are watching?'

Calum Ian doesn't answer. He jangles a hollow cowrie shell in his hand like it's a dice.

'I can paddle the boat,' he says. 'I think I can do that. But it looks too dangerous to put anyone in the hatches.'

'But we can't *all* fit in the middle big hole.'

'Correct.'

Calum Ian stands and faces us. He clears his throat. He maybe wants to appear adult, but with his too-big wetsuit and dirty face, he doesn't much.

'Two of us need to stay,' he says.

We all listen. Alex's breathing is mixed with the sound of the waves.

'Maybe Alex is too sick to go?'

'*Come on* – it can't be Alex staying. He's the reason we need to go in the first place. He goes – that's final.'

Mairi sits up. She starts to cry. Then she runs to the kayak and gets in – right in deep.

She looks back at us, shaking her head. She beckons Calum Ian forward. She looks stern, or scared.

Calum Ian holds his head like he got the worst headache ever. He doesn't want to look at me.

To begin with I don't understand what his not-looking means. And then I do. And it makes me embarrassed, because I want to cry just like Mairi did.

'Can't be left alone,' I say.

'Alex *can't* stay,' Calum Ian says, then in a shout: 'Look. He'll die, Rona. And Mairi won't stay. Look at her. Look.'

Mairi has disappeared in the boat.

My eyes give up. I wipe them on my sleeve.

'Can't be alone.'

'You won't. We'll come back. Soon as we find help. I don't know why people haven't come looking. Only we can't stay, Rona, we can't. It might be another six months: and then what? Alex needs his medicine. But just as soon as we can I'll send help. I promise.'

'First you said you'd come – now you say you'll *send* help – it's not the same!'

'OK, OK. I'll come. I promise.'

'Cross your heart and hope to die?'

'On my mum and dad and Duncan and Flora and Elizabeth's souls. I promise.'

The waves flap, splash.

'Can we do One Potato? What about a competition to see who can go without blinking the longest? Or we could pick straws, like Elizabeth did when—'

'*Stop it.*'

He turns around, showing his back to me, not looking. Maybe that makes it easier.

I go back to the boat and empty out my remaining things. My treasure trove, my best drawings. They got wet. My book of understandings of the world. My one clock that keeps true time. My oldest teddy.

*   *   *

When it's done, nobody looks at me. Calum Ian coaxes Alex back into the main hull, beside Mairi. But it's still too much of a jam, especially when they've got their lifejackets on. I hear Calum Ian swearing for a better idea.

In the end, one person has to go back in a hatch. Because Mairi's smallest, and was the quickest to fall out, she has to go in the backwards one.

When she eventually gets seated inside, her lifejacket goes so high it nearly covers her face.

I try to climb into the main hull. But there isn't any room for me beside Calum Ian and Alex.

So I get back out, and I go back to the sleeping bag, and I wear it, and I get ready to push them off.

The boat looks fine. It's not too sunken. I nearly didn't want it to float, but it floats OK.

Alex and Mairi hold up their arms when Calum Ian tells them to, to show that they understand.

They push off, not wobbling.

Calum Ian turns the boat so I can see him. He stays in the shelter-water beside the pier.

'What's going to work?' he says.

I should say teamwork, but I don't want to.

He hides his eyes, then he paddles nearer to the edge and talks up close: quick, firm.

'Get some other dry clothes. Remember Elizabeth's safety rules. Top of the list: keep warm. Always keep warm. Keep your jacket zipped up. Three layers for insulation. Eat from tins – but remember, never *ever* eat anything that smells bad. Remember the adult leaflet saying: smell a lot, taste a little,

250

wait, eat. And always, always keep your radio turned on. OK?'

I give him my affirmative.

'We can start some new rules when you bring the adults back. Today, right? Tomorrow?'

I didn't mean it to sound like a question – especially not a truly desperate one.

'Maybe tomorrow,' he says. Then his eyes screw up and he adds, 'In case we do take longer – you need to be thinking about water. Elizabeth showed you how to sterilise, right? If you count up more than two days, and we're not back, go back to your house. It's the safest place. There's water in the bath. Only one drop of bleach, OK? And remember to mark with food colouring.'

I tell him over and over that it won't even get to two days. In the end he just says 'OK, OK,' then paddles backwards a bit so Alex can see me.

'Never thought much of boys,' I say. 'I've got to think a lot more of them since I met you.'

Alex gives me the double thumbs-up.

'For bravery you get to the top,' he says. 'I'll tell everybody. You'll get a medal for it.'

Mairi is in the boat facing backwards. As it goes she's facing me.

She's a face getting small; smaller.

She waves to me, then has to concentrate on keeping her balance in the right place.

I hear Calum Ian calling out instructions, checking everyone's all right, not tipping the boat.

Past the pier there's more waves. He gets pushed about a bit, but then he gets it under control.

They stick to the shore, and I run alongside, tripping a few times because I'm not watching where I'm going.

Sometimes there's rocks and I can't get close, and it makes me sad; other times they're right beside.

Then they're pulling away, far away.

I see the tinsel on the sides of the boat shining as the boat bobs when he paddles.

Then it's just me and my belongings.

I collect them up. I wave until my arms are sore, until all I can see is a paddle, going up and down like a swimmer's arm on the water. Then nothing.

Rona Aonranach

Last week

Calum Ian did not come back that night, or the next, or the next. I made a hundred bargains with the sea to bring them home, but the sea never listened.

The first night a shiver went through the air, and it began to rain. The water got moving shapes on it, which I thought were rescuers, but they were only waves.

I stared at the sea until I saw boats, whales, faces. When the rain came I walked to the ferry slip to save Elizabeth and Duncan's bags. Duncan's fiddle had got wet, and the strings sounded wrong.

I ate the packed lunch that Elizabeth made for us: oatcakes, pineapple juice, jelly vitamins.

Stuffed beside Duncan's lunch were other things. The fiddle book he was learning last year: *Fiddle Time Christmas.* Also clothes, pencils, chalks, a packet of cards, a conjuror's set, jotters, felt-tip pens.

I made a cairn out of stones to remember them by. I threw

flowers in the water and begged the sea to change its mind, to be kind to my other friends.

When a plastic bag flew past I thought it was a person, but then I saw it was just rubbish blown from the lines of junk along the shore.

There were big birds – flying, circling over the next beach along. I didn't want to look too close at them in case they told me where Elizabeth and Duncan were.

At night I went on lookout, for lights on the sea or maybe from the next island. I looked for Calum Ian flashing his torch. He might have a flare: he could shoot it up to tell me they were safe. But I saw no lights.

I sat on a rock to watch. I imagined a genie, giving me three wishes. I could use all three wishes to make the sea go away, like Moses. Then run to the next island to join them. But each time I imagined the sea bottom it was full of mud, or wrecks, or the bones of whales, and then the water came back anyway too quick, and I didn't have a raft or armbands to stop me from drowning.

I slept in the ferry waiting room. The sleeping bags they left behind had the smell of them. When I closed my eyes I imagined that everything was back to normal.

'Why was six scared of seven?' I asked a bird outside. 'Because seven eight nine.' The bird flew off.

Behind the metal screen was the waiting-room café. I tried the door and it was open, so I went in and opened up all the cupboards: but the only thing I found was a giant tin of coffee, plus a stack of plastic cups.

Calum Ian was right, though: I did need water. Being thirsty started to take up all my thoughts. Especially as there'd been rain and I never collected any. I knew you couldn't drink from the sea – that was a rule no one ever attempted to break – but what about rock pools? No one mentioned if rock pools were in or out. Maybe not the ones nearer shore: but what about those higher up?

But it was hard to be certain, so I tore open the cartons of pineapple juice and licked the drops from the bottom of them, then from the shiny insides. The taste only lasted as long as it took to unpick the seams.

I looked for puddles, then for water in the cracks of the wood of the pier. There was a rusty crumpled can, but the water in that had gone gritty, sharp-tasting.

I looked in other places: the drain, the toilet inside, the cars in the car park. I remembered from somewhere that you could suck moss, but where would I find that?

I stared and stared at the sea. At the islands. Until my breath misted the glass of the window. I tried to lick the wetness off, but my tongue was too dry to do it.

Sadness came like a pulse in me. Every few seconds I'd remember, and it would be sharp, and I'd have to turn away from the thought, scrub my mind of it. There would be a second without, before the pulse returned.

I thought for a long time, until it got hard to know if I was thinking or talking.

'This is me talking *now*,' I said to the world. 'And now, and now. And now and now. And now.'

*   *   *

257

It helped to imagine where they were. How tall were the adults? Were teenagers taller? Did the ladies have soft voices? Hopefully they wouldn't mind that our clothes were dirty, that we had scars on our faces (except Mairi), but anyway, Calum Ian would do a quick job of telling our story. And Alex would be all right once he got his medicine. And Mairi would begin to speak again.

It got to three days: then I had to leave. I packed my teddies and clothes, and took Duncan's fiddle. Then I used his chalks to write a message on the slipway:

HERE IS RONA

But it didn't seem clear, so in the end I changed **HERE IS** to **RESCUE**. Then after that I used Duncan's jotters to write a message, which I stuck inside the window of the waiting room. The message was: my name, age, parent, the class I grew up in, the family of children I belonged to.

The road was dotted with grass and sheep shit. There were trees blown into tangles. I didn't want to look at them, because their shapes made me uneasy.

Every hundred steps I chalked a new arrow to show the way I was going for everyone to see.

It didn't matter that the arrows wouldn't last, because they'd be coming soon enough.

Her front door was open. Somebody broke it. There were trails of sheep shit going into the hall, which made me think they should've taken better care. Once animals get into your house then it stops being a home.

I thought I saw an old green blanket spread out on the stone steps. It was only when I got up close that I realised: it was the body of a somebody.

Then there was another person: just inside the hall, seen through the broken door. Normal brown hair, but with the face shrunk to a skull. A hand with black fingertips.

I ran away to the far edge of the garden.

Counted twenty.

Watched the bees on the flowers, the seagulls miles away, the slow clouds, to help my eyes forget.

I went around to the back door, and found that they didn't need to break the front one: the back was open. Or maybe Elizabeth opened it later? But the instant I put my head in there was a smell – a very bad smell.

I didn't have a perfume-hanky, or goggles, so I decided to run in and out quick, so the stink wouldn't stay.

The kitchen: a big mess. Cupboards open, drawers crashed to the floor. Plates smashed, tins of food under the table. I had to get out – to breathe.

I went back. Checked under the sink. The water wasn't where Elizabeth said her mum and dad kept it, so somebody must've taken that.

I found one empty bottle, that's all. I had to get out.

I went back. Found a tin of kidney beans on the floor. Plus a jar of beetroot. And a card on the fridge which said: **Jesus loves you — but I'm his favourite.**

I tore the card into tiny pieces, not caring that for the time it took I had to take a breath.

Back outside, I drank the juice from the jar of beetroot. The taste was very queer. I opened the can of kidney beans with my opener, but the juice was like glue.

I remembered Elizabeth's rule for food: *smell a lot, taste a little, wait, eat.* Only maybe it didn't matter the same for the water that you got in food?

'It's hard without a sidekick,' I said to the world. 'It's not easy to tell yourself you're thirsty.'

After wrapping a T-shirt and scarf around my nose I went back in. I ran upstairs.

Elizabeth's bed was made. She had a desk, a CD player. Her pencils stacked neat, in the correct rainbow order, waiting for her to come back and use them.

She kept her achievements on the wall beside her desk. **Learn to Swim — Level 5.** Beginner's Gaelic Gold Prize. Well done! *You Kept our island Tidy.* Summer Star Pupil. RESPECT AWARD PRESENTED TO ELIZABETH SCHOFIELD FOR SHARING HER STORY WITH CLASS P1 READING GROUP.

Just beside, a picture of Elizabeth on the wall. Her skin looked normal: it was from the time before. She looked young. But the main thing was: she smiled. I'd never seen her smile with her eyes taking part.

I took the picture, to show the others when they came back. To show them how strong her smile could be.

So I knew what happened. The people came. 'They ransacked,' I said, remembering the exact word.

They were looking for medicines, not food. But Elizabeth's

mum and dad were gone: they were sick at the gym. And anyway, they didn't have medicine. It was all on the boat, which nobody knew about.

Then I knew why Elizabeth didn't want to go to her home: because it had been spoiled. We all had clean homes, perfect homes, but she didn't.

Her home had strangers who had died in it, which was why she never wanted to take us there.

Past World

The metal shutters are down at the surgery, even though it's daytime. There's a lot of people waiting outside, standing at the front entrance, looking cold and wet.

Mum drives past and parks on the going-down shore road. She checks nobody followed her, then sends a message on her phone, then waits.

In ten minutes someone opens the side door. It's Morven, who works on reception. She doesn't say anything or get too close, just shows us in.

As soon as the door's locked we hear a person running up to it and banging on the other side.

'Will ye at least *look*?' a man, shouting. 'I'm not sick, you can look can't ye? Need our son's medicine.'

Morven asks the man to be quiet, not to draw attention to himself. Then she goes upstairs ahead of us to ask the doctor what to do.

She comes back – and unlocks the door, lets him in. It's Mr Gillies who works on the ferry.

When we get to the waiting room Dr Schofield is there. She's wearing strange clothes: a white paper suit, with blue gloves and covers over her shoes something like the covers they wear at the fish factory.

I see her daughter, Elizabeth, from the big class P7, looking out from one of the nurses' rooms along the corridor: watching us, her mum.

Mr Gillies looks impatient when he asks the doctor about deliveries and boats and rations. Then he says, 'Much can I take?' with a voice that sounds too keen. 'Away with me, right now? How much?'

Dr Schofield takes off her glasses, rubs at her eyes. 'You could have all of it.' Then: 'But I don't know, would have to check—'

'There's a boat coming day after tomorrow. I could get more to boost up your stock, right? Fair enough? There's nothing here, you know as well as me. If you give me a note for your supplier—'

'Look, there's a dozen others – same as you, same situation. Then the others, with chronic illnesses. Everyone has their own want. We're trying to provide for everybody. There needs to be some reserve . . .'

Her voice goes small, until it's less than a whisper. Mum is trying to listen in: I can see by the way she tilts her head, not looking away for one second.

Dr Schofield goes back into the dispensary. Finally, she returns holding a white paper bag.

'This needs to be kept cool,' she says. 'You know about cold chain? You have a generator – no. Outdoors, then. These are mixed – long- and short-acting. You can dose twice, same units. Or if you want to ration: fine, as long as maybe half is going in each day? If there's some insulin that stops ketosis. You know about that.'

Mr Gillies holds out his hand. His voice is broken up, jagged, when he says, 'Look: Alex needs his medicine. I had to take this chance, OK? He's at the Cròileagan. I'm not allowed. Can you get someone to hand it in there for him?'

Dr Schofield looks at Mr Gillies' hand for a long time, then doesn't shake it. 'I will see,' she says.

Mr Gillies leaves: then Morven goes downstairs to make sure the door is locked behind him.

We hear Dr Schofield calling on Elizabeth.

Then we hear her explaining about the boy. She talks about pens: how to dial up numbers. How to inject into a person, where to inject, how often.

Then she comes to talk to us. I notice her hands are shaking, as if she'd been out too long in the cold.

'How's Dr Schofield?' Mum asks.

This confuses the doctor: because it's her name, too. When Mum adds, 'Your man? Your husband?' Dr Schofield closes her eyes and says, 'He went to hospital.'

'I am so—'

'Really need not to think about this just now.'

She goes away, then returns with a box. In the box are lots of smaller white boxes, plus leaflets.

'One each house,' Dr Schofield says. 'If they open the door

get back to your car. Don't touch the gates, the letterboxes, the handles. Use gloves, always. Keep your mask on. Hand hygiene – you've got scrubs? There's a recording on our answering machine. Let them know about the D.E.C. Also world service, long wave.'

'We couldn't get the computer—'

'Get a wind-up radio.'

'They've all gone from the store . . . Doctor, do you need more help? Will I come again, deliver again?'

'Stay in after.'

Mum goes to take her hand, but Dr Schofield doesn't reach out for hers.

I see Elizabeth once more before we go. She's not looking at us, but at her mum: at the woman who usually walks so tall, now sagged down in a seat.

As the crack of the door closes I see her girl Elizabeth standing and waiting.

It's not a normal delivery. For starters, Mum has to do every single house. Usually I'd get to help but today I'm not allowed. It's raining extremely hard, and Mum is wearing her waterproof jacket. The inside of the van gets steamed up with her coming and going.

Mum wears gloves and a mask, just like Dr Schofield said. She wraps each box in a leaflet, then puts it in a plastic bag and puts that through every letterbox.

She runs to each house. She's a smudge in the rain.

My back gets sore from sitting too long. Mum gets out of breath, plus fed up with wearing her mask. We share a flask of tea she's got, only I can't be bothered with tea, especially when there isn't sugar in.

At one house the door opens. A man comes out.

He's not got his mask on. He walks towards our van: so Mum gets in and rolls her window up, quick.

She presses down the lock of my door, her door.

The man has red eyes. But his skin got too white, even the skin of his hands. He looks like a tired ghost.

'You put only one box in,' he says.

He bangs on the window. Mum puts her hand on the keys to start the engine.

'There's four of us in here,' the man says.

Mum doesn't look at him. She keeps looking ahead, like he isn't really there.

Mum says, too quiet for him to hear, more to me: 'One per house. That was my instruction.'

The man keeps his hand on top of the car. His breathing is fast, like he's at the end of a race.

'Come on,' he says.

Mum looks at him, shakes her head. Then she turns on the engine and drives off.

I watch the man's hand drop down. Otherwise he just keeps standing in the rain.

Back Bay

It's no fun staying up if you can't be blamed for it.

I've just one clock to tell the time, now. I put all the rest in the garden – which turned out to be a mistake, because the electric ones stopped working after it rained. Then the wind-up ones stopped because I forgot to wind them up.

So my last clock, with its true time, is precious.

I'm dressed first. Everyone else is bleary this morning. 'Rise and shine, time to dine,' I shout out. Alex wanders out to the toilet. Mairi gets dressed and just sits waiting at the table, holding her spoon up.

Breakfast is wafer biscuits, then the powder from chocolate sponge mix, mixed with water. It looks like mud at first but be patient, it will come right. Alex has a fierce hunger and eats while it's still powder-dirt. Mairi has the least appetite of us. I tick her off and she bunches shoulders but it doesn't make her eat good.

After breakfast, we pile up the plates and get ready for school. First there's fly-killing time. I'm the winner at that with twelve. After this we check the radios. Static. Then the light switches. No lights. Then I write up our shopping list for today: *Batteries. Sweets. Gaelic stickers for remembering. Fizzy cans of juice. Better water.*

Then it's calendar time. That's next door. I'm in charge, so the others have to wait. The calendar has pictures of trucks with blown-up wheels. We found it at a house in the village. It's just me that gets to mark the days.

I put a cross over yesterday. I used to use circles, but circles can mean red-letter days so I stopped, in case it made a confusion for rescuers. Last week I even drew circles on days ahead to make things happen. So I wrote on the 23rd of June: 'When the radio will start working!!' Then on the 26th: 'Electricity working again!!!'

But I passed those circles. And when you pass too many circles you get fed up with doing it.

At the door it's my job to check everyone has their bags. Plus pencils, felt-tip pens, mid-morning snack.

Me: 'Ready?'

There has to be a rule about not answering.

I wait for the leaves to settle in the corridor. I don't like to look at them in case they're true ghosts.

We started to use the P4 classroom now. It's the brightest, plus there isn't any broken walls or ceiling. Plus it's as far as can be from the big school, which helps.

The kids in here were making shields out of cardboard, tinfoil. On the front of the shields there's coats of arms.

They never got started on their December projects in P4. Which is why I prefer to use this room. Because everywhere else is always stuck on Christmas.

Today's lesson is Gaelic speaking. This is especially for Mairi, who's only learning. In the teacher's cupboard I find Gaelic weather labels and reward stickers.

Even though I'm not sitting at the front, I'm the one in charge. It's the new rule we have to follow.

'*Tha I garbh*,' I say. 'It is windy.'

Everyone has to write it down. I wait until there isn't any more sound of pencils scratching.

'*Tha I frasach*,' I say. 'It is rainy.'

I listen for the time of their pencils stopping.

The classroom fills up behind me. Calum Ian comes in, then Duncan. They are quiet getting to their seats.

Then Mum takes a seat. She's at the back, sitting beside the classroom assistant.

'I've forgotten how to say "It is sunny",' I say.

Nobody helps. They all just wait, including Mum, who could be the biggest help if she wanted.

Feeling nervous, I eat my mid-morning snack. Even though it's still early. Nobody tries to be helpful. They don't join in with eating their snacks, either.

'Did you read what it says on the wall?' I ask everybody.

Nobody answers, so I have to read it:

'Be honest. Be responsible. Be trustworthy. Be respectful. Be kind ♥ – and see the love heart after kind. That's emphasis.'

Nobody says anything, so I have to put my head on the desk. Have to listen to the sound of the floor, the hissing sound that's near or faraway.

'What's under the floor?' asks Alex. 'Ground. Then under the ground? Dirt. Under that? More dirt. Under that? Lava.'

But his voice isn't true. It's mean and scary. So I cover my ears and do *lalalala*s until he stops.

It's been fifteen days. He never said what to do if it was longer than five days. I checked the rules, but it doesn't say.

Sometimes it's easier to pretend they're here.

There are no small dogs left. Also, the sheep stopped coming near the village. I never knew what happened to the small dogs, until I saw one of them being chased by five big dogs, and then I knew.

Yesterday I left the school door open. Now it's off its hinges. That was a daft thing to have done. I write the rule on my hand so I remember it for later: No doors left open.

Shopping got harder. I can only go shopping the old way for now, because it feels safer.

In the Co-op, some of the lights fell down. Also part of the roof, where the wind got in. Now I go to the back store instead, where there's tall shelves, no windows. A big stack of wooden squares which I forgot the name of, beside the world's biggest roll of clingfilm. Plus a machine that looks like the crusher at the back of a rubbish truck, only it's indoors.

I find a packet of orange jelly down the back of the shelves. Beside, a buckled tin of sweetcorn.

When I tear open the pack of jelly I find it's gone mouldy. The tin, though, is a good result.

I open the tin, sit out on a bench to eat it.

The wind isn't blowing too hard. There's kid-spots of rain, but also sun. I look for a rainbow, don't see one.

Sometimes I cry just when I didn't think I was going to. Like now. I mean, the food is just stupid sweetcorn. And there's not too much wind, or rain. So why?

Up on the road I meet three big dogs. They stop to sniff. I keep an eye on their tails to make sure they're friendly.

I also make sure I've got my knife.

Mostly the big dogs are friendly. But after what happened to the little dogs, I'm not playing with any chances.

In the butcher's shop I find something we missed before. It's called a mood-ring. It tells you how you're feeling. Right now I'm passionate and sad but also with a hint of mixed emotions. But maybe that's because I've been holding the ring for too long. Still, I think it might be true magic, because when I woke this morning I felt a mixture, and that's what the mood-ring has shown.

The sea got something bad in it. Maybe that's what happened to the world. Maybe I remembered it wrong. What truly happened is – the sea got greedy. It wanted everyone, so it sent poison into the air. That made everyone walk towards it. Except for only a few, like me, and the people who'd already gone. It's like the opposite of the zombies that Alex worried about: the ones that could walk across the seabed to get to him. The ones that walked up out of the sea.

Maybe that's why Duncan and Elizabeth, and Calum Ian and Alex and Mairi, all left. The sea wanted them. Because it was greedy then and it still is now.

*   *   *

My tooth hurts. At first it hurt just a little, but now it hurts a lot. Can't put my toothbrush anywhere near it because it's too sore. I should've remembered to brush before now, but I forgot and that was a lot of my fault.

Can't remember if it's not all right to eat toothpaste. Or the best way to brush? Was it around, or up, down? Plus my toothbrush got yellow and chewed. But that's easy to sort: there are about a hundred toothbrushes still on the shelf at the Co-op. Enough to last for years.

I add *Toothbrush* to my shopping list. Then beneath that, *Medicine for tooth hurting.*

Now I wake up and it's been ages and I've fallen asleep but forgotten when. The light is different in the window, so it's been a while. Hours? Days? My head feels sweating hot. My mouth is truly very sore. My gum feels like it grew, like it belongs to a bigger person.

Elizabeth's books are no good, they don't tell toothache. It's too sore even to drink.

I look for Elizabeth's medicine bag, but she took it, it's not there. Then I remember – ice cubes might help: but there's no fridge plus no electricity so no ice cubes.

The best plan is to sleep beside my teddies. I gather all the teddies of mine plus Alex's and Elizabeth's, and I just hold them. It's a bit of relief, especially if I pretend they all have sore teeth, and I'm the one helping.

In the morning it's less sore. My mouth tastes yuck. When I try to speak my gum feels sore but less big.

There's yellow water, sterilised. It hurts to drink at first but I'm thirsty so I don't mind too much.

My tooth comes out. I almost wrap it in tissue and put it under my pillow, but that's stupid.

'There's no tooth fairy,' I tell myself in the mirror. 'You knew that for ages, stupid *dummy*. What – you going to expect the Easter bunny next year as well?'

After this it's too sore to talk, so I shut up again.

Past World

Mum honks her horn. We're in a car jam. I never saw a car jam before, not on our island. In films, maybe. Never in real life.

It's nearly dark. The telegraph lines are whistling. The sea looks stormy, white. The cars are in a long line.

After ages the red lights go off the car in front, and we move along one, and then the lights come on again.

Me: 'Why's it taking so long?'

Mum: 'They have to ask questions, that's why.'

Me: 'I remember we did see a car jam before, once. Getting on the ferry. You remember?'

Mum smokes. She turns off the van to save diesel.

They've put orange and white fences across the road, which means that just one car can get through at a time. Next to the fences, there's a lorry. On the back of the lorry are the big metal baskets they were using to strengthen the cliff road. Now the workmen have changed their mind; they're using them to narrow the road instead.

'Keep down,' Mum says.

Seonaid, the nurse from hospital, is standing at the fences. She's wearing a white all-over suit, like the one Dr Schofield wore, plus a mask and eye protectors.

She looks cold, she bounces, jumps to stay warm.

Mum gets me to curl up on the floor as we get closer to being the frontmost car.

When it's our turn Seonaid shines a light inside and finds me hiding. She hands Mum a piece of paper. I want to look at it first but Mum won't let me.

'Rona, then,' Mum says.

Seonaid comes around to my window. She taps politely and I roll it down.

'Can I just pop this in your ear, love?' she asks.

She reaches in and presses a white plastic gun into the hole of my ear; it beeps. Then Seonaid reads the number. After this she rips off her glove and puts on another one.

'Did very well.'

When she goes around to Mum, they talk first. Mum has questions. One of the cars behind starts to honk its horn. Mum still has questions.

'We're trying to keep a safe haven.' Seonaid waves to the men at the gates, to say everything's all right.

Then she leans in closer to Mum and whispers: 'Mary, you need to, otherwise I'll have to pull you over.'

'But which side is this safe haven? It's not clear, is it behind or ahead? Are we in it right now?'

Seonaid thins her mouth, looks around again at the cars. Someone else peeps their horn.

'The side you're going to. Come on Mary. I don't want to have to pull you over.'

Mum tries to ask another question, but when Seonaid walks away like she's lost her patience, Mum stops asking. Instead she rolls down her window all the way, and puts her head towards the outside.

The white gun beeps.

Mum keeps her eyes away. Seonaid looks at her number for a long time: then writes it down on her plastic card.

Then she rips off her gloves and says, 'I don't want to have to separate you right now. So can you keep your mask on?' Seonaid has to shout over the wind and rain. 'Listen Mary: keep Rona's hands washed. Wash everything: cups, bowls, cutlery, before she touches anything. The both of you need to wear gloves.'

'Been doing all that.'

Seonaid bites her lip: then gives the man at the barrier the thumbs-up. He waves us through.

'I've got us safe,' Mum says. She rubs my shoulder, picks up her cigarette packet with a shaking hand.

The house is cold and dark when we get back. Mum lights the storm lanterns and puts a candle on the kitchen table and at the window. We can't use the electric fire, but the central heating still works. It's nice with candles, and I want to put our sleeping bags next to the radiator and play shadow-puppets, but Mum's too busy to join in.

'Not now,' she says.

She asks for help, but when I try to work beside her she bosses me away. I watch as she fills the kitchen sink with cold water, then the sink in the bathroom, then the bath, which takes ages, then all of the biggest pots and pans. I worry that the world will run out of water, but Mum doesn't think it will. She keeps pressing her head, and talks to herself when she thinks I'm distracted upstairs.

'Come *on*,' she says. 'Get a grip.'

Back in the kitchen she's putting food in lines: cereals, tins, packets. After this she goes upstairs, to my room.

I get the worst fright to find she's tearing up, squashing flat the big cardboard boxes from all my games.

Even though I scream at her, Mum takes all the boxes downstairs, then she starts to stick them up on the windows, ignoring me because I'm crying too much.

After this she gets old blankets from the linen cupboard. She rolls them up and uses them to block draughts at the doors. Other ones she hangs over the blinds, like extra curtains.

Still crying, shouting for anger, I follow her around the house. She turns the radiators off, upstairs.

'We'll heat just the one room,' she says. 'We can save on oil. In case the tankers are a while coming.'

I'm fed up with her. The boxes of my games look stupid and sad on the windows. How will the sun get in? I get in my sleeping bag, hide way down deep.

Mum's trying to read the leaflet she got from the council.

'Water,' she says. 'Food. Warmth.'

277

She rubs her head. Then she goes quiet for a bit. Then I hear her moving about, going back and forth to the kitchen.

After this I don't hear anything for a time.

When I get out of the sleeping bag to go and find her, Mum is sitting at the table. Her face looks creased, old by the storm lantern. She's got – a stick? In her mouth.

She takes the stick out. Looks at it.

'What's wrong?'

Mum closes her eyes like she's in another world.

'Could ye do something for me, love?' she says. 'Could ye go to the bathroom, get the medicine box?'

Something about her voice makes me forget I was angry. I go upstairs and bring the box to her.

Mum puts one of the temperature-reading strips she uses for me on her forehead.

A car drives past outside, going far too fast.

'What does it say? What number?'

'I don't see a number.'

'What word, then?'

'Fever.'

Mum nods. She peels off the strip, looks at it. Then she comes back through to the living room and lies on her side. She holds a tea towel over her mouth.

'Thought that,' she says. When I try to hold her hand she shrinks away. 'Don't come near.'

I have a proper job now: to convince her that adults, especially parents, never really get sick. It's only us kids who get truly sick.

'Look. I have fever in me, too.'

I unpeel another tester, and stick it on the front of my head.

278

And I certainly got the right idea for getting her attention –
because now she sits up.

It's a race to see who will peel the strip off first.

'See? Fever as well.'

Mum doesn't look glad that we're the same. In fact it's
opposite-day for her looking glad.

'Oh, my wee girl, no, no, no,' she says.

Then she holds me. She sways me in her arms, which feels
the best, it's a thing to mend our problems.

We do shadow-puppets after all. We do it without sound,
which is best because your imagination makes the noise.

Mum's top creation is a dragon. Mine's, a dog.

She keeps shining the torch at me, even when it's meant to
be her turn, and won't let me shine it back.

'To see your face,' she says. 'My love.'

After this Mum starts to shiver again, and so she takes some
tablets from her medicine box, then she strokes my hair until
I fall asleep.

When I wake again Mum's already up. The place looks
different; strange. She's taken down all the cardboard from
the windows, plus all the blankets she put up on the blinds.
Instead, she's put up the Christmas tree. The lights don't work,
but Mum has set the lantern nearby, plus candles, and that
makes the tinsel shine good.

I find Mum in the kitchen. She's cleaning everything: the
table, our cups, even the chairs. Plus she's put away the pots
and pans that we filled up with water earlier. She's wearing
her big jacket, the one for when it's very cold.

'It's all back to normal,' she says.

'Except for my game boxes.'

'Sorry about them.'

There's three envelopes on the kitchen table. Mum picks up one of them, seals it, puts it in her pocket.

'This letter tells you how to work the heating,' she says. 'That one there is all the phone numbers for emergencies, with your auntie's number at the top.'

'What happened to your face?'

Mum's face has bumps on it. And on her hands. She looks at them as if they don't belong, as if they're on the skin of another creature.

'We need to be going away now,' she says.

We drive around the island. It seems to take all night, but how can it when our island is only small? Mum keeps having to stop the van. I climb over to the back space to get some sleep.

When I wake up her jacket's on me.

Then it's light outside. How did it get light and I didn't notice?

Mum's trying to use her phone. It doesn't work, no matter how many times she presses the numbers. She puts on her glasses to see better, but they don't seem to work, either.

From my window I see a bird in the sky. To start with I don't know it's a bird. How could it be up in the air?

We're at the car jam again. Mum's shivering like she came back from the outside. I can see the bumps on her neck, her ears, even the tips of her fingers. Now she has red bits instead of white bits in her eyes.

A man in a white paper suit puts her in the passenger seat, and drives us home. Then we're allowed to go through the place with the orange and white fences. This time they don't even want to check our ears.

I keep dreaming about the bird. It has red eyes, white feathers. It's big. Somehow it looks like a dog. It runs and flies too fast to get away from. It lives for ever.

Then I wake up: and I'm wrapped in a blanket. I feel cold-hot-cold. It's a strange room. Too dark. There's a bottle of juice and a plate of biscuits next to my pillow.

There's a baby next to me. It breathes with a fast snoring sound. My clothes are all damp.

I don't see Mum.

Back Bay

The real reason I didn't put Mum's letter back together was because she wrote three of them.

One telling me how to work the heating. The next, a list of emergency numbers.

But the last one: what was it?

If I'd seen the other two envelopes as well, it would've been easier. But I never found them.

There was just this one, the one she posted back through the door. Paper gone pale on one side, from the sun.

Try not to look at the words as I tape the torn pieces back together again. Dirt-marked but readable, only her signing-words blurry from when I dropped it that day on the wet ground:

Mo luaidh Rona,
This is for when you get home. I'm sorry they didn't let me stay. As soon as I get better I'm coming back, that's my promise.
If I don't get better then I want to tell you I love you with all my heart and always will.

Aunt Moira said she will take care of you. There's money put away by in the kitchen.
Don't hide yourself, be bright in this world.
Your mum, who loves you.

I say it out loud. I hear, or imagine I hear, Mum saying the words. I put the letter against my cheek. I don't care if there are germs of illness on it.

I write the whole thing up on my wall. I colour around the words in rainbows. It takes me hours, and my hands get numb, but it's worth every second.

I want more. I look at the letter side-on, in case she pressed into it a secret message. I look inside the envelope, unpeel its glue. It's just plain.

What else? I get hungry for other messages. So I go back to my old home and do a complete search.

Some of the cards on the mantelpiece fell down since we came in. But there's still dirty washing in the sink, Mum's grey pants and bras on the clothes horse still.

I rub the pen-marks off the tablecloth. Then I use Sellotape to stick down the wallpaper I peeled.

I peel off the stickers I shouldn't've put on the wall upstairs. But I have to stop, because the wallpaper rips underneath.

'Sorry,' I say to Mum.

She's not answering today.

I look around for anything of her: and after a strong search I find a shopping list at the bottom of a plastic bag, in the cupboard. It says: *Carrots, Lentils, Eggs, Tomato sauce, Milk, Breakfast, Rolls, Juice, Treats.*

283

Her writing isn't hurried, and even though it's only a shopping list, I want to keep it: because it's of her.

NEW RULES BY RONA
1. Watch 4 times a day.
2. Send messages.
3. Collect from beaches.
4. New Shopping.
5. Old Shopping.
6. Water – collect rain.

Six becomes one, when I remember that water is the most important thing. So I put loads of plastic cups in a fish crate on the stone wall of the house, with green nets over the top to stop the cats getting in.

After this I wait for rain. Still: I know that if you wait too hard then it never comes. So I pretend to the sky that I was busy doing something else instead.

It works for a day before the snails get in.

I never got to see where they came from. There had been a spot of rain at night, and I went straight out in the morning to find there'd been an attack.

When I shouted the dogs started to bark. There was only a couple of cups spared, so it became a battle: me against the snails. I crushed and smashed them: threw them against the wall, flattened them under rocks.

But then I saw a snail try to slide off, with its sad cracked shell. And all the world hated me, because I was the worst person for hurting this creature.

*　　*　　*

Draw imaginary people. The family I'll become part of. A kind dad with glasses, beard.

The sailors who come. They look like pirates. They keep their parrots on long string. One has a wooden leg, the other an eye-patch. The next one a hook for a hand. It was unfair that Long John Silver had all the injuries, so I spread them more evenly around his shipmates.

Talking becomes the new rule. 'Use it or lose it,' Mum used to say. My big worry is I forget to speak, like Mairi did; that my tongue shrivels and disappears and it's gone for good. So I practise. I talk out the words I remember from DVDs. *'Quiet, you fools. She's in the oubliette.'* And, *'Look for the, bear necessities; those simple bear necessities!'* Also, *'When a zebra's in the zone, leave him alone.'* Then pages from any kids' book with pictures: especially the ones Elizabeth used to read to Alex, where I can imagine her voice: *'The night Max made mischief of one kind, and then another . . . Please don't go, we love you so, we'll eat you up . . .'*

Still: my voice sounds too buried inside. So I try adverts, even though I can only remember the most annoying ones: *'Go Compare! Go Compare! When you hear that sound, look around, Go Compare!'* But though the adverts are usually short, I never seem to know them exact. Then I try reading Gaelic learning books: but I'm never very sure that I'm saying the words proper, or that I forgot how to without a teacher or Mum to correct me.

It starts to be nursery rhymes. I lie in bed and sing. If I shut my eyes I can pretend it's Mum doing the rhyme. I can nearly make myself think it's her voice.

It's difficult, but nearly possible.

The cats begin to follow me. The kittens want to follow most, rather than go to their mothers. To start with I encourage them, but then a big dog runs from nowhere and kills one kitten in a bite, which is so terrible to see and hear that I never let the kittens near me again.

I befriend two big dogs, who both act friendly. One still has a collar on: her name's Elsa. Elsa only ever wants food. She's a brown and white dog, with middle-long ears. She's friendly and sleeps beside me at night, which is a good help.

Elsa eats the dog-meat I open. In exchange she snarls at the night-time rats. It's a fair partnership.

If she keeps being friendly she'll become my sidekick.

Sometimes the sea roars. You can't listen to it for too long because it turns from a quiet rumble to the biggest sound in history. It's like watching the clock. The ticks get louder and louder until you're not sure they're bigger than you.

Other times I worry I'm not alive. So I do a routine of checks to guarantee I'm still here. First: press myself all over. Then I shout to hear the sound of it coming out from my own mouth, so it's not just air. Then there's the mirror, though sometimes the mirror lies. Then there's the dogs, who are friendly and treat me like I'm an actual being.

Then there's giving myself a Chinese burn. Or pouring cold water from the sea down my neck.

With the mirror I count my scars: check they're the same as before.

Sometimes I count wrong and have to start over.

But even after the checks I start to feel light. Like I'll blow away on the wind. Like I'm made of nothing. The mirror helps, but the worry is one day it'll show me going invisible, or thin like a person made of paper.

I try to make more friends with the dogs. If I manage to coax a dog or two in with biscuits then it helps my heart. And when I talk to them they listen patiently, so it gives me the warmth that people once gave.

The dogs aren't so scary, not when there's biscuits. Needs must, Mum used to say, about things you did because you had to. Some of them growl, but then I understood Mairi's trick: you spray them with paint and they learn from then on who's boss.

The worst thought is if there never was people. It's like disappearing, just the other way around.

I only have to go to a bad house and smell to know that's not true. And seeing the dogs, cats, birds helps to prove that other living things exist besides me.

They tried to rub off the curly **G** I did on the door, but it only went smudged.

The air got cold inside. I'd remembered it looking different:

newer, maybe, or bigger. There isn't much of a smell, just the damp most houses get in the end.

The living room is a bigger mess than before. There's a new black bit on the carpet. They had a fire, maybe it was an accident? Maybe not. They didn't tell about it.

In the kitchen I find shrunken jelly cubes. Sometimes shrunken things taste stronger, but mostly they just taste worse. I take them in case it's the first kind.

In a plastic bag on the floor beside the table – maybe hidden from Calum Ian – I find the library books about sailing and boats that Duncan took.

He was making notes. His writing looks very bad.

I miss other people, seeing the words.

Their bedroom. They took away the sleeping bags. We left them at the ferry waiting room. The clothes they left are in two neat piles on the floor. Calum Ian must've washed them: they smell damp, but clean.

In Calum Ian's drawer I find his notebooks, from before. He tore out the pages about Elizabeth and him being the parents of a family.

Lastly, I go to Duncan's room, his old room from before, to lay his fiddle on the bed, with flowers.

'Knew why you were scared of mirrors,' I say. 'It was when they checked us, right? Checked we were alive, Elizabeth told me. So I'll tell you right now: I don't blame you for being frightened. I got bad dreams about it, too.'

Duncan keeps his own opinion.

'You were becoming my friend. We were getting on with each other. That's all I want to say for now.'

I scatter the last of the flowers on his fiddle.

'Why did I come here? Would you even answer? Would that be all right?'

Duncan doesn't say.

But I get the idea why: looking out from the window.

I pull Duncan's dusty curtains right open. Then I turn the handle, open it right up.

In the garden is their plan.

The plan they were busy at, every day. The plastic bottles they kept. The petrol they sucked and collected in the plastic bottles.

The fire they were going to make.

I get less and less strong for remembering. It's like a talent you took for granted until it got too late. When did I get up today? Don't know. What was my dinner last night? Forgot. Which dog did I pat last? Can't remember. What day is it? Who knows? My clock, my best ever clock, ran out of batteries when I wasn't paying attention.

Mum's voice used to have a colour. It was warm and red at the edges. Now it's only shadow-black. There isn't even a sound to it.

I watch films to remember other voices. But they don't sound like real voices, not really. Real voices always take you by surprise. With films you know the words.

I special-covered Mum's letter. I used cellophane from the

big roll in the Co-op to make glass. Then I made a frame out of brown card, which I coloured with glitter.

She said, *Be bright in the world*. So I will. Only it gets hard when the rest of the world can't see.

My head gets sore when I forget to drink. There are only two things on the shopping list for today:

1. WASHING LINE
2. MATCHES

Before I do it, I drink the last of the coloured water. Then I read the list of two over and over until I know what it is I'm going to do.

There's a hoodie crow too lazy to fly.

Their road lost its scorch-marks after it rained. And the grass is beginning to grow back again normal.

Some of the dogs are interested. They cuddle in, which is nearly enough to put me off the plan because it's a break from loneliness, but I tell them to go away.

I changed Elizabeth's rule 8. It was the one about matches: how they could hurt very much.

Changed it by turning the 'Do not' into 'OK to' touch, so it meant that I could go ahead with this.

I remember now how Calum Ian did it at the ferry terminal: that night when he made a torch, to look for Elizabeth and Duncan. Even though they were already ghosts. Even though we knew they'd already died.

His routine was: you make a fuse. Just like in cartoons. Then you dip a washing line in one of the petrol-milk containers. Then lay and lay out, back past the side of their house, out and away to the busy car park.

The dogs are not so interested in the smell of petrol any more.

They keep back, mostly.

Unwind, unwind.

I don't have a box with a handle to make my explosion. I've just got the one match.

But it works—

Past World

Daytime. A man stands over me. He holds a mirror up to my mouth, then looks surprised to see me waken.

He holds a mirror over the baby's mouth.

I notice there are three other blanket-shapes in the room. The man goes around them all with his mirror, coughing, doing the same thing he did with me.

When he leaves, a lady comes in. She takes away two of the blanket-shapes, then the baby.

She leaves more biscuits and juice, even though we didn't eat much of the earlier stuff.

Use all my strength to sit up. Thought it was night, but it's not: somebody just covered the windows.

I make a peephole. Window looking out on the school. Lorries keep coming. I see the ambulance flashing.

See the doctors, then just one doctor.

Nights and days come like a light switch going on and off.

Then I wake up, to a smell.

A smell like the taste you get biting your finger: but all around me, in the air.

Another kid has appeared beside me, lying on a camp bed. Eyes puffed up so there isn't any white or colour to see. Red bumps so his skin looks like pebbles. He stays for a while, but then goes off somewhere else.

I never see the faces of the adults, just their shoes.

Feet with blue shoe-covers on. The covers torn through. Spotted with black, red.

I want to see their faces, but they're always way up in the sky, too far away.

No adult has come for two days. But someone beside me is singing – *Huis, huis air an each.* The words come cracked, then loud, then cracked.

When I wake up proper it's a surprise to find that the singing voice is mine: was mine all along.

Dark. Then light.

Somebody calling my name. It's a girl's voice, maybe even older than me.

I recognise her from the school. She's Elizabeth, the girl from Bristol who came to live on our island.

Her arm stretched out to me.

'Don't be scared,' she says. 'Come out from there. I've got some water. Come out.'

For now I'm too scared to come out: because that's when my new life has to start.

Back Bay

The *boom* is at the back of the house. Then I'm lying down: there's a flash of light racing over—

Then I'm not hearing.

That's fire: big fire. I can't hear any sound of it.

Dogs run past. Their mouths go big, shut, big.

I run away to the fence, to the back of the next house, to behind the neighbour's bins.

It's like the sun came up again. Light that makes the sky seem dark everywhere else.

Now I start to hear again. My one ear hurts. The dogs, barking. The roar of an angry giant.

All the sound turned up again. A roar of fire, twisting up above the roof of their house into the sky.

Arm wet. Face wet?

Glass in my arm. It makes me gasp for seeing it.

The whole street catches fire. Sparks go up in the wind making islands of fire in the gardens and houses.

I go away, far away to my street. Far away from where their burning street looks like a volcano. Sparks go up in a curtain, along with smoke which rubs out the sea, the big hill, even the top of the sky.

Next morning there's still smoke. There are birds? No: silver flakes going up and up in the air. It's ash.

The smoke goes up; the ash sideways.

I go and sit on the wall. I can hear the wind, the birds, with one ear only. My other ear doesn't work.

The street looks like when someone runs a black pen over your drawing: there's squares of blackness where the houses of Righ a Tuath used to be.

Calum Ian and Duncan's house is the worst. It's burnt down to ribs, rafters.

There's still some flakes of burning ash. I watch one single flake singe a patch of grass, then go out.

It's when I get off the wall that I feel how my arm is sore. My sleeve feels thick, heavy. It's stuck like glue to the skin just beside my wrist.

I try to peel it away, but it hurts the worst.

One of the cars exploded. I remember. The glass came from there, or from one of the houses? I never knew that glass got smashed when there was fire.

There's still a proper fire in one of the faraway houses along the street, so I don't go there.

Ash dropping around. It goes up in swirls along the road, collecting in piles in the gutters.

*   *   *

Elizabeth sits beside me. I show her all the ways of moving my arm which hurt.

'Never meant to do it so big. The fire.'

She raps the top of my head: 'Killed your brain cells.'

'Stop doing that, *please*! Would you be really mad at me this time?'

Elizabeth: 'Don't be a stress-cadet. Seriously, you shouldn't be worrying about things you can't mend.'

'Mum used to say Hell mend them. Or was it Heaven mend them? I forget.'

Elizabeth: 'You can only be mended by God.'

Me: 'I don't believe in God.'

Elizabeth: 'Hell mend him, then!'

Then she skips away, singing a happy tune.

When the soreness comes it's like a person breathing: or a drum going *bang-bang-bang*.

Elsa comes with me to the hospital. For some reason I can't get my balance on the bike, so it ends up I leave it at the fence beside the playpark on my way.

Elsa trots beside, my sidekick. I don't even have to give her biscuits or sweets now to keep the bribe going.

'*A bheil on t-acras ort?*' I ask.

She closes her mouth for attention, also to tell me she understands, she's a Gaelic dog.

We walk from the road, up to the grassy sticking-out land. Everything got further than I remember. My arm is bigger, or maybe feels bigger? Elsa waits while I get comfier by putting my fingers, my arm inside my jumper.

296

'*Tapadh leat*,' I say to her. 'Stay patient.'

We get to the door for the link corridor between the old folks' home and the hospital. There's the same old smell as before. Dust, dried-out floor, unused air.

'*Dè thuirt thu?*' I ask Elsa.

Elsa waits. She doesn't want to come in, not even for a biscuit, not even after a pat or any friendliness.

'Stay on lookout,' I tell her.

The white room is still a big mess. Maybe even more so, which makes me wonder if Elizabeth or Calum Ian came back when I wasn't there. It looks like an animal got in – there's splodges of cat shit in trails – though where a cat came and went in by I don't know.

I find about six different packets. I line them up. I try my absolute hardest to remember which ones were medicine, and which ones were poison. The best attempt comes with closing my eyes: to remember the day me and Elizabeth came here. Her words, her instruction. What she did. What I did while she was being the adult.

I look for the medicine book she used, but it isn't here. With no better ideas I line the tablets up in alphabetical order: AMIODARONE. ATENOLOL. DIGOXIN. FUROSEMIDE. GLIPIZIDE. HEPARIN. IMDUR. OMEPRAZOLE. TRIMETHOPRIM. WARFARIN.

Still, it doesn't make the memory of things clearer, so I read the packets. They all have long lists of side effects and actions and characteristics, but nothing that gives any clues as to whether they could be poison or not.

I look at my arm. The bit showing beside my sleeve is red,

297

like Duncan's face was. The red bit hurts when I don't even press, though especially when I do.

'Colour in the edges. Did you not see Elizabeth do it with the cut on her leg? Good remembering. Are you going to do it now? Don't force – I will!'

But I'm too much of a coward. Plus the pen hurts, even over the skin that's meant to be normal.

In the end I collect up all the tablets, poison or not, so I can check them in the dictionary later.

Elsa is waiting for me outside. She wags her tail like crazy, like I was gone her whole entire life.

'Wouldn't leave you,' I say, to soothe her. 'We're buddies, sidekicks. Remember? What's going to work?'

Elsa's eyes flash at me: Teamwork.

The air got hot, or is it me? Either way Elsa's the best at patience with the time it takes me getting home.

I try to push the bike, but it gets too heavy, so we dump it beside a paint-peeling boat.

Elsa leaves me at the gate. Some big dogs go past, making small yelps and running – then she's gone.

I shout and shout on her – but I guess dogs are her true world, better than being a sidekick.

I look at the islands: past the trawler, past Snuasamul. The islands where the sun goes down in winter. Nobody lived on them when I was little. Not even before I was true. But hundreds of years ago, people lived there.

So there must've been a last person there too. Maybe a girl, like me? So if there was then it's a shame we never lived in the same time. Because if we did, we could've been sidekicks. We could've helped each other, with the teamwork you get in humans.

Back home. I don't like cold hands. Or cold feet. Mouth dry: lips too. I put down all my shopping, which is really just the tablets. Then get wrapped up in my duvet.

How can you feel cold when it's sunny outside?

I hold the picture frames, with Mum's picture and her letter in them. For seeing better I take down the cereal packets that Elizabeth stuck to the skylight.

Mum has a good smile. Her photo got faded, but not her smile. In fact this makes it better. Brighter.

Her letter is losing its tape-creases. And now I think I know what *be bright in the world* means. It doesn't mean make a fire, or noise, or act to reach people. All it means is: just be a part of all the stars you can see in the sky.

Because the world is just another part of the sky.

I could take just one tablet for safety – then wait. Duncan couldn't wait when he needed his. But it doesn't matter, because I know which one's the poison. It's the one called WARFARIN. I remember Elizabeth saying that now.

Sometimes my memory works better.

Do the checks: radio, same old noise. Tucking into bed, smell of fire on my jumper, trousers. I feel less thirsty, so maybe that's a good thing.

This morning I spoke to you Mum, explaining things. Asking for some answers. Telling you where to look.

You don't have to reply if you don't want to.

There's enough clothes on the island. Of all different sizes. I could grow and still find clothes to fit.

Plus there's shoes. And trousers, in the second-hand shop. Plus clothes left in the Cròileagan.

I could keep teaching myself to read. The library has all its books. I could borrow all the books from people's houses to make it even bigger. I could teach myself sums, though that's harder than reading.

And for food. I miss milk, miss cereal. I miss bread and I miss bananas and apples. All types of fruit.

In the spring we found tiny strawberries in the polytunnels. They tasted the best ever, but they were only a nibble. There's no apple trees on the island. Or at least if there was any I wouldn't know where.

There's a new light in the rainbow Elizabeth made. I've never seen it since the sun turned into all-day.

Could go and check? But not before I've had a rest. When I get up again I'll check what it was.

Make another list tomorrow: of all the skills I got, so I know the best strengths of mine to use.

Last day

From the roster we could see the last runs had gone through late-Feb. Four, five months ago.

There was a shorter run: shorter than the removals, taking in towns, any open harbour. Anchorages a nightmare, frequently: wrecks up and down the coast, cos nothing got tied proper for the weather.

Shipping lanes: empty. Told us about the last. Belfast picked up a man – a farmer – on Colonsay. Guy had set fire to his fields and was brought mainland in April.

By consensus he was a one-off. Oldest by a mile, how'd he lived? All the rest was for clean-up.

Murdo saw first. There was an early front: low coming in from sou-west. Punching through that, over above: smoke. Stood out hardest at dusk, then we lost it. Too far, not Morven, not Mull, not even Inner Hebs.

So then we get off shift. Inverness said they'd pick up in the morn, otherwise not keen to send out a search, conserve this, conserve that, usual story.

Calum goes on his VHF, runs up and down the channels. Got a bit of stick from Donnie: said there was something like half a boat between here and Newfoundland, so he was better off shelving it and focussing on salvage.

Admit I couldnae sleep – thinking about that smoke. Set me thinking on everyone I was missing.

Family. Pals. All the older folk.

When ye meet or hear of someone from before it's like: no way. Can't believe there's an auld-lifer.

Skip, he has a nephew who's survived. So Skip has his family. That's pretty remarkable.

Kept asking him, what's it like? There's someone from your before. What does that feel like?

He's a dour bugger though. Hard to get a word out of him for what went. Nor any word of outlook.

Where did my kind go, I think, when I'm not guarding against thinking too much. Where are they?

Stayed up late, blethering to Donnie. Why'd I come to the coast? he asked. All the way up here?

Had tae think. Know something: clearest answer, crazy but. It's hardest being in the city. Even the towns. When ye're there it hits ye, ye cannay escape it.

Empty streets. Whole districts: empty. No cars on the roads. No folk in the town centres.

Here at least, looking out where there was never much in the first place, ye can pretend no much changed.

The wool over yer eyes, Donnie said.

302

So what? I answered back. Better that than getting to see how bad it did us.

Plus in the city there's all the eyes on ye: all the time, so ye feel like a museum piece. Some type of freak.

Hundreds – no thousands – of kids, looking at ye like ye're the faither and mother they need. Because it was the adults that got it worst: which makes us, the few survivors above the age of twenty, truly remarkable.

I won't say lucky. Remarkable will do for now.

Next morn, the front in. Overcast, rain. So you take the chance, or what? Plus we had a fix, or maybe no. Western Isles, southern end? Donnie thought it was off the map and a waste of diesel. I didnae.

Cleared a bit on the way out. We could use the trip for salvage, I said to Skip, laying it thick. He didn't have much to say to that. Anyway, it was a chance for fishing, and we'd maybe get the fuel back good from cars.

Basking sharks halfway. Idled for a bit, watched them: until they dropped and disappeared.

Boat never got into the bay last time. Big Spanish trawler holed on rock-reefs at its entrance, buoy to beacon, so too risky. She was slicking terrible in Jan when we came, which put us off anchorages closer.

She'd broken up, now: rudder, hull, one side, radar, mast the other. Skip navigated the channel, face like thunder. I kept out his way meantime.

Already binoculars on the beach, three of us.

Nothing doing. Nobody.

Murdo looked fed up, like I felt. But it was on the map for salvage: so it wouldnae be a waste, no really, we could recce here for a bit, then run a lorry up the Uists. Maybe work the chain, make some dough? Skip said nothing.

Dogs, gulls setting off a racket. No place to tie, pier-boats wrecked side-on against each another. We dropped the dinghy, which took long enough, Skip too crabbit, or lazy, or both mebby, away to sleep in his cab.

Murdo's bet was for a whin-fire. But that couldnae be right: the smoke was coming from inside the village, far side of the bay. Then we saw something on the pier.

An SOS in stones. Plastic bags, kids' clothes.

Radio said nothing. Skip ran the channels. We started shouting, but it made the dogs bark like crazy.

Murdo used his loudhailer. We waited on the boat. Blew the air-horn. Gulls didnae know what hit them.

Then Skip sent up a flare: and when nobody came he said, 'Check out what's burning.'

Saw straight away that someone started it. Radioed to Inverness. They said we should stay put. It was a drag, for sure, what could we do? Told us to get masks and gloves on, report back, keep them updated.

Row of three houses: burnt. Blast area, smaller fires set about. Nothing that'd go up on its own though. Two of the houses gutted. Somebody had lit up a bunch of milk bottles, probably petrol or diesel, for the blast.

We shouted, blew our whistles. Nobody came. So we stopped for eating. Clearly were survivors: Murdo found what looked like petrol-gathering: cars sprayed, caps open. Doors of houses marked up: G, B. Had to be kids.

So now everyone interested, even Skip.

Plastic bags on the shore, close to the pier. Had they set a fire for a beacon and then left? No sign on the road. The dogs weren't cared for, cats feral, half-away.

Ended up house-to-house. Lots of dead at home, they never had time. Checked the mortuary, field hospital at the school. Children's refuge: someone covered in stones and flowers. The hospital, only the early dead. GP surgery: doors forced, empty. Supermarket: empty. Coastguard's office: empty. Council offices: empty.

Kids are great trash-gatherers; they build nests just like birds. Seen it on the other islands. Just follow the trails of rubbish, tins, plastic. So there was this one house.

Kid tried to hide at first. Scared. Murdo reminded me to stay wee, kneel down, let the kid come.

There was a marine VHF – not cabled. She wanted a drink. Drank and drank. Face pocked, so safe enough. Scrawny, bad teeth, not starved. Somebody cared.

Asked if we were real. Here to take you home, Murdo says, and the kid goes: I am home. Nice start.

Slow to give her story. Kept asking if we were real.

Scabbed burns to her arms. Gave her a shot of penicillin and tetanus when we got back to the boat.

She started to talk. That's when we found out about the others. Skip radioed Stornoway: a band of us there – about half a dozen adults – who still had access and could sweep south to look for the kids. Problem was, they reckoned in Stornoway they were further off than us, plus their boats were dry, so any rescue was gonna end up ours.

We filled up from the cars. Settled her by the cabin. Rucksack, toys. Tatty letter she wanted to keep. Then as we motored away the kid said she wanted to stand free.

Watched her as she watched the sea-churn, the bay, the birds. Kept asking me: When will you know?

Said I'd keep radioing Stornoway. Gave her a jumper, oilskins for heat if she was going to stand out like that.

One thing she said – boats of the fishermen came out with us. Tailed us. That gave Murdo his fright, but he's soft in the head that way, he believes in spirits.

Held onto her, and we both watched. And that made things better – I guess – because when we got out the sound, out past the trawler, she said, 'They're gone.'